Franco leaned toward her and gazed intently with his steely eyes. "I'd like to know, Ms. Andersen, why you're behaving like a spoiled brat?"

"You're mistaken. I'm behaving like a businesswoman who's been kept waiting for an appointment I didn't—"

With his free hand he reached out and touched her cheek, running his index finger down the curve of her full lips. As her lips parted, he slipped his finger slightly inside, touching the soft flesh within. She felt filled with an unexplained longing, a raw, burning, nearly primitive feeling.

He looked deep within her eyes. "Your eyes have yellow flames in them, *cara.*"

"That happens when I'm near the sea."

"Only the sea causes you to flame?" he questioned invitingly.

Swiftly he was next to her, then all over her, and she wanted to lose herself with him and be found again and again. . . .

Dear Reader,

It is our pleasure to bring you a new experience in reading that goes beyond category writing. The settings of **Harlequin American Romances** give a sense of place and culture that is uniquely American, and the characters are warm and believable. The stories are of "today" and have been chosen to give variety within the vast scope of romance fiction.

Barbara Bretton has the hair of her heroine, Stacey Andersen—thick, wavy, and tawny. They also share a background in computer science. *Love Changes* takes place in the very romantic area of Montauk Point on Long Island Sound. Franco Borelli, Stacey's hero, is an Italian-American who spent his childhood summers in Florence. As an adult, he has the combination of the drive of America and the Old World charm of Europe.

From the early days of Harlequin, our primary concern has been to bring you novels of the highest quality. **Harlequin American Romances** are no exception. Enjoy!

Vivian Stephens

Vivian Stephens
Editorial Director
Harlequin American Romances
919 Third Avenue,
New York, N.Y. 10022

Love Changes

BARBARA BRETTON

Harlequin Books

TORONTO • NEW YORK • LOS ANGELES • LONDON
AMSTERDAM • PARIS • SYDNEY • HAMBURG
STOCKHOLM • ATHENS • TOKYO • MILAN

To my parents, Mel and Vi Fuller,
who taught me how to dream
and to my husband, Roy,
for showing me
that dreams *do* come true

Published April 1983

First printing February 1983

ISBN 0-373-16003-8

Printed in Canada

Chapter One

With a twist of her wrist, Stacey Andersen turned the steering wheel of her sleek black Corvette and zipped into her parking spot. She let out the clutch and turned off the engine, too absorbed in her thoughts to notice the way the two young workers admired the sportscar as they hoisted the newly painted "Andersen-Bradley Data Processing, Inc." sign into position on top of the low brick building.

She grabbed her pocketbook from the passenger's seat and her briefcase and bakery package from the floor, then swung her long slender legs out of the car. Unfolding her tall frame from the low-slung sportscar was no mean feat, but her movements were spare and elegant.

Unaware of the admiration of the workers on the roof, who were surprised to see such a lovely driver in such a powerful car, she leaned to her left and adjusted the hem of her almond-colored linen skirt, exposing just a touch of shapely thigh.

A long whistle pierced the April morning air, followed by, "Lookin' good, baby!" She was startled and looked up in the direction of the voices.

One of the men, young and very blond, waved and smiled. Suppressing a grin, Stacey shook her head and went in the front door of the office, marveling again at the size of the entry hall. It was nearly as large as her whole office had been in the old building, she thought. Andersen-Bradley had come a long, long way.

She winced when she saw how the light blue carpet in the reception area showed footprints. She never should have let her partner John Bradley talk her out of that nice level-loop tweed she'd picked out for this heavily traveled part of the office.

She paused at the glass window of the receptionist's office and tapped with one long manicured nail. Chris, her brown eyes dancing behind wire-rimmed glasses, looked up and smiled. She pushed the entry buzzer to let Stacey inside the main offices.

"I have the bagels," Stacey said. "Did Dee start the coffee?"

Chris finished labeling some disk packs and gestured toward the rear.

"She and John are in the kitchen arguing about caffeine consumption."

Stacey laughed. "I'd better go along and referee the battle. Are you coming back for your tea?"

The older woman nodded. "As soon as I finish packing the McCord job."

"Don't overdo, Chris. Aren't you supposed to take it easy in the beginning?"

Chris laughed, some of the worry lines around her mouth disappearing as she did. "I'm pregnant, Stacey, not sick. Besides, I've been down this road three times before. Don't worry so much." The older woman's smile was soft as she looked at her young employer. "Really, Stacey. I'm fine."

Stacey hesitated, her eyebrows shooting down in a slight frown. Because it could never happen to her, a normal pregnancy seemed like a miracle, a feat of magic that the slightest imbalance could destroy. Unconsciously, her hand touched her own flat stomach. She sighed.

"Okay, I promise, Chris. No special treatment." She

wagged a finger at the woman. "Now, you'd better get yourself back to the kitchen fast. I'm so hungry I can't guarantee the safety of these bagels if you don't."

With a grin Stacey turned and hurried along the narrow corridor toward the kitchen in the rear of the suite of offices. Her high-heeled shoes made hushed sounds on the thick emerald wall-to-wall carpeting. She passed the tightly closed doors to the computer rooms, behind which the obscenely expensive—and heavily financed—keys to the success of Andersen-Bradley whirred and rattled under the watchful eyes of the operators.

Stopping in front of a massive wooden door with her name on it, she fished in her leather pocketbook for her keys. Balancing her parcels in her arms, she unlocked the door and opened it, flipping on the overhead light switch with her left elbow.

Thank God she hadn't allowed John to influence her decision on inner-office decor! She removed her jacket and tossed her handbag and briefcase on top of the enormous walnut desk, then hurried across her office and pulled open the pale gold draperies. As always, she was struck by the beauty of the Long Island Sound some two miles away.

Laughter and the sound of tinkling coffee spoons snapped her out of her daydream. She glanced at her desk, then saw an envelope where it had fluttered to the floor and bent to retrieve it. For a moment she stared at the California postmark and the name "Quenzer" above the return address. It took a full five seconds before she recognized her mother's latest married name. She tossed it back on her desk with the rest of her mail. She didn't have time right now to read one of her mother's semiannual duty notes. Clutching the bag of still warm bagels, she hurried to the kitchen.

Dee's voice, high-pitched with excitement, greeted her as she pushed open the swinging doors.

"He's impossible!" Dee, a short, slightly plump woman in her early fifties, threw her arms in the air and whirled to face Stacey. "Can *you* drum some sense into John? He's been drinking enough coffee to float the Russian Navy."

John Bradley leaned over and spooned another teaspoon of sugar into his already sugared cup of coffee, laughing at Dee's moan of disgust.

"I've always said there's nothing worse than a former fat person," he teased.

"How would *you* know?" Dee retorted, eyeing the man's waistband. "You have a spare tire Goodyear would envy!"

John straightened up and sucked in his stomach, then cast Stacey a conspiratorial glance. "Will you give Dee her two weeks' notice or shall I?"

Stacey put the bag of bagels down on the yellow Formica table and poured herself a mug of steaming black coffee, her early-morning vice.

"I'm going to give *my* two weeks' notice if you two don't quit this bickering," Stacey said.

Dee handed her a sliced bagel, then went to hand one to John.

"What are you doing? Are you kidding?" He stared at her in wide-eyed astonishment. "How about some butter, Dee?"

The woman clasped her hands behind her and moved away from the table, shaking her blond curls. "Never. You would think a man with a heart problem like yours would start worrying about things like cholesterol levels, fat intake—"

John groaned and spread a heavy layer of sweet butter on his onion bagel. "Dee, if I wanted a lesson in nutrition, I'd call Richard Simmons."

Dee wouldn't budge. "Go ahead—don't listen to me. Why should you? You don't listen to your doctor, either. Just do me a favor"—she pointed toward the butter—"don't ask me to sign your death warrant for you."

"Can you believe the abuse I take from our employees?" John sat down at the table and looked at Stacey, who did not return his smile.

"You may not want to hear this," she said to her partner, "but I agree with Dee. Come on, listen to me," she said as his hands flew up in disgust. "You really should take better care of yourself. You've been under a lot of stress lately." In the past year John had lost his wife and teen-aged daughter in a plane crash and had suffered a mild heart attack.

"Are we talking about John's awful diet?" Chris popped into the kitchen for her tea and soda crackers.

"Not anymore we're not." John pushed his chair back and stood up. "Ladies, if you'll excuse me."

Chris stared at his back as he left the room. "Was it something I said? I was only kidding. . . ."

"We were giving him a hard time," Stacey said as she sat down at the round table and poured a second mug of coffee. "I should have known better."

"Do you think I should apologize to him?" Dee seemed abnormally subdued.

Stacey shook her head. "No. You know John—in a few minutes it'll be like it never happened. He's just tense lately since Margie and Jill. . . ."

The three women fell silent, remembering the horror of his rigidly controlled grief at the funeral. A chill ran up Stacey's spine and involuntarily she shivered.

"Should I turn up the heat?" Chris asked.

"No way! We have enough bills with this new place and the new system." She gestured toward her deep peach silk blouse. "I'll put my jacket on when I get back to my desk."

She stood up, ran a hand across her flat stomach and groaned. "I'd better skip lunch today."

"I don't want to hear it," Dee answered. "You don't have a spare ounce."

Stacey laughed. "Oh, yes, I do! I just keep my cellulite under wraps. I'm a master of camouflage." She turned to leave the room when Chris called her back.

"You can't skip lunch today, Stace. You and John have a lunch meeting at the Four Square Inn with a Mr. Borelli."

"Borelli?" Her lovely features wrinkled in a puzzled frown.

"The prospective investor."

Stacey's frown slid into a scowl. "Does John know about this?"

It was Chris's turn to look puzzled. "He set it up. Why?"

Stacey stormed toward the swinging doors.

"Hold my calls!" The door swung shut behind her.

How dare he make an appointment like that without consulting her. Especially after the argument they'd had the week before on the same topic. He knew her feelings about bringing a third partner into the company: She'd rather take a cut in her salary than give up any control in the firm they'd worked so hard to establish.

The door to John's office was closed. Without knocking, Stacey flung it open, grabbing the door just before it smacked against the paneled wall.

"I hope you have Borelli's number so you can cancel—'' She stopped and looked around. He wasn't in there and, judging by the closed draperies and unlighted lamps, hadn't been in there yet that morning. She backed out of the office and closed the door behind her.

"Is Mr. Bradley in here?" she asked Charlie, one of the computer operators, as she poked her head into the computer room.

"No, Miss Andersen," he said, never taking his eyes from the program he was running. "I haven't seen him at all today."

"Thanks, Charlie."

"I'll tell him you're looking for him if he comes in."

She nodded and, stepping carefully over the maze of wire that ran across the doorway, left.

She tucked her hands into the pockets of her slim skirt and walked down the corridor back to her own office. So, John had done it again, slipped out with no one seeing him. The anniversary of the accident was next month and the faster it approached, the more elusive he became.

Her head was down as she entered the office and her mane of wavy blond hair fell across her face. She slumped into her oversize chair and rummaged in the top drawer of her desk for a tortoiseshell barette to clip back her unruly hair.

"John!" She looked up and saw him standing by her enormous picture window, nearly obscured by a cloud of cigarette smoke.

"I was wondering when you'd track me down."

For the first time in the eight years that she'd known him, John Bradley looked every one of his fifty years, plus ten. A cold fist grabbed Stacey's heart as she looked at him, slouched by the window, a cigarette drooping from between his lips. He had never been a snappy dresser, but his shirts had always been pressed, his suits in good repair. She swallowed hard as she took in the button missing from his pale blue shirt, the way his gray pants were getting shiny in the seat.

She crossed the room and rested her hand on his forearms for a second. He was trembling slightly. She sensed his embarrassment and quickly removed her hand.

"Is—is anything wrong?" Her voice was soft, concerned.

He took a long drag on his cigarette and exhaled slowly, staring out at the Sound in the distance.

"Beautiful view," he said.

"It should be. We pay enough for it."

He chuckled.

She hesitated a moment about bringing up the lunch appointment, but then he turned to her with a sheepish look and said, "You're steamed with me, right?"

Her laugh was humorless.

"Oh, you're right, Mr. Bradley. You're *so* right! Why the hell did you make that appointment with this Bolero—"

"Borelli," he corrected.

"Bolero, Borelli—what's the difference? I don't want to keep the appointment no matter *what* his name is."

John sat down in the big leather chair in front of her desk and crossed his right leg over his left.

"Stacey, listen: Borelli is looking for a good investment and we're it. He's just right for us. He has a Master's in computer engineering from Princeton and a real eye for sound investments. The fact that he wants to invest here means he thinks we're moving up."

"I'm honored," she drawled.

"You should be. He has a lot of capital and he needs a place to put it."

She sat down in the chair behind her desk and leaned back. "I could give him a place—"

"Stacey!" John sounded shocked.

She looked at him with innocent green eyes. "Hasn't he heard about Individual Retirement Accounts?"

John sighed and ground his cigarette in her clean marble ashtray, then lit another one immediately.

"If we're going to continue expanding, we're going to have to bring in another partner, Stacey. It's that simple."

"Who wants to keep on expanding? I want Andersen-Bradley to be good, not big. Why can't we just stay the way we are?"

John shook his head. "Nothing stays the same for long, Stacey. We need more capital to do the job we're capable of. And I don't think we should go to the bank again for it. It's time to join the big time."

She fiddled with a green felt-tip pen, doodling on her notepad. "I'll take a salary reduction. We can let one of the operators go."

He raised his hand to stop her. "Forget it, Stace. If anything, with the volume of work we're doing, we could use a third operator. You shouldn't be doing the graveyard shift. You deserve your salary and more." He shook his head. "You know the problem—and the solution—as well as I do, kid."

She looked up at him, her brows rushing together in a frown.

"And what is my problem, Mr. Bradley?"

"Yourself. You're terrified of change and you know it."

Stacey felt her face flame. John knew her so well that she could hide nothing from him. He'd known her from the time she was a frightened eighteen-year-old girl working in the accounting office of an electronics firm. He had seen her through serious surgery, through a broken engagement, through a whole maturation process that had led to the poised, successful young woman in front of him. He had recognized her tremendous drive and ability, and had trained and nurtured her like the father she'd never known. She'd worked her way up from junior assistant to backbone of the company until, two years ago, he had offered her a full partnership.

She sighed.

"Have you nothing to say besides a sigh, Stacey? No angry denials?"

She shook her head and a curl of hair escaped her clip and bobbed around her right shoulder.

"I can't deny the truth. Change gives me the creeps." She looked at him. "Do me a favor and cancel with Borelli, please? I just can't face it today."

"Even if I wanted to, I couldn't. He's coming up from Princeton for this." He glanced at the Swiss watch the office staff had presented him on his last birthday. "Borelli's probably somewhere on the Jersey Turnpike right now."

"Okay, you win this round. I'll go to lunch with old Borelli, but I won't make a deal. Okay?"

"*That's* a deal." He grinned at her, some of the weariness leaving his face.

She tossed her pen at him.

"Out with you! Someone around here has to get some work done."

The rest of the morning raced by in a blur of printout deadlines, format changes, and ringing telephones.

John had said their reservation at Four Square Inn was for 12:30, so at a quarter to noon, Stacey took her makeup kit from her bottom desk drawer and went into the small bathroom that adjoined her office.

The lighting around the mirror was good—it didn't magnify nor did it conceal flaws. Quickly Stacey inspected her face. She never felt comfortable looking in a mirror and rarely did so unless she was putting on makeup or brushing her hair.

Her fair skin tended to dryness and she used a thin foundation more as protection than cover-up. The brown eyeshadow sculpted and delineated the unusual slant of her clear green eyes, which were framed by long thick lashes. Satisfied that the makeup she'd applied earlier that morning was still fresh, she dipped a fine brush into a pot of coral lipgloss and lightly touched it to her mouth, holding true to the well-defined short upper lip and the full, sensuous lower one. She dusted her cheekbones with a tawny blusher, pleased that the overall effect was natural and understated, yet polished.

She reached back and unclipped her barette, shaking her hair loose. It was too thick and wavy to run a comb through, so she brushed it into shape. The bangs and sides of her heavy blond hair were beginning to curl and she frowned at the slightly wild look it gave her. No matter. With the humidity rising, pretty soon she would have a headful of curls like Harpo Marx. She chuckled as she returned to her office and tossed the brush in her leather bag. After a quick check of her blouse and skirt, she slipped her jacket on and hurried outside to start the Corvette.

Traffic was light, and she and John made it to the Four Square Inn by twenty after twelve. The restaurant did a brisk luncheon business, and they had to leave the sportscar with the young parking lot attendant, whose eyes sparkled at the sight of the sleek auto.

"I'm getting too old to ride in that car," John grumbled, massaging the small of his back as they walked up the stone driveway toward the inn.

"You're not that old, John," she reassured him as she accepted the assistance of his arm. The steep driveway was rutted after the harsh winter, and walking in flimsy high heels presented a few problems of balance.

The noon sun was shining directly down on the restored Colonial mansion-turned-restaurant, emphasizing the graceful lines of the two-story building.

"Oh, look!" She pointed to the glossy black shutters on the enormous double-hung windows. "They've repainted since last time. How lovely!" She repeated her compliment to the hostess who greeted them inside at the dimly lit entrance to the bar.

"We appreciate the kind words," the woman said, her blue eyes twinkling. She checked her ledger for their reservations. "Can you believe my boss nearly put up aluminum siding?"

"That would have been a crime," Stacey said as she and John followed the woman to the Three Villages Room off to the left of the bar.

"This is one of the rooms from the original structure," the hostess said as she showed them to a lovely window table. "It dates back to 1752."

"Did George Washington sleep here?" John asked with a grin.

"As a matter of fact, he did," the woman answered with a good-natured smile. "When he was in New York, he often came out here to Long Island."

As the hostess took their drink orders—wine spritzer for Stacey, Scotch on the rocks for John—a busboy handed her a message.

"Mr. Bradley?" John looked up from the menu.

"Mr. Borelli regrets he's been delayed en route and won't be joining you until one P.M."

"Of all the—"

John stopped Stacey with a quelling look.

"Thank you very much," he said smoothly. "We'll have our cocktails while we wait."

The hostess hurried off with the bar order.

"Why did you shut me up?" Stacey hissed when the woman was out of earshot. "You know how I hate lateness."

"*You* know how *I* hate scenes."

"What makes you think I'd make a scene? I was just furious over this Bollino's inconsiderate behavior."

"Borelli, Stacey, Borelli. B-O-R-E-L-L-I. Will you please get the man's name right?"

Her jaw set in a stubborn line as the young waitress placed their drinks down on frilly white doilies.

"What difference does it make anyway?" She sipped the light rosé wine-and-seltzer cooler. "Mr. Bo-rel-li"— she said each syllable slowly and deliberately, grinning at John—"is probably a senile old man with tons of money and nothing but a dachshund to leave it to."

John chuckled and they both fell silent for a few minutes listening to the piano music filtering in from the bar. The Three Villages Room was a Colonial beauty: dark paneling, the wood lustrous and glowing in the light of candles that burned in brass sconces on the walls. Crisp white curtains framed windows that overlooked the formal garden. Outside, hundreds of tulips—a rainbow-riot of blazing yellows, reds, and oranges—ringed the white gazebo in the center.

The table was set with deep ruby ironstone dinnerware and heavy pistol-handled silverware that Stacey recognized as a pattern designed originally by Paul

Revere. In the center of the navy linen tablecloth sat a fat round vase filled with white carnations and baby's breath.

It would have been perfect if only John hadn't arranged the appointment with old Mr. Borelli. She checked the slender quartz watch on her left wrist and frowned.

"I'll give him until one fifteen," she said, "then I'm diving headfirst into a bowl of vichyssoise."

"I don't care if you swim laps in the punchbowl, just as long as you don't call him old Mr. Bolero."

She started to flip him a smart remark when she noticed the playful twinkle in his tired brown eyes—a look she'd not seen for a very long time. Instead, she broke into a delighted grin. Her happy laughter as they bantered back and forth drew the curious glances of some businessmen at the next table. However, the combination of her elegantly lovely face and unaffected enjoyment drew their eyes back again and again.

At one twenty she motioned for the waiter to bring more breadsticks and warm rolls. She was convinced the entire restaurant could hear her stomach rumbling. She looked again at her watch and arched an eyebrow at her partner.

"Dependable, isn't he?"

"Traffic on the Expressway must be backed up."

"It's bad enough you set up this luncheon," she retorted, "but you don't have to start apologizing for him on top of it."

At one thirty, hungry and cranky, she called the waiter back over.

"My friend prefers to wait for our tardy guest, but I'd rather order now, please."

The waiter swiftly scribbled down her order of spinach salad and broccoli-cheddar quiche. Moments later he returned with the salad then slipped away.

"I'm sorry," Stacey said to a disapproving John, "but we've waited long enough for our ancient friend to show up."

"I'll admit he's not making a great first impression on you," he said as she made short work of her salad, "but that doesn't change the fact that this meeting is *very* important."

There was a sense of urgency in his voice that made her put her fork down and look directly into his eyes.

"Is there something you should be telling me?" A small alarm of fear made her scalp tingle. Was he hiding something from her or was her imagination working overtime?

"John?"

He was watching the archway intently and she glanced over her shoulder to follow his line of vision. A dark-haired man of about thirty waited as the hostess checked her ledger.

"Do you know him?"

"Stacey, I—"

He stopped as the hostess led the man toward the table.

"Oh, God," Stacey moaned and covered her eyes with her hand. "I can hear it now: 'I'm sorry, but Mr. Borelli is unable to attend this luncheon.'"

"Ms. Andersen? Mr. Bradley?"

The man's voice was like molten gold—deep yet melodic—a curious blend of Ivy League crispness laced with vaguely European overtones. The owner of the voice extended his hand to Stacey. She stood up and was surprised to find that, with her high heels, she was just about at eye level with the stranger.

His grip was firm yet not familiar. The handshake was brief and she found herself strangely disappointed when he turned to John. He certainly didn't *act* like a messenger or assistant. She noted the perfectly styled mahogany-brown hair, the well-cared-for hands. His dark blue suit fit his broad shoulders perfectly and tapered in to a narrow waist and strong legs. He was of average height but the impression of compact strength made him seem much larger. There was nothing subservient about his manner as John offered him a seat and she wondered what on earth was going on.

"Stacey," John addressed her after asking the waiter for a fresh round of cocktails, "I'd like you to meet Franco Borelli, president of FB Computer Investment Enterprises."

Her smile disappeared as her mouth dropped open in shock.

"I'm sorry to have kept you both waiting so long for me, but I was unavoidably detained."

John laughed. "I told Stacey you were probably caught in traffic."

"Traffic?" His voice was smooth, untroubled. "No. Actually the roads were quite empty."

Stacey waited for the explanation. When he smiled, the outer corners of his eyes, an unusual amber color, crinkled in a fine starburst of lines. She was annoyed with herself for even noticing.

"Did you have a flat tire?" She ignored the look John shot her. Her heart was thumping in righteous anger. What was the matter with John, anyway? Normally he tolerated lateness the way he tolerated weight jokes: with poor grace.

"No flat tire." Borelli's eyes seemed to photograph every detail of her face and clothing in a split second. She felt her cheeks redden with suppressed anger.

"We've been waiting over an hour, Mr. Borelli." She didn't sound like herself. Her voice was high and tight.

"I understand and I apologize. As I was about to explain"—he turned toward John—"my chauffeur took ill on the way here and had to be taken to the hospital."

John looked sympathetic. "Will he be all right?"

Borelli nodded. "He's having an appendectomy right now. He'll be fine."

She looked down and sipped her wine. What an arrogant, self-serving man! Why did he turn to John when it came time to offer explanations. He acted as if she were here as John's date, not full partner. And the fact hadn't escaped her that he'd made very sure they knew he had a limousine and driver.

The men ordered strip steaks and salad. They talked about baseball and the future of indoor soccer while waiting for their food. Stacey ate her quiche in stubborn silence. Borelli glanced at her plate and looked surprised to see her already eating lunch. But he said nothing.

Obviously Franco Borelli was a game player par excellence. Nothing about business was brought up; he politely ignored her pointedly cool behavior and allowed John to direct the conversation. She stabbed the last piece of quiche with her fork.

"Mr. Bradley?" The hostess stood next to John. "There's a phone call for you in the lobby."

John groaned, put his napkin on the table, and stood up.

"You two get acquainted," he said and left Stacey and Franco alone.

"I'm sorry," she said with a sarcastic edge to her voice, "but I don't know what we'll be able to talk about. I don't know a thing about baseball *or* soccer."

"That's fine, Ms. Andersen. I have no desire to talk sports with you. There are other topics to discuss."

Oh, she could see it coming: What's a woman like you doing slaving away in data processing? Haven't I seen you somewhere before? How about drinks? Dancing? A night of love?

She looked deep into his caramel-colored eyes. "And what other things do you wish to discuss?"

She may have had *his* number, but he'd never get *hers*!

He leaned forward and returned her look. "I'd like to know why you're behaving like a spoiled brat."

Chapter Two

"*What* did you say?" She was too surprised to be angry.

He leaned back in the plush chair, his gold cuff links catching and reflecting the sunlight that streamed through the window.

"I said," he repeated with his curious accent, "you are behaving like a spoiled brat."

"You're mistaken. I'm behaving like a business-woman who's been kept waiting half a day for an appointment I didn't—" She caught herself in time.

"An appointment you didn't want to keep," he finished.

She looked away from his probing eyes. "I—I never said that."

"You didn't have to. You were coiled like a snake ready to strike when we were introduced." He leaned closer and peered into her eyes. Her skin seemed to register his warmth like sonar and she moved back a little. "I thought so. Did you know your left eyelid twitches when you're tense?"

Involuntarily her hand flew up to her face. He was right. She tossed her hair back and lifted her chin.

"I'm always tense when kept waiting. I hate lateness."

"As do I."

What did it take to get through to this man?

"I'm sorry if my message didn't reach you." His

voice was calm and even. "You and Mr. Bradley must have thought me very rude."

"We got your message," she mumbled.

"Well, then, I'm afraid I don't understand the problem."

"The message said you'd be here at one o'clock." She struggled to get the petulant tone out of her voice. "You didn't show up until one forty."

He stiffened and sat up straighter in his chair. A curtain seemed to drop over his eyes, extinguishing the glow that had been there moments ago.

"As I explained, there were external factors over which I had no control." He took a sip of his amaretto and soda. "Are you as demanding of yourself as you are of your associates?"

She met his eyes. "More so."

He nodded as if he had expected as much.

She breathed a sigh of relief when John returned, effectively ending this uncomfortable exchange.

"I'm sorry I was gone so long." John eased his large frame into his seat.

"Any problems?" Stacey asked.

"Oh, yeah."

"Serious?" She was aware, from the corner of her eye, of Borelli watching her profile intently.

"Only if you think losing two million names into the system is serious."

"What on earth happened?"

"From what Charlie said there was a fifteen- or twenty-second flutter in power—just long enough to lose that data."

Stacey groaned; then, on some wicked impulse, she turned toward Franco. "You may not know it, but if the heads on the disk crash due to a power failure, you can lose everything on the disk at that moment."

"I know," Franco answered with a smile. "I have a Master's in computer engineering."

John laughed. "You're getting forgetful, Andersen. I told you that before."

She was too upset about the computer foul-up even to be embarrassed. The community college account was supposed to be completed and sent out by messenger that night. She didn't dare look at John for she knew what he was thinking: If they had financed a better system, this might not have happened.

She picked up her leather handbag from the floor.

"I'd better get back to the office," she said as she stood up. "It must be a madhouse."

"There's not much you can do, Stace," her partner told her. "You may as well stay for lunch."

"I've had mine already. Remember?" She tossed him a sly grin then turned to Borelli. She liked the fact she could look him straight in the eye, although she had to admit he wasn't the slightest bit nonplussed by it. "Enjoy your lunch, Mr. Borelli," she said as they shook hands. This time he seemed to prolong the handclasp a second more than necessary and the touch of his warm broad hand made her feel slightly off-balance.

It was a relief to escape into the bright late April sunshine. She was almost tempted to walk the mile and a half back to the office but the parking attendant was already zooming across the asphalt lot in her Corvette.

"Man, what a machine!" he said as he hopped out.

She smiled and tipped him, then climbed into the car. She shifted from neutral into first gear then merged smoothly into the traffic on Jericho Turnpike. Automatically she maneuvered the car around large potholes, the reminders of another rough northeastern winter, not really noticing the slightly tawdry commercial look of the road. Burger King and McDonald's, discount supermarkets, and boarded-up gas stations rolled past her line of vision as she headed back toward the office. The mechanics of driving freed her mind and as she sorted out the computer problem she realized John was right. Neither one of them was needed back at the office immediately. The system could ingest just so much information at a time and she knew she'd be there well into the early-morning hours running the program through.

The traffic light turned red and she rolled to a stop. The entrance to the eastbound Long Island Expressway was just a hundred feet ahead and impulsively she turned on her left-turn signal. Just for half an hour, she told herself. Then she'd turn around and go back to Andersen-Bradley and all of its problems.

Once on the Expressway, a barren flat three-lane highway that was as crowded at dawn as at dusk, she shifted into fourth gear and headed east. She could feel the engine's power in her bones as she zipped into the left lane and easily passed a young man in a pickup.

The sunroof was open, and with the tape deck blaring some Billy Joel music and the sun warm on her shoulders, she felt eighteen again, filled with the hope that all things were possible, that happiness was within reach. It was a luxury she'd never really felt when she was eighteen.

This incredibly powerful car was her refuge, one of the few places she felt completely in control. Supporting it took a healthy chunk out of her salary, but she chalked it up to her mental health. Although she held a responsible position as co-owner of a growing company, inside she was still the same young girl she was eight years ago—afraid and vulnerable, ready to run for shelter when the winds of change blew rough.

A few years before when it had become very clear that

the suburban life of wife and mother wasn't going to be her lot, she'd traded in thoughts of a station wagon filled with kids for the two-seater Corvette of her high school dreams. In the black sportscar she could disappear behind the tinted windows and become one with the roaring engine. There were few enough things in her life she'd ever been able to control—including her ability to have children—and she relished the way the Corvette responded to her command.

She was also aware that the car made a certain statement about her life-style that, true or not, was a plus for Andersen-Bradley. She was a woman on her own, it said, successful, accustomed to power on all its levels.

Camouflage, she thought as she checked her rearview mirror and changed lanes to get out of the way of a highballing truck. Pure camouflage.

In fact, the meeting with Franco Borelli, although brief, had reminded her of all the many things she had forgotten about: that special chemistry between men and women. She had succeeded so completely in burying her emotions in business that it surprised her when she felt a tingle again. It made her vulnerable once more and that frightened her.

She shook her head and pressed her foot down more firmly on the accelerator. The car swiftly ate up the road until she realized she was already into the flat wooded areas of Medford. She sighed. She knew it was time to turn back for the office.

By 3 P.M. she was back behind her desk, up to her elbows in stacks of green printout sheets. She had rolled up the sleeves of her peach silk blouse because the black ink smudged fingers and clothing with streaks of charcoal. Charlie had converted as much of the salvaged information as he could on to the disk and Stacey was giving it a once-over. From the look of these papers, she would be there for a week.

She reached for the phone to call her sister, Dianne. There was no way she'd be driving up to White Plains tonight. She had just started to dial when she was interrupted by a series of four short knocks at her door.

"Come in." She brushed her hair off her cheeks and adjusted her blouse. It was probably one of the operators with another problem to add to the growing pile.

"You were late getting back."

She looked up, shocked to see Franco Borelli in the doorway. Her first instinct was to come back with a smart crack but she squelched it. Standing there in his shirt-sleeves, he looked less arrogant, less a member of the privileged class. Despite the impeccable tailoring of the dark blue pants and the ivory shirt that flowed like heavy cream, there was something appealing and human about him.

She hesitated, then grinned at him, showing the dimple in her right cheek. "You can come in if you promise not to tell my boss."

His face relaxed into a smile that was easy and natural. As he crossed the emerald-green carpet she was better able to look at him. He moved with grace, his obviously muscular legs taking large strides. Although he was a few inches under six feet tall, the large bones and wide shoulders suggested athletic ability and strength. The startlingly golden brown eyes were set in a face dominated by a prominent nose and sensual lips, a combination she found very appealing.

She motioned for him to take a seat on the plush black leather chair. Instead, he perched on the edge of her desk, crossing his arms across his chest. He was so close she could smell the faint citrusy tang of his cologne and she couldn't help but notice the way his biceps strained the fine fabric of the shirt.

"John showed me some of the system you've set up. I'm impressed."

"It's been a tough three years since we started buying our own equipment, but I think it's been well worth it."

He nodded and flipped through some of the printout sheets on her desk then frowned at the ink smudges on his fingers.

"I was about to warn you." She reached for a tissue and handed it to him. "Cheap ink."

He wiped the ink off onto the white tissue. "Perhaps you need a new supplier."

"Perhaps."

"Let me have another tissue."

She handed him one. In a swift move he leaned forward until his face was inches away from hers. He was so close she couldn't even focus on his eyes; they blurred before her. She swallowed, waiting, aware of the loud silence in the office. Then, before she knew it, he took the tissue and gently drew it across her right cheek with a slow, sensuous motion. She found it impossible to breathe normally with him so close.

"You had some on your cheek." He looked at her with an off-center grin. "I haven't offended you, have I?"

"No, of course not." She cleared her throat, trying to rid her voice of the sudden quiver. Had it really been so long since she'd been close to a man?

As if he sensed her discomfort, he moved to the chair on the other side of her desk. She straightened her papers, arranged all her felt-tip pens and pencils in a neat pile. She felt his eyes on her and finally she looked up. He was smiling slightly.

"You are a hard worker, aren't you?" He watched her intently.

She kept her face composed. "Why do I get the feeling I'm about to be insulted?"

His thick brows drew together in a frown.

"Saying you are industrious is insulting to you?"

"Usually when a man like you says a woman is a hard worker, you can be sure it's not a compliment."

"You've spoken perhaps ten sentences to me. You're most remarkable if you can judge my character on that basis."

She flushed again.

"Mr. Borelli, perhaps we should dispense with the amenities and discuss why you're here." She shifted in her chair, unable to get comfortable under the scrutiny of those amber eyes. "I know John has spoken with you about investing in Andersen-Bradley."

Franco nodded.

"I'll be honest with you, Mr. Borelli; I think John's wrong. I don't believe we need a third partner."

"I saw your books," he said with his elegant accent. "You *need* a third partner. The truth is you don't *want* to let anyone else in."

She leaned back in her chair, drawing strength from her anger. "I don't know what John's been saying to you, but I can assure you we're in good fiscal shape. We don't really need any dilettante investor telling us how to run our company, thank you." She chuckled. "You probably don't know Fortran from Fort Apache. Why, I—"

There was a rap at her door and John walked in.

"Glad you two are getting along so well." He beamed at them. "I hate to interrupt but your party in Rome is on the line, Franco. You can take the call in my office."

Franco stood up. "Thank you." He nodded toward Stacey. "If you'll excuse me."

She watched him as he left her office. When she heard the door to John's squeak shut, she wheeled angrily at her partner.

"You tell me our finances are in trouble and then you let that man place calls to *Rome*? What in hell is going on around here?"

John hesitated a beat before answering. "Would you believe me if I said he reversed the charges?"

Her right eyebrow shot up. "Would you believe me if I said I could leap tall buildings at a single bound?"

"Listen, Stacey, things have changed. We're playing with some of the 'big boys' now and there are new rules you have to learn. One of them is the art of bestowing small favors in order to reap large rewards."

Her lovely face turned to granite. "Whatever happened to hard work reaping its own rewards?" She collected her jacket and pocketbook and stood up. "I think I've had about as much of this kind of talk today as I can handle." She crossed in front of John and shut off the lights to her spacious office. "I'm going home to take a nap and change. I'll come back around six and work through until I finish the run."

"That's the third weekend in a row you've had to work." John placed a fatherly hand on her shoulder. She backed away. "I'll take it for you, Stace. Besides, I don't like the idea of your being here alone all night."

She sighed. "Listen, I want to do it. I'll never rest if I know the work has to be done and I'm not here seeing to it. Besides"—she softened her words with a slight smile—"I really have nothing better to do with my Fridays anyway."

"You know Stu has been dying to remedy that situation."

She groaned. "I'd rather spend my weekends with the computer than Stuart Halsey."

He tried again. "I thought you were going to see Dianne and Al this weekend."

"I'll leave in the morning when I'm finished here. One thing about my sister and Al: They never push me." She emphasized the last three words with a meaningful look at her partner's tired face.

He laughed with good grace. "I get your drift. How is Dianne, anyway? Does she still seem depressed?"

Stacey nodded. "I'm getting a little worried about it too. When they took me out for my birthday last month, she sniped at Al from the appetizer through the after-dinner drinks."

"Spring fever?"

"I wish it were." Stacey's tone was serious. "But this started around Christmas."

She slipped on her linen jacket and fastened the narrow leather belt. "I'd better go."

John touched her arm for a second, an odd look in his tired eyes. "See you Monday?"

She looked at him, faintly puzzled. "Of course you will."

As she left the office she turned and called back over her shoulder, "Give my best to our Mr. Bolero!" and, laughing, slipped out the rear entrance into the late afternoon sunshine.

The high school kids were already gathering in the parking lot of Burger King across the street from the office. She could hear their car radios blaring the loud, crashing music, nearly drowning out their laughter. As she started her Corvette and pulled out of the lot, she noticed the usual stares and comments her sportscar elicited. She had been like those teen-agers once, not too many years ago, thinking of all the luxuries adulthood would bring. She chuckled and slowed the car into the curves of Larkfield Road as she wound her way toward the South Shore of Long Island where she lived. Yet she was the one who was envious—they seemed so young and carefree, so affluent, and she wondered what kind of woman she would have been today if she'd had a privileged adolescence like those North Shore teen-agers.

She crossed Jericho Turnpike, then merged onto Sagtikos Parkway to continue south. The north and south shores of eastern Long Island were divided by much more than degrees of affluence and life-style. The terrain, as she crossed Jericho Turnpike, changed as dramatically as if the massive glacier that had formed the land millions of years before, still ran the length of the island. The sharp densely wooded hills threaded with narrow curving roads of the North Shore abruptly leveled off into the low plains of the South Shore with its flat farmlands, scrub oaks, and marshy acres of beach land.

The North Shore was elegant, cultivated. John had insisted they locate Andersen-Bradley in the more established business area of Huntington on the Long Island Sound, rather than in one of the upstart industrial areas on Route 110 in Farmingdale. "Clients like it," he'd told her once as they argued the point. "It makes them feel they're in 'Great Gatsby' country."

She rolled down her window and took a deep breath of salty sea air. Who needed Gatsby country when she could be close to the ocean, feel the spray sting her cheeks, and watch the gulls swoop into the choppy surf in search of fish. From the window of her small apartment in a sprawling complex in the town of Brightwaters, she could see the gray-blue waters on a clear day and see the rolling mists cover the lawns on a foggy one. It was worth the forty-minute drive each way to be able to live near the ocean, to be able to renew herself in its power and beauty whenever she needed it. Like today.

She made the left turn into the Bay View Apartment Complex. Her apartment was one of three hundred similar one-bedroom apartments in the complex, a series of thirty long two-story buildings built at the top of a man-made hill. The complex offered a rutted asphalt driveway, and as yet unpaved parking lot, and treeless walkways, yet it had a fifteen-month waiting list for prospective tenants. Like everyone else, Stacey had fallen in love with the incredible view of the ocean the location offered, and had been enjoying it for over a year and a half now.

The bedroom was dark and sleepily she reached to her right and switched on the small pale yellow ginger-jar lamp on her night table. The room was instantly bathed in soft light, adding a warm glow to the lustrous antique pine dressing table and chest of drawers across the room. She looked up at the ivory canopy and ran her hands across the wooden bedpost. The effect of the canopy, the intricately crafted Colonial furniture, and the thick, celery-green shag rug was both romantically old-fashioned yet uniquely modern, a perfect expression of Stacey herself. She let few people see her bedroom for she felt it exposed too much of her inner self. Everything in it—from the collection of unicorn figurines on her rolltop desk, to the needlepoint pillows on the rocking chair, to the tiny exquisite oil paintings on the walls—had a place deep in her heart.

A glance at the alarm clock told her it was well after eight o'clock. She got up and grabbed her lemon-yellow robe, fully enjoying the way it slipped across her full breasts and slithered over her round hips and long legs. So much of her life, it seemed, was spent fulfilling someone else's idea of who or what she should be. Her office at work, as much as she liked it, was designed to represent a certain "look" that would promote her position at Andersen-Bradley. Her clothes too were a symbol. Many prospective clients looked to her and mentally calculated her style on an inner computer to judge exactly *how* successful a business she and John had going for them. Even her car was a barometer of success. In fact, she felt like she were on center stage all the time and she was not a person who liked center stage.

She sat down at her dressing table and ran her brush through her honey-blond hair. It flew up and around her brush, an incredible mass of waves and curls rising around her face like golden fire. Controlling it was impossible. It would spring up at the strangest times, resisting all attempts at taming, a wild force with a life of its own. Grinning, she tucked it off her face with two tortoiseshell combs and walked barefoot into the kitchen to make a pot of tea before going back to work.

While the water was boiling, she dressed, then picked up the kitchen wallphone and dialed her sister's number. After her marriage to Al Shearman eleven years ago, Dianne had been living north of New York City in White Plains some forty miles away from Stacey's apartment.

The customary two rings sounded, followed by a cheerful " hello."

"Hi, Dianne. It's me."

A small groan, then, "Don't tell me, I already know. You're not coming. I *told* Al you would never show up for this party. Why, for God's sake, Stacey, you have to start getting out into the world again. You can't work constantly. You have to—"

Stacey started to laugh. "If I wait for you to stop for breath, I'll never get in a word. Just listen, Di. I have to run another program. We had some problems this afternoon, but I *will* be there by tomorrow afternoon and I *will* be there for the party. So you can tell Al you were mistaken."

Her sister sighed with relief. "Well, I can't say I'm not surprised that you're coming, because I am. Do you know this is the first one of our parties you've come to? In three years, you've never once been at one."

"I remember the parties you gave when we were kids. I'm not stupid!"

"You louse!" Dianne laughed. "If I recall, some of your parties were stinkers too. Seriously, though, Stace, I need to talk with you. I'm glad you're coming."

Stacey swallowed a sip of bracing tea. "I have a few minutes now," she said. "Want to talk?"

Dianne was silent a moment. "No," she said finally. "It'll wait until tomorrow."

They chatted lightly for a few minutes, then after a few last-minute "Don't-forget-to-brings" from Dianne, Stacey hung up and sat down to finish her tea. By 9 P.M. she had put her few dishes in the sink, run hot water over them, turned off the lights, and double-locked the door behind her.

The night air was brisk with a slightly damp wind blowing up off the ocean. The salty smell of the sea-water filled her with an inner joy.

Some people found it in yoga, some in music. For Stacey, just knowing she was near the sea soothed her in a way she could not explain. She tossed her pocketbook into the Corvette and, zipping her red sweat shirt over her T-shirt and faded jeans, pulled out of the parking lot and headed back to the office.

Andersen-Bradley shared the small industrial park at the top of a winding hill in Huntington, overlooking the Long Island Sound. During the day the employees of the local clothing manufacturer and the record distributor kept the area rumbling with activity; however, come six o'clock, the lot emptied as quickly as if someone had yelled "Fire!" Even the fast-food restaurant across the road was closed by nine. John had said if she'd half a brain she would be afraid to return to the office after-hours, but she wasn't. In fact, if she could have her way, she would always work nights. A loner at heart, she loved the feeling of being the only person around, loved the sense of full control she had over the machines when there was no John running in to add his two cents, no Charlie or Roy to share time with. Without distractions like ringing phones and distraught clients, she was able to devote herself to the more mechanical aspects of running a data-processing firm and she enjoyed the picayune details that drove John to threatening homicide in seconds.

It was after midnight when she finished scanning the first of four dupe-elims for the community college account. It was a tedious process, going over thousands of names and social security numbers to pull out the duplicated ones before reentering them into the computer for the master disk. She half-jogged down the corridor to the kitchen, swinging her arms overhead to loosen her tense shoulder muscles. She plugged in the kettle, then bent over to peer into the tiny refrigerator for the strawberry yogurt she was certain she'd hidden in the back.

Damn! Except for a shriveled lemon and one half-carton of milk, it was empty. She'd had her heart set on it, could almost taste the tart-sweet tang of the berries in the thick yogurt. It was ridiculous, but she felt like crying. She sank into one of the metal chairs and rested her chin in her hands. She glanced around the kitchen, trying to remember if there weren't some cookies or cake somewhere when her eyes landed on a small white box on the Formica counter. She leaped up and crossed the room in three steps.

It was a bakery box, all right, tied up with the familiar thin red string. A square blue envelope was tucked under the knot and she drew it out and turned it over. In an unfamiliar left-slanted handwriting was her name.

"What on earth?" She slit the envelope with one fingernail and unfolded a heavy piece of cream-colored stationery. She whistled in appreciation. Whoever bought stationery like this certainly knew his stuff. The heft of it, the beautiful watermarks on the bond, all spoke of taste and sophistication. It shouldn't have surprised her when she saw the engraved initials "F B" in the upper left-hand corner.

"Ms. Andersen," read the bold navy-blue script, "my apologies if I offended you this afternoon. It was not my intention. Accept this as my token of peace. Franco."

She slipped the string off and opened the lid. Nestled in a bed of wax paper were two of the most delectable Linzer tarts she'd ever seen. Liberally covered with confectioner's sugar, the double-layer round cookies, oozing with red raspberry jam in the middle, begged to be eaten. How on earth had he known that her passion, her most wicked indulgence, was Linzer tarts? But of course he couldn't have known. He probably had wanted to make amends for that strange interlude in her office— though now she wasn't exactly sure why he needed to make amends—and John, being John, had advised him about the tarts.

She checked her watch. Not quite 1 A.M. She knew he would still be awake. Since losing his wife and child, John had been plagued by chronic insomnia. She picked up the phone and dialed.

"John Bradley here."

"You nut! Thanks for telling Borelli about the Linzer tarts. I'm about to dive into them this second."

"Slow down, Stacey. I don't know what the hell you're talking about."

"The Linzer tarts in the kitchen. You *did* tell Borelli about them, didn't you?"

There was a long silence. "Have you been drinking, Andersen?"

"Didn't you know he left me a peace offering in the kitchen?"

"Oh, now I get it. He'd said he thought he'd offended you and when you left early, he got upset. I knew he'd gone out and come back again around five, but I had no idea what he did. I assumed he sent you flowers or something and checked your address with Chris or Dee."

After a few well-placed jibes from John about Borelli's "gift," Stacey hung up and poured a cup of tea. With a twinge of easily overlooked guilt, she sat down to her surprise dessert.

Although she had a terrific figure, it didn't come easily for her. She wasn't blessed with natural slimness and had to watch what she ate and compensate for indulgences like these sinful tarts with hard exercise. *My God,* she thought as she washed down the last crumb of cookie with tea, *I'll have to swim from here to Florida to make up for this!*

She was remarkably cheerful considering the hour as she went back to the computer room. Her mind was only half on the job at hand as she labeled the disk packs and kept her eye on the one currently rolling. That was such an odd gesture of Franco's—it struck her as more intimate somehow than sending flowers or a bottle of wine. Obviously he had taken the time to discover she was working late that night and had come up with a surprise to delight her during her owlish hours. She smiled as she packed the disks into an enormous corrugated carton and rummaged around for the packing tape and mailing labels.

Maybe he wasn't so bad, she reflected. There was a courtliness to him, a strange mixture of sensuality and sophistication laced with tenderness that had shaken her facade. If he only weren't interested in joining their company. . . .

He was never far from her thoughts as she whizzed through the rest of her work. By 7 A.M. she had everything packed and ready to go, had arranged for messenger service to take the cartons away, and, suitcase already stowed in the car, she headed her Corvette up to White Plains and Dianne's party.

"Dianne, why didn't you *tell* me Michael was coming?" Stacey's voice was filled with fury as she faced her sister in the privacy of the bedroom.

"I didn't know myself until he and his wife walked in with Al's boss." The anguish in Dianne's face was so intense that Stacey knew she was telling the truth.

"I can't go back in there." Stacey sank onto the bed, her hands clenched in front of her. "Especially not with her like that."

Dianne knelt in front of her younger sister and took her hands in her own. "Listen," she said, her eyes, so like Stacey's, heavy with empathy, "you *must*. You know I don't care if you stay in here the rest of the evening if that's what you want, but I do think you would be making a tremendous mistake if you did."

Stacey forced herself to look into Dianne's eyes. "I know what you're saying is right, but—Di! Did you see her? She was radiant." She chuckled grimly. "I used to think what they said about pregnant women was a myth—but looking at Carla, I believe it." She buried her face in her hands.

Dianne watched her sister carefully for a few moments. "Stacey, you have to go out there. You have to be warm and charming and even congratulate them— yes, I mean it—on the baby. It's the only way you'll ever exorcise those awful memories."

Stacey straightened her shoulders and stood up. "It hurts so much sometimes, Di," she said as she adjusted the metallic cinch belt on her black silk jumpsuit. "Everytime I'm sure I've gotten over not being able to have children, I see something like this and I hurt all over again."

"I can't minimize what you're feeling, Stacey—no one can. But, believe me, there are men out there who want a woman for herself, not her baby-making potential. They're not all like Michael." She gave Stacey's shoulders a quick squeeze. "It's been five years. Make your peace with him and let it all go."

How could Dianne understand? Stacey sat alone in

the bedroom after her sister went back out to her guests. Dianne didn't understand how it felt to be different, how the simple fact of her condition had pulled Stacey out of the mainstream of man-woman relationships.

What was supposed to have been a minor bit of gynecological surgery had tragically developed complications that left Stacey irreversibly sterile. Five years ago. Five long years. And yet she could still see the look on Michael's face when she'd turned to him in the hospital for comfort. In her heart she had known the truth even before he gave it voice: The fear and sorrow in his eyes were all for himself. Her chance for marriage and family had been shattered the moment her doctor said, "Stacey, I'm sorry, but. . . ."

She stood up and quickly checked her makeup in the beveled mirror that hung over Dianne's dressing table. The facade was in place: No one could possibly tell by looking at her just how hard it was for her to go back out into the living room and pretend it still didn't hurt.

Michael and Carla were standing by the living room window, talking with a group of Al's friends from the bank. Stacey poured herself a glass of white wine and watched them from the corner of her eye. Despite the fact that these people were his wife's co-workers, Michael dominated the conversation, his voice loud and animated. She suddenly remembered how his need to be at the center of things had always made her squirm, as if he were trying to compensate for some lack in his personality.

He patted his wife's stomach absently once as he spoke to the man next to him. It was clearly a gesture he had made so often that it was second-nature to him. Stacey felt a surge of pain as she saw the look of contentment on the woman's face and she turned away, rifling through some stacked record albums near the stereo, trying to stem the tears that threatened to fall. It was funny how over the past five years only the fact of Michael leaving her had remained clear and vivid in her mind. Time, in one of its perverse tricks, had clouded the very real doubts that had cast shadows during their engagement. All that she had remembered was her own shortcomings, the yoke of guilt she had readily grown accustomed to.

As she stood by the stereo, lost in bittersweet nostalgia, Stacey became aware of a prickling sensation at the back of her neck. She turned around and her gaze was drawn straight to Michael's. Even from fifteen feet away, the clear blue eyes were startling in his angular face. His mouth stretched in a wide grin, and with a word to his wife, he headed toward Stacey.

She moved the wineglass to her lips as she watched him—still lanky and slim—stride across the room. A lock of straight, silvery blond hair fell across his forehead in a manner so casually attractive that it seemed calculated.

He stopped two feet in front of her and grinned. "The years have been good to you, Stacey," he said, then leaned down to kiss her. His breath was moist and smelled faintly of whiskey and tobacco.

"It's been a long time, Michael." Her fingers tightened around the stem of her wineglass.

He laughed. "Is that all you can say after five years, Stacey? No compliments for me?"

She looked up at him. His eyes seemed to glint like chips of pale blue ice. "You're looking well," she answered finally, annoyed to be pulled into her old role of ego-stroker, a role she suddenly remembered with a fierce clarity.

"Thanks. I've been running"—he patted his own flat belly—"to keep the flab down."

Stacey's left eyebrow shot up and she took another sip of wine. Michael had never had an ounce of flab to keep down and probably never would. She knew it was a ploy to make her notice the flat, nearly concave abdomen and the long, sinewy muscles that ran down his tanned arms.

"Michael?" Carla, a small auburn-haired woman with freckles that matched her curls, slipped an arm through her husband's in a wifely gesture of territoriality. She looked at Stacey, a cloud of suspicion darkening her narrow face. "Introduce me."

He looked at Stacey. "This very pregnant lady is my wife, Carla." He started again to pat her enormous belly then, looking at Stacey, stopped just short.

"It's nice to meet you." Stacey extended her hand, then removed it awkwardly when Carla made no move to release Michael's arm to shake her hand. "I'm Stacey Andersen."

"I know." Carla's fingers tightened around Michael's forearm. "I've heard about you." She paused for a moment, then said, "Dianne's sister."

Stacey blushed and became aware of Michael's uncomfortable shifting. Carla, although not a beautiful woman, had the ripe glow Stacey had seen before in pregnant women. She saw the jealousy in Carla's brown eyes, the flaring of worry over her husband's beautiful ex-fiancée. Stacey suppressed an urge to tell Carla not to worry—there was nothing Stacey had to give that could compare to the gift of a child. Nothing at all.

"Congratulations on the baby," Stacey said, trying to ease them out of an awkward silence. "Dianne said you're due next month. You both must be excited about it."

"The first two times it's exciting," Carla said as she eyed Stacey's slim figure. "By the third time you just get impatient to get it over with."

"Your third baby?" Stacey was stunned. "I had no idea."

Michael grinned. "We're getting separate rooms after this," he said. "If we even breathe the same air, she gets pregnant."

Inwardly, Stacey flinched with pain.

A few other couples joined in as the conversation turned to talk of third-trimester discomfort and post-partum blues. Stacey gratefully used the cover of animated talk to slip away to the kitchen, ostensibly to get more ice.

She was submerged deep in a well of bittersweet memories, tempered by an enormous rush of compassion for Carla. She envied the red-haired woman her experience of pregnancy—no one knew how much Stacey would have liked to know the thrill of giving life. Yet, instinct told her that Michael's basic shallowness had widened with the years, and for that, she nearly pitied Carla. More than ever in the past, his eyes reflected nothing but Michael.

She shook her head as she remembered her grandmother Lillian's words when Stacey first broke the news of her engagement. The old woman had tried to make her granddaughter see him without the gauze of infatuation over her eyes. "Think carefully, child. Michael will give you children but he'll never give you a family. His concern is limited to the width of his mirror."

Stacey, however, determined to rush into marriage rather than back out of her engagement—shades of her much-married mother—had resolutely stayed fast. Only Michael's defection would have stopped her from entering into a very bad marriage.

She sighed and put some ice into her empty glass and picked up an almost empty bottle of Chablis from the counter.

"Still a daydreamer?"

She looked toward the door and saw Michael leaning against the doorjamb, muscular arms blocking the way.

"Some things never change," she answered, matching his light tone of voice perfectly.

"I wasn't surprised you left," he said. "That talk about pediatricians gets pretty dull."

She poured herself more wine from a carafe on the table. "No, it wasn't that." She gestured toward the wine. "I needed a refill."

He drained his shot glass. "Same here. Where's the Seagram's?"

She moved away from the table. "I don't know. You'll have to ask Al or Dianne."

She went to walk past him to go back into the living room, but he stopped her by placing a hand on her arm. She looked up, one brow arched, into his frosted blue eyes.

"Isn't Carla waiting for you?" she asked as she pulled her arm away from him.

He reddened. "Stacey, you don't know how often I— Listen, I'm sorry if what I said out there hurt you. It's just—I always wanted to be able to explain why I—"

"It's a little late for explanations, don't you think?" She found it impossible to believe they were even having this conversation. Was he going to tell her he made a mistake after all this time? Now that he had his children? They heard Carla call him from the next room.

He glanced toward the sound of her voice and cleared his throat. His words came out in a rush. "Stacey, I'm sorry. I really am." He pulled his hand roughly through his blond hair. "I *did* care for you, Stace. If things with you had just been different, you know, I—"

She stared at him in a kind of embarrassed anger, then ducked under his arm and went back inside to rejoin the party. While she tried to pretend to enjoy the joking and the dancing, Michael's words to her of five years ago pounded in her brain. "I owe it to my family to carry on their name. A man needs his own children. . . ."

Time had changed nothing, she realized. It still mattered. Even now, her sterility still mattered.

Somehow she got through the rest of the evening. After the party was over, she lay on top of the bed in the guest room and stared at the skinny shafts of moonlight that spilled through a crack in the venetian blinds. Vivid scenes of Michael's hand on his wife's fertile belly taunted her, replaying in her mind like a bad movie. It dredged up pain she'd kept buried beneath the surface for years.

Lillian had been right about him. Everyone had been right about him. But, no matter how despicable Michael's actions had been, she had to thank him for one thing: honesty. He had only told her what any man in his position would have told her: Given a choice, a man wants a child of his own blood. Plain and simple. A barren marriage just wasn't enough to build a lifetime on.

Her medical condition was her problem and no one else's. She had no right to ask anyone else to share the burden with her.

Since her surgery, she'd learned to avert her eyes during baby food commercials on television, managed to schedule doctor's appointments for early evening when she'd be less likely to find herself surrounded by lustrously pregnant women with ripely swollen bellies. But, as she got older, she discovered she couldn't avoid it forever. One by one, friends married, and as night follows day, they became pregnant and the whole inevitable cycle began again. Even in the cocoon of Andersen-Bradley, Chris was proof that in the real world women had babies and nothing Stacey could do would ever change that fact.

And, tonight, she had Michael's words to her as a powerful reminder of the importance of it all.

She spent a sleepless night. Early Sunday morning she dressed and got ready to leave for home. Maybe she would be able to rest in her own apartment, away from these memories. Besides, Dianne's sniping at Al was making her nervous. All through the night she'd been aware of the low rumbling of an argument seeping through the bedroom wall that separated their room from the guest room.

"At least stay for breakfast," Al said as Dianne fixed some tea for her before she left.

"Thanks, but no. I'm exhausted. Besides, I have a lot of work to finish at the office, so I'd better get going before traffic builds up."

"You're running back to bury yourself in that tomb you call Andersen-Bradley." Dianne's voice was accusing. "A friend of Al's is coming over this afternoon. Why don't you stay and meet him?"

Stacey laughed and shook her head. "Forget it, matchmaker. I'm a lost cause. I'm the one in love with a computer, remember?"

"What about this Borelli guy you were telling Di about?" Al asked. "Any possibilities?"

"For God's sake, Al! Don't get so personal." Dianne's voice was harsh.

Stacey felt sorry for her brother-in-law. "That's okay, Di. I don't mind." She turned to Al. "No possibilities with Borelli," she said. "None at all." She was surprised to hear a subtle note of regret in her voice when she added, "In fact, I've probably seen the last of him."

Al walked her outside to the Corvette after she'd kissed Dianne good-bye. He leaned in through the open window as she started the car. "Does Dianne seem a little strained to you?" He smiled to cover the oddly serious tone of his voice.

Stacey thought a moment. The whole thing with Michael had made her forget Dianne had wanted to talk with her. "Not really. Well, actually, yes, she has seemed a little—shall we say—testy the last couple of weeks but I thought it was because of her job." She blushed as she remembered the sound of their arguing late last night.

He shook his head. "It's been going on longer than that—since her birthday, actually. She seems very far away."

She patted his forearm. "That's it, then. Don't worry, brother-in-law. She's probably just depressed about turning thirty. You go in and sweep her off her feet and everything will be just fine." *It has to be,* she thought. "You two are my hope for the institution of marriage. God knows, Mother was never much of a role model!"

With a laugh and a wave, she backed the sportscar out of the blacktop driveway and roared down the sleeping street to the safety of Andersen-Bradley.

Angry suppliers, burnt-out switches—she could handle those. Even Franco Borelli and his investment company were problems she could sink her teeth into without fear.

But her visit to White Plains had been deeply upsetting. She saw Carla's face taut with tension, heard the low-grade resentment in Dianne's voice, the confusion in Al's, and shivered. As long as she kept her heart securely on ice she had nothing to worry about.

After all, it had been working for five years now, hadn't it?

Chapter Three

"John won't be in until after noon." Dee looked up from the CRT, and relayed the message to Stacey, who had just gotten in.

She exhaled in a long, slow breath. "What happened? Car trouble?"

"He said he has an appointment with that gorgeous Franco Borelli who was here on Friday." She rolled her eyes heavenward. "Now, there's a man I could leave home for."

Chris, standing by the file cabinet, laughed in agreement. "I can agree with you on that one, Dee. He has being sexy down to a fine art."

The two women looked at Stacey, waiting for her to add her two cents to the conversation. She looked down at some notes on Dee's desk and pretended not to hear the comments. As a matter of fact, she was thinking more about the meeting between Franco Borelli and John than of Borelli's good looks.

"Where is this meeting taking place?"

Dee shrugged and looked at Chris.

"I don't know either," Chris said. "John just left a message with the answering service before we opened up this morning."

Dee started a rundown on Borelli's finer points but Stacey stopped her short. "I'm going to take care of the end-of-the-month billing. Let me know when John gets back, please."

Dee and Chris exchanged glances as their employer turned and left the room.

Stacey was deeply absorbed in the bills, watching the outgoing funds outpace the incoming, when the intercom buzzed.

"Pick up line three," Chris's efficient office-voice told her. "It's John."

Stacey pushed the lighted button the telephone panel and lifted the receiver. "John. . .? Where are you calling from?"

"I'm on my way back from Borelli's office," he informed her. "Now, don't get upset, Stace, but I had a little fender-bender and I have to wait for a tow truck to take me to a station for a new front tire."

"Are you all right, John?" She was frightened by the hollow sound in his voice. "Listen, you sound exhausted. Why don't you stay in Jersey overnight? You could check into a hotel while they work on your car, and get some rest."

He wasn't thrilled with the idea, but promised to take it under consideration.

"Call me if you decide to stay," she said. "I worry about you."

He was silent for a moment. "Listen, Stacey, I'm sorry about all this." She was confused. She'd never thought he'd deliberately had a car accident, for heaven's sake! "Take care of yourself," he said. "Don't let things get you down."

"John? What in hell is the problem? Are you *sure* you're—" She stopped at the sound of the line being disconnected.

She couldn't concentrate. All the numbers merged into one illegible blur before her eyes and her hands shook so that she couldn't hold the pencil steady. A quick glance at her calendar confirmed her fears: Tomorrow was the anniversary of his wife's and daughter's deaths. She paced the office. Why hadn't she asked him exactly where he was calling from? She had half a mind to jump into her car and head for the Jersey Turnpike, praying she might find him by his Chevy, waiting for her. Her muscles were tight with fear; the contained frustration was ready to explode.

She walked to the reception area to speak to Chris.

"Did John sound all right to you?"

Chris thought for a second, then shrugged. "I guess so. Did he say something to upset you?"

"Nothing concrete." She hesitated before going on. Except for Dianne and John, Chris was her closest friend. She could be trusted. "Don't tell anyone, but he said he had a small accident and was waiting for a tow truck to take him to a service station."

"What!" Chris's voice was loud and shrill. Stacey had to motion for her to be quiet.

"He says he's fine—the car just needs a new tire or something." Her hands fluttered uselessly at her sides. "Oh, Chris, I just can't explain it." Her voice shook and she sank onto the hardback chair near the desk. "I think there's something terribly wrong. Do you know what tomorrow is?"

Chris looked confused then Stacey pointed to the large wall calendar and the older woman's face turned ashen.

"Oh, God," she breathed. "Margie and Jill...."

"And he's all alone." Stacey was distraught. "I had wanted to be with him, try to keep his mind off everything."

Chris put an arm around the young woman. "Did you ever think that he might want to be by himself today? Maybe he has to work out some things on his own.''

''But he was always around for me when I needed him. All during that awful time after my operation, he was there teasing me, keeping me from feeling sorry for myself. I wanted to do the same for him.''

''He knows it, dear. But you have to allow him the luxury of grieving in his own way.''

''I know you're right, but why do I keep feeling that he needs me?''

Chris shrugged. ''Listen,'' she said with a glance at the list of appointments for the afternoon, ''you have a block of free time up 'till two P.M. Why don't you run over to the spa and swim a few laps?''

''No, no, I can't. What if John should call?''

Chris snapped her fingers. ''Easy. I'll call the spa and have you paged.'' She firmly pulled Stacey out of the chair and gave her a gentle shove toward the door. ''Out with you. You know you're too restless right now to be any good to anybody. Go ahead.''

Stacey leaned down and gave the woman a quick kiss on the cheek. ''What a way to talk to your boss. Have you no respect?''

Chris laughed. ''Oh, go soak your head! Just make sure you're back by two.''

When Stacey returned to the office after her swim, the ends of her hair were still slightly damp and she could smell the faint scent of chlorine from the pool. A steady hum of peace ran through her as once again she sat down at her desk and checked her messages. Tim had called about the catalogs. Cathy wanted a price on 50,000 college names pronto. Dr. DeMartino needed his work tomorrow or he'd cancel the rest of the state university's order. She sighed. Just the normal disasters, nothing that couldn't wait until after her meetings this afternoon. She was about to finish the billing when the intercom buzzed.

"Mr. Borelli is here to see you, Sta—Miss Andersen. Shall I send him in?" Dee's voice was high-pitched with excitement.

"Yes, please, Dee."

She jumped up and hurried into the bathroom to try to straighten out the ends of her damp hair. She had planned to hot-roller it before her meetings, repair her makeup.... What on earth did Borelli want? Why wasn't he in New Jersey where he was supposed to be? She heard the door to her office open, smacking sharply against the paneled wall.

She came out of the bathroom and saw Franco Borelli.

"Don't you believe in knocking?"

He quickly crossed the room and took her by the arm. "Where's John?"

"Let go of me." She yanked her arm away from him and rubbed the skin through the taupe sweater. "I thought he had a meeting with you today. He's still in New Jersey."

Borelli raked his hand through his chestnut hair.

"Is something wrong?" Stacey reached out and touched his arm, her anger replaced by fear. "What's going on?"

He shook his head, eyes deep in thought. "I don't know exactly what it is, but I have the feeling he's in trouble."

"Oh, my God." Her knees wobbled like rubber bands and she sat on the edge of her desk. "I knew it. I was sure something was wrong." She looked up at Franco, her green eyes wide with fear. "I—I thought you two had a morning meeting."

"We did."

He moved closer to her. She suddenly felt her skin grow clammy and she lowered her head to her lap to let the rush of nausea pass. He raised his hand as if to rest it on her shoulder to comfort her, then apparently thought better of it.

"He got there about twenty to ten—half an hour late—and just stayed long enough to tell me he wouldn't be *able* to stay." Franco walked over to the window and looked out at the Sound, then back at Stacey. "I don't want to upset you, Ms. Andersen, but I think he'd been drinking."

She shivered and wrapped her slim arms around her chest, unable to control the shaking. "This makes absolutely no sense." Her voice trembled. "Why should he drive all the way down there just to say he couldn't meet with you?" She jumped up and faced Franco. "Do you think something's happened to him? He called me before and said he'd had a little accident on the Turnpike and wouldn't be back this afternoon. He said your meeting went fine."

She picked her blazer off the coatrack in the corner and grabbed handbag and car keys but her hands shook so badly that the keys clattered to the floor. She stared down at them. "I'm going to try and find him. That's what I should have done in the first place."

"No, you're not." His voice was like a whip as he bent to pick up her keys. "You're in no condition to drive that distance. You couldn't even react quickly enough to pick up these keys."

"Don't tell me what to do, Mr. Borelli. You may be trying to—"

He grabbed her shoulder. "Shut up and listen to me."

His strong fingers burned into her flesh, branding her. The shock of his rough words stopped her in her tracks.

"I have to be in Princeton tonight anyway on some family matters. Let me look for him. I know the area much better than you possibly could and I have men who could comb motels, hotels, and the like."

She bent her head for a moment; her forehead lightly rested on the fine wool of his Harris Tweed sport coat. He loosed his hold on her. It subtly changed from a demand to a near-caress as they stood for a long moment. He put a hand under her chin and raised her face to his.

"Doesn't it make sense, Ms. Andersen?"

She swallowed. He was so close to her—his nearness was making her feel disoriented. Finally she nodded.

"What can I do? I feel so useless."

"Stay by a phone," he ordered. "I'll check in every hour or so. If I can't get you here, I'll call you at home."

She wrote her phone number on her business card and gave it to him.

"I'll be in touch." He took her hand in his and covered it with his other hand, imprisoning it there.

"Please." Her voice was just a whisper.

He started for the door.

"Mr. Borelli?"

He turned, a questioning look on his face.

She looked at him, tossing her hair off her face with a quick shake of her head. "Thanks for the cookies."

He broke into a slow grin, then bent low in a courtly bow.

"At your service."

Franco turned out to be true to his word. He called her at four o'clock from a point just past the Outerbridge Crossing in New Jersey; at five from New Brunswick, and at six from Jamesburg, outside Princeton.

Stacey pressed a hand against her scratchy eyelids while she listened to him explain where he'd looked up to that point.

"We're breaking for dinner now. I'll start checking motels by about eight. Do you have any ideas?"

She hesitated. "I'm almost afraid to say this, but maybe you should check the hospitals."

"I was planning to."

They talked a minute more. "Why don't you go home?" he finally suggested. His voice was deep and warm with concern, and his unexpected tenderness brought tears to her eyes. "I'll call you there after eight," he said.

She didn't argue. She felt drained of all emotion. Before she left the office, she called Chris with the latest news, then headed home.

By six forty-five she had showered and dressed, pulled her wet curly hair into two ponytails, which she'd fix later, then gone into the small kitchen to make a cheese omelet and toast. When the meal was ready and the tea brewed, she settled at the maple kitchen table, her elbows seeking the familiar depressions in the old wood. She loved this old table, felt somehow that years of use had given it a patina new furniture could never duplicate. The table had belonged to Grandma Lillian who had raised Stacey and Dianne from childhood, while their mother made a career out of getting married. Stacey sat there, the omelet congealing on her plate, and stared out the window at her tiny slice of backyard as her thoughts rushed backward in time.

The pretty kitchen, with the lush asparagus fern in the corner and the copper molds on the wall, became the crowded narrow one of her childhood with the chipped porcelain sink that backed up once a week. The room filled with ghosts of a younger grandmother and the sad little girls she and her sister once were.

Late at night, when she and Di could hear the light snoring, like a low whistle, coming from the sofa bed in the living room, they would weave their own fairy tales about the loving couple who'd adopt both them and their grandmother and take them all to a wonderful old house bursting at the seams with apple-cheeked cousins and kind aunts who baked chocolate chip cookies and big furry mutts who tracked muddy pawprints through the kitchen. She chuckled. It had been years since she'd thought of that old dream—years since she'd let herself.

She sighed and pushed the plate away from her. Reaching back, she turned on the gas jet to boil water for fresh tea. She looked over at the round clock above the sink. It was only five after seven.

When her tea was ready, she wrapped her fingers around the heavy, bright red earthenware mug and went into the living room. It was almost dark outside; the streetlights outside her window switched on and she crossed the room to close out the world. With a flick of her wrist, she twisted the rod to close the narrow-slatted blinds, then pulled the gold draperies across the window.

Seven-fifteen. She had used up all of ten minutes. She could feel the rapid pulse in the side of her throat as the adrenaline worked overtime. She still had forty-five minutes until Franco called again with—she prayed—news of John.

This pacing of hers, she told herself, was doing nothing but wearing tracks in the ivory carpet. But she simply had to keep busy. She pulled a plastic bag from the catch-all closet in the entry hall, then curled up in a corner of her couch. The needlepoint canvas was rolled loosely and tied with a piece of yarn. Her long fingers deftly stretched it out full-size. The body of the silvery unicorn was filled with a slanted basketweave stitch. She held the blunt needle to the lamplight and threaded it with pale gold Persian wool to work the maiden's gown. The intricate work demanded concentration and soon her mind was free of all but the needle flashing through canvas as the gown took shape.

She didn't realize it was now a few minutes past eight.

"Ouch!" The sudden buzz of the doorbell caused her to prick herself with the needle. She popped her index finger in her mouth and stood up, knocking the needlepoint to the floor by her bare feet. The buzzer sounded again—three short staccato bursts followed by a long insistent one.

She flew to the door, straightening the collar of her plaid cotton shirt as she unlocked the two deadbolts and undid the chain.

"John! Where in hell have—"

Franco Borelli stood there, leaning against the doorjamb, a light stubble of dark beard on his face, circles under his golden eyes.

She stared at him as she hung on to the doorknob for support. Her knees suddenly seemed unable to support her full weight.

"May I come in?"

She jumped as the sound of his voice pulled her out of her trance.

"I'm sorry." She opened the door wide. "Please do."

He stepped into the tiny foyer and stood by the hall

closet, hands plunged in the pockets of his raincoat. Stacey closed, then locked the door, breathing deeply in an attempt to calm herself. She turned to him and saw the pain in his amber eyes and she knew. She wrapped her arms around her body, trying to physically hold back her shivering.

"You found him, didn't you?" Her voice was thin and weightless.

Franco nodded. "Yes, I did." He stepped toward her, frightened by her drowning green eyes, hating to be the one to have to tell her. Would she have the strength she'd need?

She willed herself to lift her head and look him straight in the eyes. "Is John dead?"

"No, he's not."

Her breath rushed from her body in a long sigh. She went limp with relief, sagging against his broad chest. Until that moment she hadn't fully realized how frightened she'd been for John.

Franco put an arm around her waist and led her to the sofa. She sat in the corner, her elbows on her knees, her head bent low.

"Is that brandy?" He pointed to a decanter on the flip-out shelf in the center of the wall system opposite the sofa.

She nodded.

He picked the decanter up, removing the stopper, and poured two fingers of the blackberry brandy into a shot glass.

"Drink this."

She wrinkled her nose. "I hate brandy. It's too powerful."

He sipped the sweet liqueur and made a face. "God, this is vile. No wonder you think you hate brandy." He sat next to her and handed her the glass. "Take a few sips anyway," he said. "Please."

Something in the tone of his liquid-gold voice made her obey him. Mentally she held her nose and took a swig, shivering at the fiery aftertaste.

"What happened?" she finally asked. "It's bad, isn't it?"

He nodded. "I'm afraid it is." He hesitated, searching for the way to tell her that would cause her the least pain.

She touched his forearm. "Tell me," she urged. "I won't fall apart on you."

"He's in the hospital. He'd checked into a motel a few blocks from the service station where they'd towed his car. The motel manager said he'd started walking down the highway to a McDonald's and apparently was struck from behind by a truck driver."

She flinched under his words as if they were physical blows. She drooped against the sofa; she felt as if her bones had melted. He saw the effort it cost her to straighten up and ask the next question, the one he dreaded having to answer.

"How bad is it?"

He captured the fluttering hands between his own, offering himself as an anchor. The plain truth would be the kindest cut.

"It's very bad, Stacey. Has he family here?"

"No, no one. Just a cousin in Brooklyn—in Bay Ridge, I think." She yanked the rubber bands from her hair and rubbed her scalp where the skin had been pulled taut. "Is he permanently injured? Paralyzed?"

He took a deep breath. "I'm sorry, Stacey, but he's dying."

As completely as if someone had thrown a switch, her

mind shut down, protecting her from the unthinkable. Weeks later, all she remembered about the next few hours were small things: standing in her hall in her shirt and worn, patched jeans; the feel of the carpet beneath her bare toes; Franco looking under a chair for her sneakers, then tying the laces for her as if she were a child.

It seemed like moments—years—later when his big black car roared into the hospital parking lot, incongruously located in the middle of rolling New Jersey farmlands, where tragedy seemed alien. They ran full-out across the dew-slick gravel toward the Emergency Room entrance.

"Mr. Bradley is in surgery." The young red-haired nurse at the information desk eyed Stacey curiously. "Are you a relative?"

"Friend and business associate," Franco answered for her. She clutched his hand like a lifeline.

The nurse waved a sheaf of forms. "We need releases signed."

He looked at Stacey. "Did he give you power of attorney?" She nodded and mechanically signed the papers at the spots he indicated.

The nurse pointed to a small waiting room behind a large glass door. "You can wait there," she said, friendlier now that the legal papers were completed. "There's coffee in the machine."

Franco led her into the waiting room. She winced as the garish fluorescent lights stabbed at her eyes. Even though it was just April, the air-conditioning unit was on. She huddled inside her old blue trench coat, pulling it more tightly around her trembling body. He got coffee to warm her, and she wrapped her fingers around the cup, trying to draw the heat into her fingers and

Love Changes

through to her bones. He stood there looking at her pale, shivering face and took off his London Fog raincoat and draped it across her shoulders.

She sank low into it, burrowing under like a frightened animal. At every squish of crepe-soled shoes, she looked up, waiting for the worst. A middle-aged couple, dressed in the understated way of the long-rich, sat across the room, whispering intensely with a young woman in a white lab coat.

Stacey's nostrils quivered as they picked up the stinging scent of pain. Lowering her head, she buried her face in the fabric of his coat, blocking out the medicinal smells. She inhaled deeply; the coat held the tang of a citrusy cologne and a warm, comforting musky scent of life.

The swinging doors squeaked as a lanky, fortyish doctor with a shock of silver hair loped into the waiting room. He was still in his surgeon's "greens," that absurd little hat half on, half off his head. For some stupid reason she couldn't tear her eyes away from that hat.

He approached them, shook Franco's hand. She stood up, had to crane her neck to see the doctor's face.

"How is he?" Her words seemed to come from very far away.

"We did everything humanly possible, Miss Bradley." His lean face looked genuinely pained. "Your father's injuries were simply too extensive." Neither she nor Franco corrected him. "The operation was to stop the hemorrhaging but we just couldn't do it."

Dr. Sarnoff shifted position, then pulled off the surgical cap, letting it dangle from his right hand.

"This whole accident is tragic enough, but there's a police procedure we have to comply with." He cleared his throat and stepped closer to Franco, speaking quietly and directly to him. "We need someone to identify the body officially."

"I'll do it," Franco answered with hesitation.

Stacey had been listening to their words but up until that point nothing had registered. However, now something clicked inside and she straightened to her full height and lifted her chin.

"I think I should do it."

"Are you sure?" Franco put an arm around her shoulders.

She nodded, her wild mane of curls wreathing her face, unaware of the uncommon beauty sorrow gave her. "I owe it to him."

Franco nodded. "May I come with you?" It would be a grisly business; he had read the traffic officer's accident report earlier and shuddered at the memory.

She forced a wan smile. "Thank you."

When they left the hospital it was nearly sunrise. A rim of violent sunlight had started to outline the adjoining buildings on the east side of the main part of the hospital. They walked through the deserted parking lot quietly, holding hands. The sights and sounds seared her memory; she knew the images would always be with her. In the pasture across the highway from where they were, a herd of cows, content after an early-morning milking, grazed in the wet grass of a huge farm. Long shadows from the red clapboard barn fell across them, darkening parts of the pasture. It was neither night nor day; the parking lot seemed gray-blue and ghostly, suspended in time.

He unlocked the passenger's door and helped her into the sedan, then got in the other side. Her head was pressed back against the headrest. His fingers drummed a beat on the steering wheel as he watched her. Her closed eyelids seemed so delicate, so fragile.

Her eyes fluttered open and she saw him watching her. For a second she was confused. She passed a hand across her eyes, then a soft moan broke the heavy silence.

"It's not a dream, is it? Not some lousy, stinking nightmare?" Her voice strangled on the words.

"No, *cara*," he answered, "it's not a dream."

She couldn't help the tears that rolled down her cheeks and she made no attempt to wipe them away.

He started the car. The roar of the massive engine was a loud intruder in the early-morning stillness.

"Try to get some rest," he said to her as he backed out of the parking space. "It's been a long night."

"You mean it's going to be a very long day." She reached into the backseat for her purse, pulled out a pad and pen, and started listing what had to be done, who had to be told.

Franco watched her as they waited at a red light. Her pointed chin was thrust forward and her jaw had hardened into a line of stone.

He shook his head and gunned the engine as the light turned green.

When it hit her, it would hit her hard.

Chapter Four

The days between John's accident and his funeral passed in a dark whirling blur for Stacey and everyone else concerned. She and Dee and Chris huddled together in the office, while Stacey made arrangements for the nondenominational services. The phone rang incessantly—shocked clients calling to offer their condolences, some saying they'd be coming up from Florida or in from California to attend the funeral, others sending enormous floral tributes that made Stacey want to scream with rage.

Franco Borelli had been wonderful; that first terrible day he had made all the necessary funeral arrangements. Stacey had been numb, as numb as if she'd been drugged.

"When is Mr. Borelli coming back?" Chris asked as they sat in the kitchen of the office, drinking tea the day before the funeral.

"Tomorrow." Stacey rubbed her eyes, then grimaced at the black mascara smears on her hand. For the past few days she hadn't been wearing makeup and she'd forgotten she had it on.

"He seems like a lovely person," the older woman continued. "He really didn't have to do all that he has for us."

"No, he didn't," Stacey said reluctantly. "He was a tremendous help that night." He really *had* been wonderful to all of them, but especially to her. Her hand still seemed to hold the memory of his warmth and strength as he supported her that long, awful night in New Jersey. If only he hadn't been introduced as a prospective partner, she might have allowed herself to like him.

She shook her head. No matter—there would be no new partner. She would do her all to keep Andersen-Bradley afloat now, on her own, even if it meant working all day, every day, for no matter how long it took her. It was the least she could do for John. For his memory.

After the funeral service she opened her home to some of the mourners. Her small apartment was full of people. She had forgotten that many of them had brought spouses along, people who had shared dinners with Stacey and John or long lunches at computer-service conferences.

In her kitchen she filled the enormous rented coffee urn with cold water, added the correct amount of coffee, and turned it on. She was arranging small sandwiches on a platter when her sister came in.

"You doing okay, Stace?"

Stacey brushed her hair off her face with the side of her arm and smiled at her sister's concern. "I'm doing okay. I just didn't expect such a mob to come back here."

Dianne took another platter out of the cabinet over the refrigerator and started arranging deviled eggs and other tidbits on it. "A lot of people cared for Johnny," she said.

Stacey's eyes started to fill and she found it hard to see the platter before her. "He was a hell of a nice guy, Dianne. There'll never be another like him. Never." Her words were choked.

Dianne wiped her hands on the dish towel and put her arms around her younger sister. "Let go, Stace. You've been wonderful through this. You can let it out now."

She stiffened in Dianne's arms and lifted her head. "No, I'm fine. Really."

She was afraid if she ever did let go she wouldn't be able to stop.

"By the way, where is Al? Did he have to go out of town?" Her brother-in-law and John had been fairly friendly.

Dianne shifted uncomfortably. "In a manner of speaking." She picked up a full platter of food and headed for the kitchen door. "I'll explain it later, okay?"

"You two aren't having trouble, are you?"

Dianne didn't answer her question. Instead, she said, "Don't worry," and left the kitchen.

Stacey finished arranging the platter then returned to her guests. She had no time to think of Dianne's and Al's problems for, as she moved through the dining area and living room, she was stopped many times.

"Take your time with the new job," Jack from Hofstra University said as he sipped his Scotch. "There's no rush."

"Don't worry, I'll keep you busy with mailing lists," Rita from Gallagher Brothers School Supplies told her, smiling through ten layers of Pan-Cake makeup.

"We won't let you down, kid," they all said.

Stacey retreated back into the kitchen on the pretext of getting more ice. Once alone, she sank onto a kitchen chair and rested her head on her arms. At the touch of a hand on her shoulder she turned and looked up into Franco's amber eyes. He sat down next to her, impeccably groomed in a suit as black as ebony. He looked so in control, so in charge, that she longed to hand this whole day over to him and ask him to take care of her as he had a few days ago. She chuckled. She knew she really *must* be overtired.

"How are you doing, *cara*?"

She shrugged, then sighed. "Okay. You know, I must be stupid but it never occurred to me that some of our clients might jump ship now that John's—" She couldn't finish the sentence. "I didn't realize anyone would feel that way."

Franco was silent for a moment. "They may not realize you were the backbone of the company."

She pushed her hand through her heavy hair, holding it off her face, then chuckled. "How come *you* realize it?"

He leaned back in his chair. "John and I had some long talks the past few weeks." He smiled at her upraised eyebrows. "Yes, we talked about you. He said you were the heart and soul of the company and he was the mouth."

She laughed genuinely, the first time in days. Franco smiled again, happy to see some life in her gaunt face.

"It's true. Thank God he was good at those things. I never really liked those long lunches with boring clients, making small talk over the breadsticks—" She stopped, horrified, as she saw the grin spread across his face. "Oh, God, I'm sorry! I didn't mean it like that."

"I know. But admit you weren't exactly delighted to lunch with me last week."

She blushed with good grace. "No, I really wasn't. Was it only last week?" Her smile faded. "It seems like a few lifetimes ago. Things change so fast."

"That's a very sad truth but, unfortunately, a truth nevertheless." He stood up and, for a second, rested his hand on top of her blond head, his long fingers burrowing deep into the silky curls. A rush of warmth bubbled through her veins. "Can I be of help in any way?"

"Would you check the bar and see if I need anything? I didn't expect so many people to show up."

He smiled. "At your service, *signorina,*" he said and left the room.

She lifted her hand and briefly touched the spot on her head where his hand had been, then sighed and got up to get some ice. By now, more was probably needed.

By 6 P.M. everyone had left and Stacey and her sister were alone in a room filled with paper cups, overflowing ashtrays, crushed packs of cigarettes, and the mingled smells of smoke and perfume and food.

Hands on hips, Stacey stood near the bookcases and looked at the footprints on the ivory rug, at the wet rings on the walnut end tables, and at her sister, who was sprawled on the pale yellow-and-green couch, her head drooping against her shoulder.

"Well," Stacey finally said, wrinkling her nose at the sight, "I think the thing to do now is move."

Dianne groaned in agreement. "It will take hours to simply air this place out." She sat up and began to pile dirty plates and cutlery on the low coffee table. "Might as well get started."

The two women fell into the remembered rhythm they had shared as children cleaning up their grandmother's kitchen each night after dinner.

Finally, just before nine, the apartment was straightened, they were both showered and dressed in robes. A pot of tea and leftover sandwiches waited on the coffee table. Stacey switched on a "golden oldies" radio station and adjusted the volume so it was just a backdrop to conversation. Dianne curled up at one end of the couch and Stacey took her favorite seat in the enormous circular chair that was covered in a silky, fine-wale corduroy fabric of deep peach. By unspoken agreement they steered clear of what had happened that day: talk of the funeral and the future of Andersen-Bradley were off limits. Their chatter flitted like a butterfly from their mother's latest letter to the new car Dianne had been thinking of getting, to the high cost of gasoline.

They fell quiet when an early Beatles' song filled the room.

"I remember when that came out," Stacey remarked when the song ended. "Mother had just married that cowboy from Texas and—"

Dianne waved her hand to stop her. "No, no, small fry, you remember wrong. The cowboy was number three. That song came out when she was married to the guy with the dry-cleaning business in New Hampshire. You were only about seven years old then."

"Spoken from the privileged viewpoint of an eleven-year-old?"

"Precisely." Dianne laughed. "Just remember: I'll *always* be your older sister."

"Just *you* remember it when you turn forty first," Stacey retorted. She looked at her sister, a twinkle in her green eyes.

"Being older has had its advantages," Dianne answered with a matching twinkle in her own eyes. "Do you remember the year Grandma let me start wearing makeup and you were insanely jealous?"

Stacey groaned at the memory. "You suddenly seemed so grown-up with your pastel peach lipgloss and your blush-on. It took all my willpower to keep from throwing that shiny blue makeup case of yours in the incinerator."

"You came close, though," Dianne shook her head. "When you hid my lipstick before my big date with Kevin Reilly, I wanted to throw *you* in the incinerator."

Stacey laughed at her sister, whose voice had grown higher in unconscious imitation of her younger self. "Grandma's rule about no makeup and no dates until sixteen seemed very arbitrary to me then."

Dianne grinned. "That's because you were twelve."

"Exactly!" Stacey grew thoughtful for a moment, then shook her head, blond waves dipping across her face. "I felt like you had been initiated into a secret society where you and Grandma both knew the secret word—"

"Maybelline!" Dianne broke in.

"No, I'm serious, Di. Suddenly you'd grown up and I was left behind with a fresh-scrubbed face and a copy of *How To Meet Boys* for company."

Dianne got up and gave Stacey a hug. "Poor little sister! I had no idea you were feeling so abandoned. I thought you were just jealous of Kevin."

"There was that," Stacey admitted with a chuckle, "but everytime I saw you getting ready to go out I had this urge to lock the door so you couldn't leave."

What she couldn't say was, at sixteen, Dianne suddenly looked so much like their mother that it almost hurt Stacey to look at her. When her sister dressed for a date, Stacey would have the swift, clear vision of their mother spinning brightly through their orbit on her way to another marriage.

Dianne grew serious. "I think I understand," she said after a moment. "I felt that way when Al and I moved up to Westchester—like all my old landmarks were gone and no one had bothered to give me a new roadmap."

The sisters were quiet for a while, listening to music

and sipping their tea. When they were finished, Stacey got up and brought the empty plates and cups into the kitchen, then returned with a platter of cookies and a fresh pot of tea. As she poured them each a cup, she noticed her sister seemed a little distracted.

"You know," she said, sitting down next to Dianne, "you can call Al if you want to touch base with him. I can afford a phone call, Dianne."

Dianne said nothing, just sipped her tea and kept her eyes on the small watercolor on the wall behind Stacey's head.

Stacey changed the subject. "The office is closed tomorrow and won't reopen until Monday. I thought I'd drive out to see Grandma. Can you come along?"

Dianne nodded. "Sure. I arranged to have tomorrow off and since the next day is Saturday, I thought I'd stay the weekend if you'd have me."

"Of course I'll have you. But won't Al be getting antsy without his wife?" She narrowed her green eyes when she saw the uncomfortable look on Dianne's face. "Di! You haven't done anything stupid, have you?"

Dianne got up and walked behind the couch, running her hand along the back of the furniture.

"This may be one hell of a time to tell you, but you've probably already guessed. I left Al, Stacey."

"What!" Stacey jumped, nearly knocking her tea into her lap. "I can't believe this. I didn't think you'd be that stupid!"

"Wait a second," Dianne said, blushing. "I don't think that's fair, Stace."

Her sister stared at her. "Not fair?" Her voice was high with outrage. "Al is crazy about you." She groaned. "Is there somebody else? Another man?"

Dianne shrugged. "It's nothing like that. Actually it's

nothing concrete at all. It's just that I've been married all my life—I've made a *career* out of being married. You may not understand, Stace, but I'll level with you: Al and I have been together for eleven years now and after that long you begin not to see the other person. I need to know if I'm with him because I want to be or because I'm afraid *not* to be. Can you understand that?''

Stacey shook her head. ''I don't know... you seemed so happy, Dianne. You two were the happiest couple I've ever known. I've always wanted to find a relationship just like yours. Sometimes I think that's why I said yes when Michael asked me to marry him—I envied you your marriage so much that I wanted one of my own.''

Her sister came to sit beside her on the couch. ''I'm changing, Stacey. Just being married isn't enough for me anymore.''

''But you have your job—''

''Not the one I really want. I'm thinking of going back to college nights to get a really good job.''

''You can have a good job without a degree,'' Stacey said. ''I do.''

''You started young. I'm thirty—it's a lot harder for me. Besides, you didn't have a husband to divert you.''

''Touché.''

''I didn't mean it as an insult, Stacey, but it's true. I wanted so much to be a good wife and to make my marriage last that I put myself in last place all the time.''

''Did you explain this to Al? He's a reasonable man. He'd understand.''

Dianne shook her head. ''I tried. But he felt insulted and threatened and said maybe we should have a baby. Maybe that would fulfill me.''

''Maybe it would. I wish I had that option.''

Her sister glared at her. "That's not the answer to everything, Stacey. You just think so because you don't have that option."

Stacey's face burned. Dianne sighed and reached for the younger woman's hand. "I didn't mean to hurt you. I just want you to see that being fertile doesn't mean you'll have a good relationship or happiness or success. All it means is you can give birth to a child. The rest is still up to you to provide for yourself." She squeezed Stacey's hand. "I want a family but not until I'm sure of who I am. I don't want to end up like Mother."

"I like your philosophy," Stacey said, "but you should have made that speech to Michael when I was in the hospital."

Dianne frowned. "Michael was—and is—a fool, Stace. I think we both know that."

Stacey didn't respond to that. "Are you getting a divorce?" she asked.

Dianne shrugged. "I don't know. We're going to try it apart for a while, then decide." Stacey looked so forlorn and lost that Dianne got up and put her arms around her. "Listen, I know this was a lousy time to break it to you, but there was just no way I could hide it anymore. I'd wanted to tell you what I was thinking about doing the night of my party."

"I know. I know." Stacey wiped at her eyes. "It just seems like everything around me is changing faster than I can handle it. It scares me." She blew her nose into a Kleenex. "You're not dating, are you?"

"Not yet." Dianne shook her head. "That will certainly be an experience after all this time."

"You can spare me the details, thank you. Frankly, the thought of you with another man makes my skin crawl. Change isn't *always* a good thing, Di."

Dianne smiled and sat back down. "Well, I know one thing that never changes: Grandma. You'll get your bearings back tomorrow, mark my words."

Dianne was right. The visit to the retirement village where her grandmother lived put Stacey's feet back on solid ground. Lillian Newton, at eighty-four, still had the wit and lively personality she had at forty-four. Stacey and Dianne would have willingly taken Lillian into their homes but the old woman wanted to be totally independent and have a home of her own. When the neighborhood began to be rife with robberies and muggings, the two sisters found her a lovely retirement complex on eastern Long Island and, with their mother's reluctant assistance, convinced Lillian the time had come to move. Lillian paid rent and utilities with the social security and the pension she received from her years working for an insurance company. Stacey and Dianne helped pay the rest of her expenses.

Stacey knew her grandmother would have read about John's death in *Newsday,* and although her grandmother wouldn't have expected her this weekend, Stacey thought it best to see her and explain it all personally.

"Let's not tell her about Al yet," Dianne advised as they knocked on the front door to their grandmother's attached house. "There's enough for her to absorb without hitting her with that too."

Stacey agreed and had an enormous smile in place when Mary, the aide supplied through Lillian's pension plan, opened the door and let them in.

"Your grandmother's been waiting all morning," Mary said as they went down the hallway to Lillian's room. "Could hardly get her to do her exercises," she added with a laugh.

"Grandma, what's this?" Stacey asked as she entered the bedroom. Lillian was sitting up in bed, propped up by a horde of fluffy pillows. "Your arthritis acting up again?"

The white-haired woman, with clear green eyes like her two granddaughters, brushed off the question with a wave of her gnarled hand.

"It's this damp spring weather," she answered, sounding annoyed with the season. "It gets into my joints and gives me a little trouble. In a couple of days I'll be just fine. That slavedriver Mary"—she motioned toward the middle-aged woman who stood in the doorway smiling—"makes sure I do exactly what Dr. Bagarozzi says."

Dianne went into the kitchen to help Mary make lunch and Stacey sat by the bed, holding her grandmother's hand and talking about John.

"He was a desperately unhappy man since losing Margie and Jill," Lillian said, stroking Stacey's curls. "You must understand that. Life became a burden he could no longer support."

"You talk as if he committed suicide, Grandma." Her voice was indignant.

Lillian picked up the paper and showed her a small column on the sixth page. "It says here that the truck driver swears John saw him and heard the horn blow."

Stacey sighed. "What they forgot to tell you is the autopsy found he'd had another heart seizure and that's what probably caused him to fall into the path of the truck."

Lillian folded the paper and placed it on her nightstand. "We'll never know the truth, my dear. But I hope he'll find some peace now. Life was very unkind to him."

Stacey felt the long-withheld tears build up again and she turned away for a second to regain her composure.

"Don't be afraid to cry in front of me," her grandmother said gently. "I won't be upset. It's natural you should grieve for him."

"I'm not crying, Grandma."

Lillian arched a white brow. "It might do you some good, child. It may have helped John if he'd been able to express *his* grief. Tears ease the pain."

Stacey shook her head. "Tears never kept Mother from leaving Dianne and me, did they?" She sounded bitter. "They're not going to bring John back either."

Lillian sighed and ran her hand across her granddaughter's blond head. "Oh, child, I can see the same look in your eyes now that you used to have as a little girl each time Maryann left after a visit. Can't you cry for John and have done with it?"

"No, Grandma, it wouldn't help anything at all." She smiled. "All I'd end up with is a bright red nose and some wet Kleenex." She patted Lillian's hand. "Don't worry—I'll be fine."

I have to be fine, she thought as she left her grandmother's room. *Everything's up to me now.*

Just before dinnertime, Stacey and Dianne got their jackets and said good-bye to Mary. Lillian was dozing, an effect of the drugs her doctor had prescribed to ease the pain of her arthritis.

"How is she really?" Stacey asked Mary as she slipped into her rust-colored leather blazer.

Mary rolled her eyes heavenward. "Crotchety as ever. I'm almost glad she's in bed for a few days: it was either her or me."

The two young women laughed with her. They knew

Lillian was known as a handful around the retirement complex.

Dianne gave Mary a check for that month's groceries, then, after Stacey's promise to come back the following week, the two women hurried down the crushed stone path to the Corvette. The memory of their grandmother's warmth carried them through the rest of the bittersweet weekend until Dianne left for White Plains Sunday night and Stacey was again left alone with her sorrow.

She got to the office early Monday morning and was surprised to see Chris and Dee already there. A funereal air still lingered, although the two older women had made sure they disposed of the floral arrangements and sympathy cards before Stacey arrived.

After coffee she went down the corridor to her office, averting her eyes as she passed the closed door to John's office. Sooner or later, she knew she would have to go in there and sort through his papers and do all the things that would conjure up memories she didn't yet know if she could bear. She hung the jacket of her dark green linen suit on the coathook by the bathroom door, then went in to check her makeup.

The face that stared back at her was thin; the green eyes, above prominent cheekbones, dominated her face. She had used foundation to try to alleviate the paleness of her skin but had stopped short of blusher—the result right now would have been clownish. Her hair was pulled back into a chignon at the base of her neck; soft tendrils of honey-blond hair framed her face and cheeks, softening the stark effect. The lemon-yellow blouse, while lovely, only emphasized the fatigue visible on her face.

Her telephone was ringing and she hurried from the bathroom to pick it up.

"Is everything going well?" Franco Borelli's voice, rich with that curiously elegant accent of his, floated into her ear.

"Fairly so." A small smile played at the corners of her mouth. "I want to thank you again for being so kind to me during all of this. I don't know how I can repay you."

He was silent a moment before answering. "I know how."

She stiffened and waited for him to explain.

"I'd like to see you today," he finally said. "I have a few business questions to ask."

"If it's about the partnership, please spare us both a lot of aggravation."

"It has nothing to do with that. Give me credit, please, for a little sensitivity."

She flushed. "Sorry," she muttered.

"I'd like to talk about time-sharing on your new system."

"They don't have Compu-500's in New Jersey?"

"My family lives in New Jersey. I have an apartment in Manhattan and your system is the only accessible one within miles. The bigger companies keep theirs in use twenty-four hours a day."

"Well, I'm afraid ours is in use constantly during business hours. I don't really know when you could possibly use it."

"I couldn't use it during normal business hours anyway," he countered smoothly. "After six P.M. is better for me."

She sighed. It hadn't occurred to her that he'd be willing to drive forty miles each way after hours for the

Compu-500. "All right," she said. She had too many other problems to prolong this. "Can you come in this afternoon around three and we'll work out the details?"

When she hung up, she was surprised to notice her heart pounding at a more rapid rate. Franco had a very strange effect on her—a slowly escalating sense of controlled electricity that both intrigued and frightened her. No man, not even Michael, had made her feel so vulnerable, so exposed to life. Franco seemed to be a man she could easily become interested in and there was no way on earth she could allow that to happen.

By the time three o'clock rolled around, she was ready to call it a day. For almost four hours she'd been in conference with their corporate attorney, Joe Dumas, who had read her the very bad news on Andersen-Bradley. There were a number of unexplained losses that neither she nor Joe could account for. And, to top it off, John died intestate, which promised a tremendous legal hassle over rights and privileges concerning his estate. Much of the company was covered by virtue of their incorporation, but the situation was looking very poor.

Joe didn't need to tell her that cash flow would be tight and, in order to meet payroll, she would have to take a drastic cut in pay, provided they could pay her at all. She rubbed her temples, trying to ease the anvil pounding behind her eyes. She hadn't told Joe, but she was pretty sure John had kept the safety-deposit box they'd rented for the company papers, back when they were sharing a tiny office in Floral Park. When she could bear it, she would have to search his desk and see if she could find the key. She didn't particularly want to dismantle his office; at this point there was really no need to, since the client files were maintained in a separate area. She preferred to leave John's office intact, at least until she could gather the necessary strength to remove his personal effects.

She herself had once possessed a duplicate key to the safety-deposit box, but it had disappeared during one of her apartment moves. She smiled now, recalling the day she'd confessed the awful news to John. He'd been extremely sympathetic—after he'd chastised her for being so careless as to mislay it. The key never had turned up and she'd chalked up the experience as one of life's many mysteries. John had retained the original key, and the entire matter had been dropped.

She knew that the bank where the safety-deposit box was stored held a master key, but without the client's counterpart key, it was impossible to unlock the safety vault. Another key would have to be ordered—meaning a stack of paperwork—and Stacey couldn't be bothered with the hassle.

There was a knock on her door and Franco walked in. Involuntarily, she glanced down at her watch.

"Three P.M. and ten seconds," he said with a smile. "Do I get penalized?"

"Not this time," she teased. "But don't make a habit of it."

Suddenly she felt ill-at-ease, terribly uncomfortable with this virtual stranger with whom she had shared such a personal and devastating loss. A part of her wanted to reach out and touch him to thank him for his unflagging kindness, but another part of her wanted to hide. He had seen her at her most vulnerable, and worse, he was beginning to have too much power over her emotions.

She listened uneasily as he outlined his time-sharing proposal, reserving judgment till he had finished. He wanted to rent computer time from seven to eleven every evening and all day Sunday. Since he was working on a new way of doing payroll and inventory for his father's clothing firm, he explained, sharing the Compu-500 would save thousands of dollars each year—money that he could invest for his father.

"I don't know," Stacey said finally. "What if we need the system one night? Our workload runs hot and cold and it's hard to say in advance what our needs will be."

"Let me be blunt with you, Stacey." He leaned forward, resting his powerful hands on top of her desk, fingers splayed out on the wood. "Your financial situation is terrible." He motioned for her to be quiet. "Don't deny it. I saw your books. I know. The income you can pick up from time-sharing with me can enable you to meet some of your operating costs without going any further into the red than you already are."

She became annoyed, her green eyes flashing warning signals. "I can't see the point in fouling up our own working schedule to accommodate yours simply for a little extra money. No, but thank you, anyway."

He quoted her a dollar amount that made her sit back and emit a low whistle. He was right. It *would* make a tremendous difference. They batted amounts and times back and forth until Stacey's head was swimming with figures and her brain ready to burst from her skull.

"All right! All right! I can't take any more." She extended her hand across the desk. "It's a deal." She grinned. "For the last price quoted."

He repeated the number and she nodded, suppressing a wide smile.

"From seven to eleven Monday through Friday and half a day on Sunday, right?"

She nodded. "Provided we have the option of extra time if we give you twenty-four hours' notice."

He agreed and they both sat back, watching one another, admiring each other's business savvy. Again he was dressed impeccably in a navy blue blazer with brass buttons, perfectly proportioned gray flannel pants that skimmed his muscular legs, and a tone-on-tone white silk shirt with French cuffs fastened by discreet circular gold cuff links. On his right wrist he wore a thin gold watch that she instantly recognized as one of those pricey Baume & Mercier models she had coveted. Her eyes strayed to his left hand and she was annoyed when she felt relieved to see he wasn't married.

"I may just not wear a wedding ring, *cara,*" he said in that lazy, honeyed voice of his.

"Don't be flattered," she snapped back to cover her discomfiture. "You can tell more than marital status by looking at a man's hands."

"And what else can you tell about me?" he asked, his tone light and teasing.

"That you've probably never worked a decent day in your life." She instantly regretted her flip remark when she saw the way his face hardened, shutting her out completely.

"I'll be going." He stood and buttoned his coat.

"Don't you want—"

He spoke right over her words. "My secretary will be sending you the necessary information, and I trust Chris or Dee will forward an agreement."

She nodded. She had obviously offended him and she was sorry but the words stuck in her throat.

"Good day." Without shaking her hand, he turned and left her office.

She was between a rock and a hard place. Andersen-

Bradley needed his money to get them over this rough period, but she needed his electric presence as much as she needed the measles. He spelled danger for her, an end to her enforced isolation from the real world and she knew that was something she couldn't handle. Not now. Not ever.

The office closed at five. The first day without John's presence had been emotionally draining for all of them and by the time she double-locked the door and got into her Corvette, Stacey felt as if all her bones had collapsed. It was still light out and the sun splashed a lemony-yellow light over everything, making even the highway, with its hood-to-trunk traffic, seem lovely.

Suddenly she couldn't bear the thought of going home to that tomb-silent apartment, so she drove past her exit and headed for the health spa in the South Shore shopping center near her apartment.

An hour later she dived into the blissfully empty pool. She let the cool water buoy her sagging spirits, help her float over the rough spots in her life, wash Franco from her thoughts.

She only wished she could capture this feeling of control that she had when swimming when she she was on dry land. Maybe then she could dispatch Franco Borelli before she lost control of her emotions.

Swimming blocked out everything but the movement of her arms and legs, the smell of chlorine that reminded her of clothes on a line on washday, the rushing of the water past her ears as she swiftly, cleanly, glided across the pool.

There was no room in there for sorrow or fear, no Franco Borelli with his magnetic pull—none of the things that threatened to change her life.

Just her and the water and the swift economy of her strokes as she did her laps, faster and faster, until finally she clung to the edge of the pool, her breath coming in hard, tearing gasps, exhausted but at peace. In control of things. In the water, no one could hurt her, nothing could possibly go wrong.

Chapter Five

Charlie stood in front of Stacey's desk, shifting his weight from foot to foot as he stammered through his explanations.

"I don't want to leave you in the lurch, Ms. Andersen," he said, red-faced, "but when ITG made me that offer, well, you know—"

She sighed and rubbed her temples. "I know, Charlie. It was an offer you couldn't refuse." She looked up at the young man, who probably was no more than a year younger than herself, and forced a smile. "I appreciate your honesty, Charlie, and you know you'll get the finest references." She toyed with the felt-tip pen on her desk. "When will your last day be?"

"Friday." At the look of shock on her face, he hurried to add, "But if it's a problem, they said they'd hold the job another week for me until you can find someone else."

"Don't worry," she answered. "We can manage with just Roy in there."

We can manage better than you know, she thought as the young man stumbled his way out of her office. There just wasn't that much work to be done any longer. She flipped through the pile of unanswered letters on her desktop, recalling how five of their best accounts had recently pulled their work out and taken it to larger national companies. Oh, they'd had their reasons for leaving: "...better rates...quicker turnovers... dividends...."

With the cash coming in slower than it was going out, there was no way Stacey could bargain with the companies—with Charlie, with Dee, whom she'd had to let go the week before, or with almost anyone. Chris accepted a 10 percent cut in pay, but Stacey had reduced her hours so she could have more time with her family, especially now that the baby was coming. She herself hadn't drawn salary in the two weeks since John had died, and she was feeling the pinch in her dwindling savings account. Certain expenses were unavoidable, the most important of which was her share of her grandmother's bills.

She laughed hollowly as she looked around at her beautiful office, at the sensuous carpeting, the wall system with the stereo that played soft, almost subliminal music all day, at the paneled walls and the picture window overlooking the Long Island Sound. Oh, it was going to make a grand impression, this stylish office; it would just knock the socks off all their prospective clients. The only trouble was: There *were* no more prospective clients; there weren't even as many old clients as there used to be. There was no one to enjoy this splendor but Stacey, Chris, and the bank that had so kindly extended all the necessary credit.

She glanced at her wristwatch. Nearly noon. She stood up and stretched, then smoothed the creases in her black trousers and tucked in the back of her gray blouse. It was time to relieve Chris at the front desk so the woman could go to lunch.

As she hurried through the corridor, she couldn't help but notice the quiet coming from the computer room. Instead of the racket of whirring tapes and clicking capacitors, an ominous stillness filled the air.

She pushed the door open. "Anything wrong?"

"Roy didn't show up today," Charlie began slowly, finding it difficult to meet her green eyes.

She leaned against the doorjamb. "And?"

"He found a job in Florida and he's taking a plane out this afternoon to sign a contract."

The breath fled her body in a short gasp. "No notice, no nothing?"

He shook his head, looking miserable. "Nothing. God, I'm sorry, Ms. Andersen."

She brushed his apology aside. "It's not your fault, Charlie. Don't worry about it."

He brushed his red hair off his high forehead in a nervous gesture. "Listen, I'd be glad to stay on and help out," he said, voice filled with dismay over her situation. "They'll hold the job at ITG for me."

She smiled and felt her eyes fill. "ITG is a big, secure firm, Charlie. I want you to take advantage of your opportunity." She gave him a quick hug. "You have Marie and the baby to think about. A-B will come out of this slump." They both blushed—neither one was physically demonstrative by nature. "I'll never forget you for this, Charlie. Not ever."

She turned quickly and hurried from the room, vowing to give Charlie a healthy bonus before he left. If Andersen-Bradley was going down the tubes, she'd make sure they at least went down the tubes with class.

Forty-five minutes later, she was going through some old files in the reception area, engrossed in some of their early advertising brochures, when the buzzer sounded. Joe, their attorney, waved at her through the glass window and she buzzed back to let him in.

"You're playing receptionist?" he asked, his voice serious.

"Chris is at lunch." She kept her own voice light. "I figured I'd come out here and check the files, keep an eye on—"

He cut right through to the heart of the matter. "You had to let Dee go?"

She nodded. "I'm afraid so. She was a luxury we just couldn't afford."

He sat down on the hardback chair and opened his leather portfolio, pulling out a sheaf of papers neatly stored in multicolored plastic binders.

"You're very businesslike today," she said as she took a seat behind the reception desk. "Are all those binders ours?"

He nodded. Usually he responded in kind when she was in a light mood, but his weathered face remained somber. "Unfortunately they are, Stacey."

"What—what are they?"

"Outstanding debts."

"Heat, electricity, security?"

"Gambling, refinancing, and loans."

She stared at him. "I don't get it. Who gambles?"

He flipped through the pages, found what he wanted, and extended it toward her. "That's a photocopy of some of John's gambling debts run up this past year. Take a look at the bottom line."

She did and felt her face drain of all color. "I had no idea," she breathed.

"Neither did I." He handed her more papers, each one making her face turn paler and paler. "You can imagine my shock when my investigators turned this up."

"Why did you send out investigators?"

"With an accidental death, I knew that the insurance company would be sending out investigators of their own, so I decided to look into a few things so there would be no surprises later. It's routine.''

She waved the pile of folders at him. "And this is what you found? I'd hardly call these 'routine.'"

"Neither would I. The problem is," he said, clasping his fingers together and leaning back in his chair, "what do you want to *do* about them?"

"I thought you would know."

"There's always bankruptcy proceedings," he said, then stopped at the sight of her shocked face. "That's a last resort, Stacey. I don't think it will come to that."

He outlined a consolidation system of loans and payment structures that would eliminate A-B's profits for at least six months. From the numbers Joe was quoting, Stacey realized, it would also cut her savings account in less time than that. He advised her to immediately pay off the outstanding debts to the loan sharks "because they can cause more trouble than we can handle." She agreed. Some papers were missing and Joe believed them to be in either John's apartment or office. She kept silent. She knew there was nothing left in the old apartment, but she still hadn't dug up the key to the elusive safety-deposit box that she was more sure than ever he'd kept.

Later that evening she dragged the box of gardening tools from her hall closet and, dressed in shorts and sweat shirt, opened the sliding doors in her living room, and stepped out into the warm May air. The sun was setting over the roofs of the apartment complex, and it bathed everything in a pink-orange glow. She was beyond thought. Everytime she let her mind latch on to the facts and figures Joe had surprised her with that morning, she felt a sense of panic begin to boil over. *Keep ahead,* she told herself, *don't think too much or you'll drown in it.*

There was still a good half hour or so of daylight left and she knew that some hard work would ease her troubled mind. She had just a tiny patch of ground behind her apartment to work on, but she loved it as if it were an acre. Since she'd been raised in a third-floor apartment, the notion of land was something new to her. She realized it wasn't hers legally, but there was a stipulation in her lease that ground-floor tenants could use the backyard for whatever purposes they wished, as long as it was kept in good repair.

So, last year, her first spring there, she had tried her hand at gardening and discovered that the feel of the loamy earth between her fingers, the life-giving smell of it when it was heavy with a summer rain, soothed her the way swimming did.

She knelt down now, knees sinking into the earth that had softened after a bad winter, and pushed her trowel down deep, feeling the texture and richness of the soil. As she turned it, preparing it for the lush round tomatoes, the cucumbers with their delicate bell-shaped yellow flowers, the minty basil, and mouth-watering oregano, she saw the tiny tunnels left by earthworms. She smiled. The first time she'd seen one last year, she remembered letting loose with a blood-curdling scream.

"That ain't nothing, Miss Andersen," Mr. DeLuca, her upstairs neighbor, had told her. "Earthworms do good for you. They keep the soil loose and fertile, makes things grow real fine. You'll see."

He'd helped her plan out her tiny patch of garden to its best advantage and had steered her through the maze of 5-10-5 fertilizers, the A.M. versus P.M. watering controversy, the benefits of tomato cages. Ultimately she had been rewarded with a cornucopia of produce.

She sighed.

Mr. DeLuca was gone now. John was gone.

"Damn," she said. "Damn, damn, damn!" She flung her trowel across the yard and went back inside.

The garden went unattended the next week. It rained steadily, the skies unleashing a continuous, murky-gray sheet of water that seemed never ending. The trowel that she had flung near the barbecue lay rusting in the grass. Every evening when she closed her blinds, she saw it there, accusing her. What effort would it take to unlock the sliding door and slip out and bring it in? A minute, perhaps? Thirty seconds? But she just didn't have the energy to do even that. Each night she averted her eyes and twisted the rod to black out the rain, to lock herself into her cocoon.

She was tired beyond all imagining. The effort of doing the meet-and-greet work and programming and running the computer was taking up all of her time. She was a robot, programmed to rise at four, dress in the dark, and slide behind the wheel of her Corvette. She imagined that even the car knew her routine by rote. Coffee and doughnut from 7-Eleven, newspaper at the candy store down the block from the industrial park, and then straight into the computer room. She tried to get all mechanical work done by three so she could take over the front desk when Chris left for the day. Phone calls were made between three and six. Then she would gather up all the file folders and papers and leave the office, trying to get out before Franco Borelli arrived.

She had only seen him once since their argument. They nodded hello to one another, she told him there was coffee in the kitchen and that had been that. It was funny. She barely knew him, yet she had felt a sadness when she'd seen him, a sense of loss, though she hardly knew why.

No matter. She had no time for sadness or humor or love—they were all luxuries she could ill afford. Her main concerns were keeping a roof over A-B, her grandmother, and herself. Dianne was in the middle of changing jobs and wasn't due to begin her new one until the end of June. Since Al had been having trouble finding an apartment, her sister had decided to stay with their grandmother and let him have the house in White Plains until she returned to start work.

Stacey sighed. She missed Lillian and Dianne, but there was no time to take the hour's drive out to see them. There was barely time to worry about her wardrobe, do her laundry, or have a cavity filled. Her twenty-four hours each day were programmed for optimum efficiency and she prayed no emergency would crop up to foul her schedule. She simply had no *time* for trouble. She already had enough of it.

It rained again the Friday of Memorial Day weekend. In fact, it had been raining almost all of May. Chris's work load at this point was so light that Stacey gave her the day off so she could enjoy a four-day weekend with her family.

Stacey herself was at work by 8 A.M. and had been steadily feeding information through the computer. Around 7 P.M. she decided to break for dinner, and while the water for tea was boiling, she called Dianne to remind her she was going to see her and Lillian—finally!—for lunch the next day. It was a short conversation, and when she hung up the phone, she fixed her tea, took her tuna sandwich out of the tiny refrigerator, and sat down at the Formica table. She switched on her cassette player and was singing along with Billy Joel when she heard footsteps coming down the hallway. Heart pounding, she took her feet off the table and stood up.

"Who is it?" She tried to sound like she wasn't scared to death.

"Is that you, Stacey?" Franco's unmistakable silky-smooth voice echoed in the hallway.

Her relief was so great she felt weak.

"I'm in the kitchen," she called.

She quickly ran her hands through her hair and brushed some crumbs off her T-shirt just before Franco pushed open the door with his elbows and came into the kitchen, hands busy carrying cartons of Szechuan Chinese food that made her mouth water. She jumped up to help him.

"Do you always treat yourself like this?" she laughed as he put the white containers on the ledge by the stove.

"Not always. I was coming down Jericho Turnpike on my way here, realized I was starving, and there was Szechuan Palace staring at me, so...." He shrugged. "What can I say? I have no willpower."

She looked at him then, and a peal of delight bubbled up.

"A private joke?"

"No—I'm sorry." Her cheeks reddened and she stuck her hands in the pockets on her jeans. "It's just that I've never seen you dressed like that before."

He looked down at his own jeans and black T-shirt and smiled back at her. "Did you think I sprang from my mother's womb in a three-piece suit?"

"No, but I *did* figure you were the only infant ever swaddled in a wool blazer from Hardy Amies."

"I like *your* sartorial splendor." His eyes rested for a

quick moment on her full breasts beneath the thin cotton shirt.

Feeling unexpectedly lighthearted, she did a pirouette for him, holding the edges of the T-shirt away from her body like a ballgown. "I always dress for company."

He stepped closer to read the saying on the front of her shirt. " 'No guts-no glory.' I like that."

"It's my motto." She picked up her mug of tea and unfinished sandwich.

"Where are you going?" he asked as he took paper plates from the cabinet over the sink.

"Back to my office. I'm sure this is a private party."

He touched her shoulder, then quickly removed his hand. She had the most luminous eyes he'd ever seen. He wanted her to stay. "Look at all this." He pointed to the four cartons of food. "I bought way too much—even for a man who likes to eat as much as I do. Join me, please."

She hesitated, then melted at the sight of jade-green broccoli coated in a spicy garlic sauce with little curls of scallion sprinkled on top. "I'd love to," she relented.

In moments everything was set out on the tiny table, glasses of Pepsi were poured and they were seated opposite one another, munching spring rolls and savoring the hot-and-sour soup, as they enjoyed the music on the cassette and the easy conversation that both surprised and delighted them.

She was shocked when she looked at her watch and saw that it was a little after nine. "Can you believe the time?" She stood up and started piling paper plates to toss into the garbage. "I'd better finish what I was doing so you can get started."

"Don't rush on my account. The system can handle two programs at once."

"No," she said, putting the Pepsi bottle back in the refrigerator. "I'd better get moving. I have to leave early tomorrow morning for—"

He waved his hand. "You don't owe me any explanation about your social life."

"Oh, it's nothing like that. I'm—" She stopped abruptly when she realized he had turned away from her and was busying himself with wiping soy sauce from the Formica tabletop. What did he care about her social life, anyway? For all she knew, he had a stable of beautiful women waiting for him in Manhattan while he worked out here in the "sticks" of suburban Long Island. And, more to the point, what did she care what he thought, anyway?

She stood awkwardly for a moment, her arms dangling at her sides, waiting for him to finish cleaning the tabletop so she could say something, anything, to break the heavy silence in the room. Finally she just murmured her thanks for the meal and slipped out of the kitchen.

By 10:30 she'd finished all she'd planned to do and was zipping the front of her Windbreaker when Franco came into the computer room.

"Is it still raining?" she asked as she put some papers into her briefcase and took her car keys from her purse.

He shook his head. "Not the last time I looked out the window. But be careful on the road. It's flooding out near the overpasses."

She nodded.

"Do you take the highway home?"

She nodded again. "As far as Deer Park Avenue," she said. "The highway is more well-lighted at night than the local roads." She gave him a quick smile. "Well, see you Tuesday."

She hurried through the parking lot, car keys in her hand, and got into the Corvette. She ran through a mental checklist to assure herself she had locked her office door, left the packages in the chute for the messenger service, and was pleased she had apparently thought of everything.

Well, almost everything.

A few blocks away from her apartment she noticed the needle of the gas indicator was almost on *E* and she pulled into the only open gas station in her neighborhood.

A young attendant, tall, loose-hipped, and angry-looking, stepped up to her window.

"Fill it, please." She handed him the key to the gas tank.

She reached to her right to get her wallet from her purse, rummaged through crumpled Kleenex, small spiral notebooks, makeup, and loose change. Then, suddenly, in a clear vision, she saw her own kitchen table with her brown wallet centered near the sugar bowl.

She popped open her seat belt and leaped out.

"Wait! I don't have my wallet."

"Great!" The attendant yanked the nozzle out and splashed gasoline on the asphalt. "I've already given you six dollars' worth. Couldn't you have told me sooner?"

She apologized but he glared at her and demanded, "So now what?"

She stood there in the slight drizzle, under the floodlights on Deer Park Avenue and, not for the first time, was reminded how much she had leaned on John. There was no one to bail her out now.

"The only thing I can do," she told the boy who

stood there, hands on hips, jaw set, "is go home and get the money for you."

"You're not taking that car."

"I'll leave it here," she offered, growing frightened. "I'll walk home and bring the money back, okay?"

He shrugged and looked out at traffic, spitting toward the curb.

"I'll be open only fifteen minutes more," he finally said. "If you're not back, I'm pulling your car into the shop."

She sighed. It was dark and late, and she knew she'd never make it back in time.

She walked fast, concentrating on not being afraid, and had gotten two blocks when she heard a horn honk—once, twice, three times. She wouldn't look. Kids, probably, out looking for a good time, some Friday-night fun. She swallowed hard, preparing to scream "Fire" when someone called her name in a voice she was coming to know very well.

He leaned over and flung open the passenger door to his large black Buick.

"What the hell are you doing walking around here?" Franco sounded angry, and strangely, that pleased her.

She told him what had happened. "What are *you* doing here?" she asked.

He motioned to some papers in the backseat. "I found them under the table in the computer room. They looked urgent and I figured you might need them this weekend."

He made an abrupt U-turn on the empty road and took her back to the station, where he paid her bill.

"If you follow me back to my apartment, I'll reimburse you."

"Don't worry about it," he said, plunging his hands

into the pockets of his jeans. "Give it to me on Tuesday."

"No," she said, reluctant to let him go. "I couldn't. I wouldn't feel right about it."

It was ridiculous—to be so concerned about repayment of such a small sum and they both knew it. However, he agreed and she started her car.

The windshield wipers were no match for the rain. The few blocks to her apartment complex took longer than usual. She kept glancing back in her rearview mirror to make sure he was still there. Her car cut through the mud in the unpaved driveway to the complex and she pulled into the residents' lot, motioning for him to do the same. He parked behind her, right near the side door to her apartment. Drops of rain bounced off the slickly waxed hood of his car.

"I'll wait here," he told her as she opened the door.

"Don't be foolish. It's awful out here. The least I can do for you now is make some coffee."

He nodded and followed her into her apartment.

The brown wallet was right where she thought. "I really appreciate this," she said as she handed him the money.

He stuffed the bills into his back pocket. "It wasn't anything, Stacey, really."

She cleared her throat and pushed her curly hair back from her forehead. "Do you know," she said, trying to make a joke to break the tension in the kitchen, "I haven't been able to get a brush through this mop since the rains began? I was getting a headache from keeping it pulled back in a chignon all the time." She reached back and started to twist the thick blond hair into a knot at the nape of her neck.

He reached out and clasped her wrist, his fingers completely encircling it. "Don't," he said, surprising himself by his action. "It's too beautiful to try to control."

He released her wrist and she looked at it, amazed not to see some kind of mark there from the heat of his touch. Her hair fluttered again around her face.

They both grew very quiet, avoiding each other's eyes, acutely aware of the hour, of being alone, of the intimacy of the dimly lit kitchen with the rain splashing against the windows.

She started the coffee water, put in the filter, and added the fresh-ground beans.

"Excuse me a second." She walked through the long narrow hallway to the catch-all closet for some chocolate chip cookies. As she turned she brushed against three cans of tomato soup. They fell to the floor with a bang that was startling in the silent apartment.

"Are you okay?"

He was standing next to her, his hand on her shoulder, as she bent down to pick up the soup cans. It took her a moment to stand and, when she did, he didn't make room for her. She felt a twitch in the corner of her mouth.

"I'd better see if the coffee's ready."

"It isn't," he answered, putting both hands on her shoulders.

He was so close to her that her skin became sonar, registering his presence. She let her eyes fill on the amber wine of his, tracing slowly over the prominent nose and down over the planes of his cheekbones, the full, sensuous mouth. How easy it would be to lean forward and kiss him, she thought, if only to break this magical spell she was falling under. But she knew if she did that there would be yet more decisions to make, and everything would change. She couldn't risk it.

She averted her eyes. "You have work to do tonight."

He chuckled and stepped aside. "You're right. So we'd better rush the coffee, right, Stacey?"

"Right."

He wouldn't sit at the table at first. Instead he drank the coffee as he stood by the refrigerator. She watched him lift his right hand and look at his watch.

"You're a lefty, I see."

"No, I'm not. What made you say that?"

"You wear your watch on your right wrist."

"So?"

She shrugged. "Usually only lefties do that."

"Do you always notice such things?"

She blushed. She'd noticed everything.

Her kitchen was different with him there. He seemed too big for it, larger-than-life, adding tensions and vibrations that threatened to rock her already shaky foundations and cause problems far worse than those at Andersen-Bradley. Problems she could never fix.

He looked at her levelly and she noticed a tiny freckle on his right eyelid.

"Have you ever been married, Stacey?" His voice was golden flame and she was a candle before it.

She shook her head.

"Do you have anyone serious now?"

She laughed. "Not unless he's hiding inside the computer. I don't have time for things like that."

"You don't allow yourself time is more like it."

"How would you know?"

"John told me something about you."

A hot flame of panic seared her belly. "What did he say?"

He smiled. "Nothing bad. Just that you were a terrifically hard worker and he worried you were cheating yourself out of a personal life.''

''I'm only twenty-six,'' she laughed, relieved to know her secrets were safe. ''I think I still have time for that in the future.''

''That's what I thought when I was twenty-six. Time passes quicker than you think.''

She looked at him, intrigued. ''Spoken from the grand vantage point of what—thirty?''

He groaned. ''Thirty-three.''

It was her turn for questions. ''Never married? Married now?''

He shook his head. ''No.'' He raked his hand through his mahogany hair. ''And, the funny thing is, I wish I had been. At least I'd know I'm capable of that kind of deep commitment to someone. That kind of life-long caring must be a beautiful thing to experience. At least I'd like to have risked it.''

Her heart swelled behind her breastbone and for a second she couldn't catch her breath.

He looked at his watch again. ''I'd better go. The machine is running and it's nearly time for a new disk. I didn't expect to be away this long.''

''No, don't leave yet.'' Her words popped out like machine-gun fire. She peeked through a crack in the venetian blinds at her kitchen window. ''It's coming down in sheets. Why don't you sit and have another cup of coffee? Maybe it'll let up some.''

He hesitated a second. She touched his forearm and showed him the bag of chocolate chip cookies. ''Come on, how about it?''

He laughed. ''Okay. I can't resist those cookies.''

''Oh, that explains it. I was going to ask you how you ever knew cookies—especially Linzer tarts—were my passion.''

"It was easy," he said as he lowered himself onto a kitchen chair. "We share the same passions."

He broke a cookie in half, took a bite, then handed her the other part. She chewed and swallowed it, barely aware of the flavor, the texture, aware of nothing but Franco. She fussed around the stove, threw out the old coffee, and boiled water for fresh. He picked up a copy of *Cosmopolitan* from her countertop and flipped through it. She was humming quietly, surprised when she realized what she was doing. She was filled with emotions that terrified her, felt she'd boil over like the coffee just did.

He laughed and the sound made her turn around.

"Look at this!"

She bent over his right shoulder, her hair brushing against his cheek. She felt his warmth, felt herself sway toward it.

"She looks something like you, Stacey." He pointed to a picture of a blond model. "Did you ever think of modeling?"

"You're crazy!" She laughed but was immensely pleased.

"No, really."

He tilted her chin up with his hand. His fingers felt slightly rough on her skin, but it was a tender roughness. She held her breath as he traced her cheekbones with his index fingers.

"You really do. Same bone structure. Look."

He lifted the toaster up.

"You *are* crazy!" She laughed as she looked at her face in the stainless steel.

Although the image was wavy and distorted, a fun house shape, she could see the vulnerable look in her eyes and she looked away.

"Let me make more coffee," she said, a little unsteadily.

She turned back to the stove. She was acutely aware of every sight, every sound, in the room. His chair squeaked against the floor tiles. She turned around and saw him standing a few feet away.

"Care to dance?" he asked, mocking his request with a slow grin.

"Sure," she answered, feeling shy and wild. She moved into his embrace and lowered her head slightly to rest on his shoulder. His hands burned the flesh on her back. She felt his heart pounding violently; it ricocheted off her own. Her breasts flattened against his hard chest; the dampness of his shirt wet the front of her own T-shirt. Her breathing grew rapid, ragged, as she felt him against her hipbone.

"Cara?"

She looked up at him, into those limitless eyes. She couldn't speak. He moved his face to hers, brushed his lips against her hair, her cheek, finally meeting her lips. His touch electrified her. She gasped at the feel of his tongue inside her mouth, the way it traced the contours of her, drawing her breath from her body with its intensity and power. She tasted him, savoring the faint traces of coffee and chocolate, his own sweetness.

"You have to go back to work," she finally said when her mind was hers again. "You left the machine on, remember?"

He looked at her. She shivered. Gently he reached out and cupped her chin with his hand, caressing it.

"Stacey, I think we both know what's happening." He saw the way her lovely green eyes widened with both fear and desire. He knew she wasn't ready, but he had to say it. He couldn't *not* say it. "I want to make love to you, *bellissima cara*."

"I want you to," she said honestly, knowing no other way. "But I'm frightened."

"I would never hurt you." His voice was so tender she feared she'd cry.

"I believe that," she whispered. "But I hardly know you."

They both fell silent. The sound of the rain outside seemed almost a third presence in the quiet kitchen.

"Then we must take it from the beginning," he said, caressing her with his voice. "*Signorina,* may I have the honor of seeing you tomorrow?"

She laughed, charmed by his courtliness. "I would be honored, *Signore* Borelli, but I have a previous engagement."

The amber eyes began to cloud over until she explained about her promise to visit Lillian. She smiled inwardly. He was relieved, she knew, that there was no other man.

"You could meet me out there," she said, surprised by her own initiative. "We could continue on out to Montauk for the day."

"And you'll be mine for the rest of the day?"

"Yes." Her lips brushed against his cheek.

She opened the side door nearest to the parking lot and they stood in front of the screen. The rain blurred everything in sight and yet a heavy, swollen moon illuminated the lot. He turned his collar up and put his hands deep into his pockets.

"Till tomorrow," he said.

"Till tomorrow."

He touched her hair for an instant, then kissed her off center for she had just turned her head to fix her earring. He ran through the rain to his car. His beautiful car, splattered up to the wheel wells with mud from the driveway, sped quickly out of the parking lot and down the road. She watched until the taillights were mere pinpoints in the darkness.

As she stood by the door for a second she was sure she had imagined everything. However the side of her mouth was damp where he'd kissed her. With the tip of her tongue she touched the wet spot, savored the faint coffee taste, then, shivering in the cold night air, went inside and locked the door. She looked at the sheaf of papers he had been bringing to her when he found her walking on the road. Advertising brochures—nothing marked "rush," nothing important.

A shiver of fear and delight blossomed inside as she sat in the dark by her bedroom window and looked out at the rain and the lights and the heavy moon. She had never expected to feel like this again, vulnerable and yearning, but it was already too late to turn back.

She wrapped her arms around her chest and closed her eyes to wait for dawn.

Chapter Six

It was still raining when Stacey reached her grandmother's house the next morning.

"I don't think it's ever going to stop!" Stacey tried to shake some of the moisture from her curly hair and pin it back in a chignon to dry.

Dianne laughed and put her sister's jacket on a hanger to dry in the bathroom. "Grandma says it's time to start building the ark again."

"I think she's right." Stacey adjusted her lipstick then turned to face her sister. "Notice anything?"

Dianne's eyes widened as she inspected her. Stacey was dressed in raspberry twill pants that fit snugly at the ankles, topped by a loosely knit striped sweater in shades of raspberry, aqua, and bone, and cinched by a narrow belt.

"Fantastic! What happened to the conservative Stacey Andersen?"

She blushed and shrugged. "I don't know. I bought this on a whim last spring and never had the nerve to wear it. Today just seemed like the right day."

Dianne arched an eyebrow. "There must be more to this than coming to visit Grandma and me. What's up?"

Struggling to sound casual, Stacey explained about Franco and the afternoon they had planned.

"Do we get to meet this man of mystery?" Dianne asked as they went down the hall to Lillian's room.

Stacey hesitated. "If you want to, though I can't see that it's such a big deal. I'm supposed to pick him up at the train station in Shirley at two o'clock. I guess I could bring him back here to meet you and Grandma."

They stopped for a second at the door to Lillian's room. "Not to change the subject," Stacey said, "but how is Grandma doing?"

Dianne's face sobered. "Not that well, Stace. The pain from the arthritis seems to be worsening and Dr. Bagarozzi has been making noises about sending her to the hospital."

A cold chill ran down Stacey's back. "Is it that bad?"

"It's her age, he says. At eighty-four, even small things become potentially serious. But she just won't listen."

They opened the door. Lillian, looking paler and more fragile than she had two weeks before, said, "Who won't listen? Were you two gabbing about me out there in the hall?"

Dianne laughed and fluffed up the woman's pillows. "There's nothing wrong with Grandma's hearing, as you can tell."

Stacey hurried across the bright blue carpet and bent to kiss her grandmother. The wrinkled cheek felt dry and powdery beneath her lips and the once beautiful green eyes were clouded over with pain. "We can't even gossip without you eavesdropping, can we?" she teased, trying to hide her concern.

"It's no wonder you gossip about me." Lillian met and matched her granddaughter's light tone. "I lead an extraordinarily exciting life here in Sin City, Senior Division."

Dianne left the room to make tea and Stacey sat down

at the side of the bed, smoothing out the blue-and-white quilt, then took Lillian's thin hand in hers. "How you doing, Grandma? Really?"

Lillian smiled, her face creasing into a network of fine lines and wrinkles, none of which had succeeded in obliterating the original beauty of her elegant features. Even in pain, she retained a regal composure that Stacey prayed would be hers when she was older.

"Not that good, child. I'm feeling very tired lately."

"Haven't you been sleeping well?"

"I've been sleeping well. This fatigue goes beyond sleep. I think age is finally winning the battle."

"Don't say that, Grandma!" Stacey's voice was harsh. "I don't want to hear you talk like that."

"I'm not trying to upset you, Stacey, but I am an old woman and old women have earned the right to speak the unvarnished truth."

"If you'd spoken the truth, I'd agree with you. But that was just a pile of rubbish, Grandma. You're younger in some ways than any of us."

Lillian shook her head and squeezed her granddaughter's hand in hers. "You never have liked to see things change, have you, dear? I remember you when you were a little girl—you'd get upset if we even changed the curtains in your room."

Lillian's green eyes narrowed and her look went right through Stacey. The old woman shook her head again. "I still see that look you used to have when your mother—" She stopped and took a deep breath. "All these years I've tried not to blame Maryann for how she treated my son. I think I've been pretty successful. But, when I see that look of fear on your face whenever a door closes behind you, I feel such anger...."

The intensity of her grandmother's feelings frightened Stacey.

"Don't think about Mother. You can be sure she's too busy with her stockbroker to think about us."

Lillian smiled at her lovely young granddaughter. "Don't worry about my blood pressure, child. A little well-placed anger is healthy—even at my age. You should try it sometime."

Stacey began to laugh. "I'll remember that, Dr. Newton." She glanced at her watch. "Well, I think my session is about up, Doctor."

The older woman laughed along with her, then closed her eyes for a moment as if to regather her strength. Stacey felt a sharp pain in her own heart as she gazed at the tired face she loved so dearly, at the kaleidoscope of lines that radiated around her eyes. Lillian looked ethereal; with her crown of white hair and pale skin she seemed otherworldly. Stacey shook the images from her mind and grinned when Lillian's eyes opened.

"I haven't heard any comments about my outfit." She stood up and modeled the bright, rather sexy clothes.

"Quite a change." Lillian's eyes twinkled.

"She didn't dress like that for us, Grandma!" Dianne bustled into the room carrying a tray of soup and sandwiches. "She's meeting a mystery man this afternoon and they're heading out to Montauk!"

Lillian looked at Stacey and nodded. "Well, I'm glad, child. It's about time you spread your wings again."

Stacey jumped up with an exasperated grin. "For God's sake! You two are making a simple afternoon with a business associate sound like a night of love."

She headed for the door of the room. "I'm going to wash up for lunch."

They declared a moratorium on Stacey's social life during lunch. Instead they chatted about the terrible weather and the price of produce, all things inconsequential. However, at one point as they talked about the beagle they'd had when the girls were teen-agers, Lillian put her soup spoon down and looked from Dianne to Stacey with a faraway gleam in her green eyes.

"Grandma?" Stacey's voice was gentle. "Is something wrong?"

"I was just thinking how lucky I am to have granddaughters like you."

Stacey caught Dianne's eye. It was totally out-of-character for her to say something like that and it took both young women by surprise.

"Oh, come on, Grandma! You used to call us brats!" Dianne's voice was light and teasing.

Lillian smiled. "You two girls have never given me anything but joy," she said seriously, "despite any of your 'bratty' outbursts in the past."

It was a companionable lunch, the three of them very happy to be in one another's company. Yet, as she sipped the creamy mushroom soup, Stacey kept stealing glances at the clock-radio on the bedstand. The closer it got to 2 P.M., the harder she found it to keep her mind on anything around her.

"Stacey!" Lillian's voice pierced her fog. "I'm the only one in this room legally entitled to bouts of senility."

She blushed. "Sorry. I must have been daydreaming."

Dianne laughed. "Clock-watching is more like it.

Why don't you leave now and spare us your attack of nerves?''

With promises to bring Franco back to say hello, Stacey grabbed her light jacket from the bathroom and ran through the drizzle to her Corvette. Two minutes later she had merged onto William Floyd Parkway, which was slick from the rain. She had to slow down at intersections and ease her way across enormous pools of five-inch-deep water that had accumulated during the last few days of rainfall. She barely noticed the familiar landmarks of shopping centers and movie theaters as she drove toward the railroad station. The thrumming excitement in her chest matched the powerful roar of her sportscar as she entered the parking lot and headed toward the fifteen-minutes-only parking spots near the platform.

The station was crowded with cars and vans; all sorts of people were waiting to pick up relatives who were spending the Memorial Day weekend on Long Island. The rain had soaked the train station, making some of the concrete supports that held the elevated tracks darker than others. She looked up at the platform, at the men and women huddled in raincoats, who stood under the overhang, leaning against the white bricks of the locked waiting rooms. She could just make out the sign for a Broadway play that hung lopsided from a billboard on the other side of the station.

She spotted a young man leaning against the wall by the taxi stand, reading a folded-up newspaper. He was wearing a tan trench coat, the belt loose and blowing at his side. For a second she thought he was Franco until he lifted his head and she saw the curly blond hair.

She swallowed and turned off the engine. Could he

have forgotten which station? Could he have forgotten that he was supposed to meet her at all? The whole episode the night before had such a dreamlike quality that she was hard pressed to remember what was real and what was fantasy. She started the car and was about to drive to the other side of the lot to look for him when she noticed Franco, shoulders hunched, hands in the pockets of his red Windbreaker, standing under an awning near the pay phones.

She beeped her horn twice. He turned, spotted the Corvette, and waved. She was about to pull out of the parking space and drive over to him, when, looking right and left, he leaped over a puddle near the curb and jogged easily over to her.

He shook the water off his hair, then got in. "God, what a rotten day."

"Listen, I'm sorry you were waiting for me out there. What time did your train get in?"

"It's my fault," he answered. "I made all the connections quicker than I thought, so I took an earlier train." He grimaced. "It just never occurred to me that your grandmother's name might not be Andersen."

She groaned and eased the car into traffic. "I'm sorry. I should have given you her number. How stupid of me."

He looked at her, amber eyes warm and alive in his tanned and handsome face. "Do you realize you've apologized twice and I haven't even been in this car thirty seconds?"

"I'm sorry—" she started, then she broke into laughter. "Okay, from here on, no matter what happens, no apologies!"

"I don't know about that," he said as she had to jam on the brakes to avoid hitting a man who dashed out in front of her. "You mean if you drive us into the Atlantic Ocean, you're not even going to say you're sorry?"

At the next red light, she turned and glared at him. "I'm insulted! You sound as if you don't trust my driving."

"Did I say that?" he teased, feigning fear as he checked his seat belt and shoulder harness, then grabbed the armrest with white-knuckled strength.

By the time they reached Lillian's home, Stacey felt totally at ease and was grinning as they went in the backdoor. They peeled wet jackets off and draped them over the kitchen chairs.

"Is that you, Stace?"

Dianne came into the kitchen, tucking in the tail of her green shirt as she did.

"Hi! You must be Franco." She extended a hand and smiled at him.

"I am. But you have me at a disadvantage, Miss..."

"Some sister she is!" Dianne shook his hand and threw a look at Stacey. "I'm Dianne Shearman, the forgetful one's older sister."

They chatted a few moments then Stacey looked at her watch. "If we don't get in and see Grandma, it will be nightfall before we get to Montauk Point. Is she awake?"

Dianne nodded. "She dozed again while you were at the train station so she'd be alert when she met Franco."

Dianne stayed in the kitchen to do the dishes and Stacey led him down the hall to Lillian's room. "She's a remarkable lady," she said as they reached the door. "She's always been the most important person in my life."

He looked into her eyes with a curious mixture of tenderness and admiration, then followed her into the lovely, feminine blue-and-white bedroom where Lillian waited for him, hands outstretched in greeting.

"Grandma, this is Franco Borelli. Franco, my grandmother Lillian Newton."

The two clasped hands, green eyes measuring amber and finding no fault there.

"I see where your granddaughters get their beauty, Mrs. Newton."

Lillian tilted her chin and flashed a saucy smile. "I see you were blessed with the Latin charm the Italians are justly famous for *Signore* Borelli. *Piacère. S'accomodi.*"

He beamed and sat down as she had invited him. He looked at Stacey. "I didn't know your grandmother spoke Italian."

"I didn't know it myself," said Stacey, flabbergasted.

"There are many things you don't know about me, child." Lillian turned back to Franco who was sitting on the chair next to her bed, leaning forward in fascination.

"E andato all'università a Roma?"

He shook his head. *"Sono andato all'università a Firenze."*

"Were you born—*nasce in Italia?*"

"No, Signora Newton, quando ero ragazzo passavo tutte le vacanze a Firenze."

Stacey cleared her throat. "Excuse me, but what on earth are you two talking about?"

Franco glanced up at her and smiled. "I was telling your grandmother how I spent summer vacations in Florence when I was a boy."

"How did you learn Italian, Grandma? This is quite a surprise."

"Remember Mrs. DeTrano, the woman who introduced me to opera?" Stacey nodded. "Well, the music was so beautiful that I wanted to understand the words. Rose helped me and, after awhile, I picked up a smattering of conversational Italian."

"More than a smattering, *signora*," Franco said as he smiled warmly at Lillian.

"If you two don't mind, I'll leave you to your mutual admiration society while I speak to Dianne." Then, to Franco, she added, "After that, I think we'd better get going."

When she returned to the room fifteen minutes later, Franco was standing in the hallway, smoking a cigarette. "She's asleep." His face looked soft and tender. "We were speaking awhile, then she suddenly grew tired and dozed off."

Stacey nodded. "That's been happening more and more. I'll just go in and check on her, then we'll leave."

"I'll say good-bye to your sister and start the car if you'll let me." Smiling, she tossed him the keys and slipped into Lillian's room.

At the sound of her feet making hushed sounds on the carpet, Lillian's eyes opened.

"I like your Franco," she said. "Now, that's what I call a man."

Stacey laughed. "Well, I guess it's obvious he's not a woman."

Lillian frowned. "Let me tell you something, Stacey. Being a man has to do with much more than the way he fills out his trousers."

Stacey blushed. "Men can't be judged quite so easily,

Grandma. Look at Michael. Sooner or later, the truth will out.''

Her grandmother shook her head. "No. Franco Borelli is made of the right stuff. Strength like his is unmistakable. I can tell. Give him a chance. You'll see.''

Stacey bent and kissed Lillian. "We'll have to continue this, Grandma. But right now I have to go.''

Her grandmother grabbed her hand as she turned to leave the room. "Just remember Michael had problems that went far beyond yours. Your problem was the catalyst, not the root of your breakup. Don't think all men are the enemy.''

"Oh, Grandma, come on now. I never said anything like that. Enough gloomy talk.''

With a wave and a promise to call her in a few days, Stacey hurried outside to where Franco and Dianne stood waiting near her Corvette. The rain was now only a slight drizzle.

"Do you want me to drive?'' He turned to Stacey, droplets of rain beading his mahogany hair.

"No, that's okay. I may not get many more chances to drive this car. I don't want to miss any.''

"Are you going to do it after all?'' Dianne sounded disappointed.

"It's coming to that,'' Stacey answered, trying to ignore the question she saw in Franco's eyes.

The wheels of the sportscar kicked up gravel as they backed out onto Neighborhood Road and headed for the highway to Montauk.

Once they had passed the Game Farm, which was a mini-wildlife zoo, they were truly away from suburbia. Farms and potato fields whizzed by as Stacey maneuvered the car along the flat, seemingly limitless highway, the scenery dotted only occasionally by a lone house or barn. When they reached the Riverhead exit she got off and headed for Route 27, the local road that wound through the historical and currently very trendy towns of the Hamptons: Hampton Bays, East, West, and Bridgehampton, Amagansett. Franco was filled with questions and Stacey thoroughly enjoyed playing tour guide.

"I'm surprised you've never been out here before," she said as they entered the picture-postcard village of East Hampton.

"I've been here before," he said, smiling at her look of surprise. "I just never had the chance to see much of anything but the beach while I was here."

"I should have guessed," she said, her voice suddenly heavy with sarcasm she couldn't control. "You were probably one of the summer singles, one-twelfth of a summer house, frying on the beach all day and sweating in a smoky disco all night."

"You make it sound pretty tawdry. It had its moments." He was baiting her, trying to see where he stood.

"I'm sure it did." Her voice was dry.

"Stacey, listen, I was young, single, no prospects, and no prospects of any prospects. I didn't even have a job. What's wrong with a summer blowout before the real world settled around me?"

She flushed. What he spoke about was normal behavior for the rest of the world. "I forget sometimes that that's how most young adults act," she relented and downshifted into second as they went up a hill and out of the village of East Hampton. "We never really had time or money for things like that. Dianne and I have been working for as long as I can remember: baby-sitting, delivering newspapers, working as salesgirls in Macy's. Grandma couldn't possibly earn enough to support all three of us.'' Her voice softened, acquiring a faraway quality, almost as if she were talking to herself. He didn't understand all of what she said but the gaps could be filled in later. He let her speak without interruption for he sensed it was a catharsis, ridding her of some stone of sadness she needed to be free of. ''My mother's career was getting married, you know. Our father was her first husband—he was the only one who died.

''I never thought of it like this before, but maybe Mother has been looking for him ever since.'' She glanced at Franco out of the corner of her green eyes. ''Though that may be too generous an explanation. Anyway, the other husbands never felt any obligation to Di and me and Mother would move wherever they moved, do whatever they wanted, and we only got in her way. Grandma Lillian was the only one who wanted us or saw any value in us. Our other relatives seemed to see us as slightly disreputable, as if our mother's sins were our own. I guess that's why Dianne and I are the way we are—she threw herself into marriage the same way I threw myself into a career—as if our two halves might make a perfect whole.'' She shrugged. ''Who knows?''

They were stopped at a red light and she looked him full in the face, expecting to see laughter, a man ready to make a joke. She was surprised by the compassion glowing in his amber eyes.

''I don't usually talk about this,'' she said. ''I don't really know why I did now.''

Her hand was on the stickshift and he covered it with his own. She could see the crisp dark hairs on his fingers. They were well-cared-for hands and for some reason that seemed to matter to her.

"I hope you told me because you feel comfortable with me, Stacey. I care what happens to you."

"Why should you?" she started to say, then stopped and looked at him, drawn deeply into his gaze, thoughts of her past disappearing in smoke. He moved his head closer, a lazy smile on his face. She leaned toward him, feeling her lips part slightly—

"Lady, I ain't got all day!"

Laughing, they moved apart, kissless, and she pulled away from the light to the grumbling horn-honking of an irate man in a Mercedes behind her.

"Have you no 'true confessions' for me?" she asked, trying to break the intimate spell in the car as she threaded her way through the town of Montauk and drove the eight miles out to the Point and the lighthouse.

"I have many, *cara*," he said easily. "But, later."

"There's a little place to get food at the lighthouse. Are you hungry?"

"Not really. Are you?"

She shook her head. "Good. Then we can park by East Lake Beach and walk. I think you'll appreciate everything more if we approach it that way."

"You're the boss."

She looked at him with a grin, one eyebrow arched. "And don't you forget it!"

They left the car on the east side of the jetties at the entrance to Montauk Harbor. Although the rain had stopped, the sand, Stacey told him, would be heavy with moisture and she recommended that they leave their shoes behind. She slipped out of her sandals, then unbuttoned the cuffs of her raspberry pants and unceremoniously rolled them up over her calves.

He looked at her. "They'll get ruined," he said, pointing to her pants.

She sighed, a brief twinge of regret flickering through her. "I know. But it's worth it to be here."

The feeling of regret quickly passed as she looked out at the limitless expanse of deep gray-green water, frothed by the wind into a meringue of whitecaps as far as the eye could see. The sky hung low, a deep pewter mottled by streaks of clouds the color of heavy cream. Thought ceased as she drank in the untamed beauty of the Atlantic, listened to the roar of the three thousand miles of ocean, smelled the melancholy, romantic scent of salt spray, and felt the way it stung her eyes and cheeks and turned her hair into a wild mass of deep blond curls as untamed as the landscape before them.

She heard a sharp intake of breath next to her and turned to look at Franco. He stared out toward the horizon and she recognized that look of awe and joy. He understood.

They walked slowly over the sharp dune grasses that tickled the bottoms of their feet and he helped her down over the rocks and shells to the smooth wet sand. They were the only people there. Gulls swooped down, heads dipping into the water and coming up empty, only to be swept skyward again on currents of air. Their strange, mournful call joined the ocean's roar in an eerie and beautiful harmony. The beach was unusually broad from shoreline to dunes, an enormous stretch of wild nature. They started walking east where, four miles ahead, the lighthouse rose above a foundation of swirling mists. They didn't touch one another as they walked, two very separate persons, yet Stacey felt a connection running between them as they became one with the sea at the end of the island.

A small boulder jutted through the water just a few feet past the shoreline. "Are you game?" she asked him, hiking her pants up over her knees.

For answer, he bent over and rolled his khaki trousers up the same way. Then he took her hand and they plunged into the cool surf, scrambling up the rock to perch four feet over the water on the slippery surface of the boulder, a relic of the Ice Age that had formed Long Island millions of years before.

As they sat, shoulders touching, hands now clasped, she was engulfed by a serenity that surpassed anything she usually felt when she came to the beach. The expected solitary joy was there, but it was intensified. Rather than being diminished by his presence, it was enhanced. She saw the beauty of Montauk Point not only through her own eyes but through his as well. Her hand in his felt natural, yet flowing with electricity. An unspoken question had vibrated between them since that unconsummated kiss in the car; now it crackled like undischarged current searching for ground.

He said something to her but the words were lost in the wind. She leaned closer to hear him and her breasts brushed his forearm. Their gazes caught and held; she felt suspended, caught in the depths of those amber eyes.

With his free hand he reached out and touched her cheek, running his sensitive index finger down the curve of her high cheekbones, then across her full lips. She stifled a gasp and, as her lips parted, he slipped his finger slightly inside, touching the soft flesh within. On impulse she gently closed her white teeth over his finger, her tongue tasting the salty tang of his skin, redolent of sea air, uniquely his. The wind whipped her hair around her face, long strands obscuring her vision. The wildness of the wind as it roared in her ears matched her emotions, till she felt filled with a raw and burning, nearly primitive feeling.

He looked deep into her eyes. "Your eyes have yellow flames in them, *cara*."

Her voice was soft, almost thought, not sound. "It happens when I'm near the sea."

"Only the sea causes you to flame?" He brought his face close to hers and brushed her lips with his own.

She smiled at him and, as she did, he brought his mouth back to hers and, with exquisite tenderness, parted her lips with his tongue and sought the nectar of her mouth. The position was uncomfortable and precarious; holding each other would mean slipping to the ground. So, only their mouths were able to meet and she trembled at the power of a kiss. She hadn't remembered it like this: a searing intensity that stripped her of thought, that made her body melt like a candle before a burning flame.

She longed to wrap her arms around him, to plunge her hands into his silky dark brown hair, to meld her torso to his. Long-buried passions erupted like a dormant volcano, leaving her stunned by their power. He had broken the kiss and was now tracing a line of fire down her throat, nibbling at the sensitive cord where shoulder met throat, sending tremors of terror and delight through her body. She pressed her nose against the flesh at the side of his neck, drinking in the sweet smell of his flesh, mingled with the tang of his cologne and the lure of the salty sea.

She was dizzy with delight, intoxicated by the touch and scent of him. Her jacket was unzipped and he unhooked her belt, then slid his hand under her sweater. The muscles of her abdomen quivered beneath his touch. His sensitive fingers memorized her flesh like a blind man reading Braille, savoring contour and softness. He murmured endearments in Italian that she couldn't translate but understood by the way her breasts swelled as he neared them, by the way his fingers lingered at the top of her lacy bra, poised for one exquisite moment, then slipped between fabric and flesh to cup the round softness within.

Her hands were flat on the rock as she watched his face, burning with a mixture of pleasure and pain, as he moved his lips to the curve of her bosom and branded her. *"Bellezza."* His voice was a husky murmur as he told her of her beauty. *"Bellezza."*

Time had no meaning. They were lost in their senses, sailing into uncharted seas with no guide, no compass to lead them to the other shore. Only when the rain began again, pelting them with furious elephant-sized drops of water, did they rouse from their nearly drugged state and, putting their jackets over their heads, run the last thousand feet to the tiny restaurant at the base of the lighthouse.

"Your eyes still flame, *cara,"* he half-whispered as the waitress approached them with menus. "Can it be more than the sea now?"

She blushed and looked down at the tabletop, afraid for him to see the open, vulnerable look she knew blazed in her eyes. They sat opposite one another at the tiny wooden table, sipping from enormous white bowls of hearty Long Island clam chowder, redolent with thick tomatoes and pieces of succulent clams, while their eyes said things their words could not. His amber eyes had darkened; they were liquid caramel now, heavy with promise.

The two of them lingered long, munching oyster

crackers and breadsticks, then finishing the meal with mugs of tea and enormous pieces of rich cheesecake while they waited for the rain to stop.

The easy comfort they had felt with one another on the drive out to Montauk had disappeared, replaced by a thrumming excitement Stacey was sure was powerful enough to light the room. The atmosphere between them was dangerously electric—everything had changed so quickly and completely that they were without ground. And yet Stacey wasn't afraid.

For once, change didn't frighten her. She was ready to cut anchor and drift aimlessly, never return to reality, stay in this blissful world of half-dreams forever.

As they finished their last cups of tea, the rain stopped. It was a little after 6 P.M. The sky was still gray, a shade of pewter that was darker than when they last looked. The light mist had turned to a rolling fog that tumbled along the beach outside the window and swirled magically up the black-and-white banded lighthouse that rose from the steep seventy-foot cliff at the edge of the Atlantic Ocean.

As the matronly waitress brought them their change, she glanced from Stacey to Franco and accurately gauged them to be lovers or nearly so. "If you folks have the time, you might like stepping out to the overlook by the lighthouse over there. Every so often when we get a good rolling fog like this, *The Will o' the Wisp* sails in."

"Isn't it dangerous?" Stacey asked, looking out at the fog that nearly obliterated the shoreline. She could easily imagine a ship crashing against those jagged rocks.

"Only for those who don't believe." The waitress laughed and explained that scientists said the ship was really an optical phenomenon caused when the atmosphere contained phosphorous, something that occurred during certain fogs. "But those of us who've grown up with the *Will o' the Wisp* don't believe them. We think she passes by on her journey elsewhere."

Stacey shivered with a tingling anticipation as they went out the back door of the restaurant and leaned against the weathered fence, looking out past the lighthouse and into the distance. It was getting darker; the sky was now the color of steel, deep and forbidding. Franco's arm was around her shoulders and she marveled at how they fit: not the usual ideal of taller man, tiny woman—they were a pair, hips meeting hips, lips within reach.

"Maybe we should go," Franco said, turning to her. The wind had blown up again and it was getting raw. "We still have a long walk back to the car."

"No, wait," she said, hating to leave. "Just a moment more. The waitress said we can get a cab back to the car if we want."

Then, suddenly, passing through the beam of the lighthouse, moving so swiftly and silently that if you blinked it would be gone, was the *Will o' the Wisp*. Silent and majestic, she glided across the waters in full sail, heading toward Long Island Sound, a glowing amber lantern swinging from her mast. In the blink of an eye she disappeared into the fog that rolled thick over her prow, obliterating her from sight.

"Did you see it?" Stacey breathed, afraid it had been a mirage.

"Yes." His voice was stunned, subdued.

She put her arms around him and peered out into the fog, straining for another glimpse of the mysterious ship. "Was it real, do you think?"

"I don't know." He moved his lips to hers and kissed her deeply. "Right now I only know that you're real."

She chuckled. "I might be a mirage," she said, teasing him gently. "I may just disappear into the night like the *Will o' the Wisp* did."

His arms tightened around her. She could feel the strength of him. "I won't let you," he said. "Not tonight."

Chapter Seven

The inn had one empty room left.

"When this weather blew in, we had a cancellation," the portly innkeeper told them with a grin as he unlocked the door to their double room. "Don't happen too often on a holiday weekend." He glanced from Franco to Stacey, who moved instantly to the window and stood looking out. "Will you folks be needing a bellhop to bring your bags?"

"No, thanks," Franco answered smoothly. "We'll manage. Thank you again." He pressed a bill into the man's outstretched hand and then locked the door behind him.

Lit by just the electric sconce on the wall, Stacey's profile was wreathed by a dim golden light, making her hair seem like a curly halo swirling around her face. He could tell by the way she swallowed often and kept her hands clasped securely in front of her that she was as nervous as he was about what was sure to happen. He took his jacket off and placed it over the chair by the small maple desk. He longed to pull her into his arms, to discover the wonder of her glorious body, but he breathed deeply to gain control. She was not a woman to be rushed; she was a woman to be savored, to revel in every golden inch, to make love to in every way he knew, every way he could imagine.

"Take your jacket off, *cara*," he said, his voice husky. "It's wet and you'll catch cold."

"You sound like my grandmother," she said with a nervous smile.

Just minutes ago in the car, they had been wrapped in each other's arms, one heart ricocheting off the other. They knew they needed to be alone, to be far away from Andersen-Bradley, from her apartment, from anything that was not uniquely theirs at this moment. Yet, now, alone in this strange room, they seemed unable to manage even conversation.

Stacey opened the top drawer of the dresser.

"Look at this." She lifted out a plastic bag. "Toothbrushes, tiny toothpaste—everything you need." She shook her head. "Makes you feel kind of odd, you know?"

He frowned at her. "Just a courtesy," he answered. "Perhaps you would like to freshen up, *cara*. I think I'll call room service to send us up some sandwiches or something. Anything particular you'd like?"

She shrugged. "Just tea. I can't think of anything else."

He turned and went over to the phone. She picked up her pocketbook from the bed and headed into the large combination bathroom-dressing room. Her stomach fluttered as if a thousand butterflies had taken residence inside. Her clothing, her purse, even the face in the mirror—nothing seemed familiar to her. Her eyes were enormous, a luminous green, her expression so vulnerable that she couldn't bear to see her own reflection. It scared her to see the power she was giving him, yet it was impossible to turn back. She didn't *want* to turn back.

She started to pull her sweater over her head, then hesitated. What on earth was the thing to do in a situation like this? Clothed, she felt awkward. Nude, she would find it impossible to cross the room in front of his burning eyes. Finally she noticed the enormous, king-size bath sheets, piled on the towel rack near the tub, and stripping off her clothing, she draped the yellow bath sheet across one shoulder and around in a toga-style garment. She laughed at her reflection—it really didn't look that bad. Finally she knew she could delay no longer. She took a deep breath, switched off the light, and went back into the bedroom.

He stood by a tiny table that had been set up by the bed. With an elegant gesture, he raised the bottle of champagne toward her, then poured a generous amount of the bubbling liquid into each of the long, tulip-shaped glasses. "I hope you like champagne."

"Does anyone not?"

He held his glass out to hers and they clicked gently. He smiled. *"Intrigo amoroso."* He took a long sip, never taking his eyes from her.

"What does that mean?" She sipped her own, wrinkling her nose as the bubbles tickled her.

"The mystery of love."

Her eyes darkened as he set his glass down, then slowly removed his shirt, peeling it down over his muscular shoulders, sliding his arms out inch by inch. She could barely swallow her champagne as she saw, for the first time, all that had been promised: His physique was as well-sculpted as a statue—each muscle was defined against the bronzed hardness of his body, drawn as if by the hand of an artist. The beauty of his body filled her with a sensual thrill that enflamed her. For the first time in her life she was able to understand how a man must feel when faced with a beautiful woman.

She was, quite literally, speechless before him.

He took her champagne glass from her and placed it

on the table near his own. With infinite patience, he put his hands on her waist and pulled her body close to his. She gasped as she felt his hardness against her, a demanding, insistent force.

"Bellissima cara," he whispered, pressing his lips against the base of her throat.

She felt as if she were burning up, her mind incinerating in the fire he had started within her. She wound her arms around his neck, her hands finally plunging into his thick mahogany hair, the strands like silk against her skin. Cradling his face, she pulled it closer to her own and kissed him. He felt an inexpressible joy at her touch and responded with an intensity that filled the room. Finally, he pushed her a few inches away from him and, with a lazy half-smile, untied the knot at her shoulder and let the towel slither to the floor at her feet. She reddened, her blush coloring even her throat and breasts.

"Bellezza," he said once again. *"Bellezza."*

Emboldened by his obvious pleasure in her body, she stretched herself out languorously on the dark bedspread, unconsciously curving her long legs and torso into a graceful line of feminine beauty. He unzipped his trousers and stepped out of his clothing. She stared at him, mesmerized by the sight of his masculinity. He reached up to turn off the wall sconce when she said, "Don't."

He looked down at her, drinking in her loveliness. "I thought it would make you feel more comfortable."

"No." Her voice was so low he could barely hear her. "I want to be able to see you. I want to be able to watch you the whole time."

Her words turned him to fiery steel. With a groan, he lowered himself onto the bed, gasping at the first full touch of flesh against flesh. Their nearness to one another was an unequalled aphrodisiac. He ran his hands down over the sweet curve of her waist and hips, then drew his fingers across her quivering belly.

She stiffened as he touched the tiny white surgical scar just above her bikini line. "No, don't look. It's ugly." She turned her head toward the pillow.

He raised himself up onto one elbow and touched her cheek. "Quiet. There is nothing about you that is not beautiful to me."

Before she could respond, he moved his mouth down over her breasts and navel and gently drew his tongue along the scar, caressing it until she was giving little moans of pleasure.

His action released something in her; some icy core finally melted and her hands and mouth played him like a fine stringed instrument, drawing from him music worthy of the Masters.

Finally, when they both could wait no longer, when their bodies were crying for fulfillment, he raised himself up on top of her and looked down into the aching beauty of her green eyes.

"Now," she said, pulling him down onto her breasts. "Now."

How could she have forgotten this awesome power and beauty? Or was it ever like this? Had it ever been like this before? He was inside her and around her and a part of her; he was everywhere, everything she touched and breathed and thought. When it was over and she was lying in the crook of his powerful arm, breathing in their mingled scents, half-drunk on him, she realized that at the moment of release, he had cried her name in his ecstasy and she had answered him in kind.

They were exhausted—as much by emotion as by

their actions, and they dozed for a while. Time had no meaning, nothing mattered but that they were there together, on that bed, in that moment in space. After a while, he cupped her breast with his hand and leaned down over it, teasing the nipple with his rough tongue until she arched her back and moaned, begging for him to ease the fire again.

The first time had been sweet and sacred. This time they were wild and abandoned, coaxing one another to heights unimagined before, meeting and matching passions that she had never thought existed.

Franco winced as Stacey soaped his back the next morning in the shower. "Careful!" He moved away as she lathered over the long red marks. "I'm going to call you *La Tigre* from now on."

"Oh, knock it off!" She tossed the wet washcloth at him as she turned around in the narrow stall shower. "Come on, turnabout's fair play!"

He grinned and started soaping her, making slow, sensuous circles on her back.

"Hey! You're taking unfair advantage!" His soaping had extended down over the full roundness of her buttocks and he gave her a playful pinch.

She reached out to give him a taste of his own medicine but he slipped out of her grasp and stepped out of the shower stall.

"Take a few minutes," he said as he wrapped a towel around his lean middle. "Room service will be bringing breakfast any second."

He closed the door behind him, leaving her alone in the steamy bathroom. Thank heavens the inn was generous with towels. She bent over and wound one around her thick wet hair, then began to dry her body with the bath sheet she had worn the night before.

Not even twenty-four hours had passed since she and Franco had become lovers and already she couldn't remember how it had been without him. Her body seemed new to her as she dried her breasts and hips, remembering the pleasure she had given and received just hours ago. At Franco's hands, her body became an instrument of joy and she looked forward to the next song he would play.

An hour later they were dressed and ready to explore the town. Even in the misty rain with the skies leaden and gray, she realized Montauk had never looked so lovely to her before. They strolled down Main Street, poking into the little crafts shops, admiring macramé wall hangings and fiber sculptures done by local artisans, stopping in the late afternoon for the ubiquitous Long Island clam chowder at a place down near the docks.

For the first time in years, Andersen-Bradley didn't exist. Not once did her mind stray back to the office, to computer problems. She was aware of nothing but the moment, of the feel of his hand in hers as they scrambled up the dunes after a stroll on the beach and made their way back to the inn.

He'd asked for a menu to be left in their room, and sitting together on the bed, they read the list of entrées.

"I'm having sirloin, *cara*. Would you like the same?"

"I don't eat red meat." She looked down at the list. "I guess I'll have a Caesar salad and mushroom quiche."

He narrowed his eyes as he looked at her. "Are you a vegetarian?"

"Semi. I lapse now and then but basically I prefer not to eat meat."

"No chicken? No fish?"

"Like I said, I'm only a semi-. Maybe once or twice a week I'll have tuna salad or some sliced turkey, but I try to avoid it most of the time."

"How do you live? What the hell do you eat?"

She shrugged. "Fruits, vegetables...Linzer tarts. There's plenty to eat, believe me." She patted her hips. "I still manage to carry around a little excess."

He smoothed his hand over her lovely curves. "You're crazy, *cara*. Every inch of you is perfect—there is nothing extra."

She jumped up from the bed, straightening her sweater. "Come on, *Signore* Borelli. Quit delaying. Call in our dinner orders. I'm starving."

He got up and pulled her close to him, flattening her breasts against his chest. "I am starving too," he said as he nibbled her lower lip. "Other appetites must be satisfied as well."

She was barefoot and her eyes were about an inch lower than his. She saw the tiny freckle in his lower lid and reached up and gently traced the outline of his eyes, drawing her finger lightly down over the planes of his cheekbones, over the nose that was still beautifully shaped despite the fact he'd broken it when he was seventeen. She raised her index finger for a moment in the tiny hollow above his upper lip.

"I'm surprised you don't have a mustache," she said in a low voice. She turned her finger sideways, covering the clean-shaven area to try out the effect. "You'd look quite debonair with one, actually."

He caught her hand in his. "You prefer men with mustaches?" His golden eyes seemed lit by an inner fire.

"I prefer you," she answered, "with or without a mustache."

He brought her hand to his lips and kissed the soft fleshy part of her palm, touching it lightly with his tongue. Her heart hammered in her throat, a now familiar response to his nearness, evidence of his power over her life. His mouth curved in a teasing smile and she drew her index finger across the upper lip, then down and around the full lower one, then, watching his expression, she drew her finger across the space between them, slipping it into the warmth of his mouth. As she had done to him once, he caught her finger between his teeth and applied pressure, watching her green eyes dilate as she looked back at him.

He slipped his hand up under her sweater and, palm flat, slid it over her quivering abdomen to the valley between her full breasts, now unrestrained by a bra. She didn't break the gaze to look away. Instead her eyes focused on him and she let him see exactly how she felt, every nuance of expression on her face, as he roused her to a peak of excitement that surpassed any he had taken her to before.

Finally, as they slid onto the bed, their clothes in a tangle on the braided rug, he lifted himself up on one arm and, with a sly grin, said, "Damn! I forgot to call for dinner."

She looked at him and burst into laughter. Then, turning serious, she drew her hands up the chiseled muscles of his back and said, "I'm not hungry for dinner anymore...I'm only hungry for you." He stifled further words with demanding kisses as he lowered himself into her warmth.

Dinner was very late.

Sunday came all too quickly for both of them. Stacey was quiet as they sat in the small diner on Deer Park Avenue near the Long Island Railroad station, having an omelet while they killed time until his train to Manhattan arrived. It had been so perfect in Montauk. Every thought and movement had seemed choreographed for romance, so well had things gone between them. Things had gone *so* well, in fact, that it scared her.

She looked at Franco, who was absorbed in putting mounds of pickles and cole slaw on his sandwich plate. The imitation Tiffany light shone directly over his head, creating a circle of light on top of his shiny hair and casting soft shadows beneath his amber eyes. She noticed the way the waitress had appreciated his oddly appealing combination of elegance and masculinity, the courtly manners that were as natural to him as his heartbeat, the impression of chained strength that intrigued and frightened people.

She sipped her tea and glanced out the window at the traffic whizzing by on the busy street. Families were returning from visits to aunts and uncles, elderly couples going home after a Sunday drive, and lovers returning to the real world after a weekend idyll. The mainstream of the real world—and now she was a part of it.

Her thoughts returned to Andersen-Bradley for the first time in forty-eight hours. Andersen-Bradley—her fortress. Unfortunately, now a fortress that was crumbling around her. She sighed and checked her watch.

"We'd better hurry, Franco. Your train pulls out in fifteen minutes."

"I almost hope I miss it, *cara*." He reached for her hand and held it. "I wish I didn't have to be in Princeton tomorrow morning."

She understood. But in a way she was glad he did have to return. She needed time to examine her feelings, to adjust to the changes in her life. This hadn't been part of her plan.

However, when she stood on the platform ten minutes later and watched the big silver-gray train ease its
way out of the station and head west toward the Big
Apple, she was unprepared for the way her heart ached,
for the way she felt cut in half, as if the other part had
been snatched away.

She realized that what she felt was *alive* again; too,
she realized with sickening clarity that being alive meant
being open to hurt.

Monday, Memorial Day, she spent resting, still suspended in the fantasy world of their weekend together.
Tuesday morning she thought she'd be able to pick up
her life and plunge herself back into office routine
without a ripple. However, Chris's sharp, knowing eyes
picked up immediately on the glow emanating from
Stacey, noticing the soft sheen in her green eyes and the
secret smile that played now and then at the corners of
her mouth.

Stacey was sitting in the kitchen at lunchtime, enjoying a cup of yogurt, when Chris came in to take her
roast beef sandwich out of the refrigerator. Grabbing
the mustard from the cabinet, she sat down opposite her
boss. Stacey grinned, then stopped when she saw the
strange look on Chris's face.

"Is something wrong?" she asked, putting her plastic
spoon down. "Do I have a yogurt mustache or something?" She wiped her lips with a paper napkin.

"All I can say is, if they bottle the stuff, let me know
where you got it."

Stacey started to laugh. "Is that a foreign language,
Chris? I don't have any idea what you're talking
about."

"You, Stacey. Look at you! You're radiant. I don't

think I've ever seen you look so beautiful—your outfit, everything. It's like you're a new you.''

Stacey blushed. "It's springtime, Chris. The birds are singing, the sun is shining, things are blooming—'' She broke off and laughed when Chris glanced at her own belly, round with pregnancy. "Oh, you know all the old clichés," she said, returning to her yogurt.

Chris shook her head. "Sorry. I don't buy it. We just had a rainy, awful Memorial Day weekend and we don't have enough work to fill one floppy disk in the computer room. There's got to be another reason."

Stacey stood up and tossed the empty container into the garbage. "Maybe I'm crazy," she said to the older woman. "Maybe I just happen to like rainy Memorial Day weekends and a business that's sliding downhill on a bobsled."

Chris shook her head again. "Is this contagious? Should I call a doctor?"

Stacey gave the woman a quick hug. "If anyone wants me, I'll be in the computer room packing the order for Leader."

So it showed. She wasn't surprised. She smiled as she entered the computer room and got down to work. When she'd got up that morning, she had noted the twinkle in her eyes, the peachy glow on her face and she knew she couldn't face putting on her sober, dress-for-success clothes with the button-down look. Instead she chose a linen jumpsuit the color of buttered cream and topped it with a full-cut red linen blazer worn with sleeves pushed up to her elbows. Her hair was loose and full—as Franco liked it—tamed only by two tortoise-shell combs on either side. Not exactly the image for the young female executive.

Since John died, most of the major accounts had disappeared. "I'm sorry, dear, but you're just *so* young..." and "We need a bigger firm to handle our accounts...." However, her attorney, Joe, had told her the unpleasant truth: The rumor was out in the closely knit data processing trade—Andersen-Bradley was in hock up to its computer terminals and Stacey was in big trouble.

She flipped on the switch to the memory bank and sat down on a wooden stool to wait for it to print out the information she needed on the Leader Business School account. She used to really love this work, hadn't she? When John was alive and the office hummed with the sound of Dee's CRT unit and Chris's typewriter and the computer room rumbled with activity thanks to Charlie and Roy, she had really loved this place. It was her family, her home. Her apartment had just been where she slept each night. Every morning she raced to A-B, eager to see those dear, familiar faces, and took hold again of a world that was manageable, a world that promised her fulfillment and no pain. Only pleasant, slow progress.

Now that A-B rested on her slim shoulders, the magic had worn off and, deep down, she knew the truth: She had loved the atmosphere and the work when they'd been a team. Being captain *and* crew was a lonely, miserable business. The work, what she had of it, seemed boring and repetitive. She didn't have the formal computer background to be able to coax from the computer all it was capable of. She couldn't take on new accounts without that ability and she couldn't *get* that ability when she didn't have time or money to go to school.

The intercom buzzed.

"A Mr. Martell is here to see you, Ms. Andersen."

"Show him in to my office, Chris. I'll be right there."

She sighed. Another change. She felt the pocket of her blazer for her car keys, then, straightening up, headed toward her office.

Mr. Martell's eyes lit up when he saw Stacey, tall and blond, enter the room. He was well built and fairly attractive, but he seemed too aware of it, too concerned with how to present himself to the best macho advantage. She had apparently passed some little sex appeal test of his and it made her nauseated to see the way he actually turned on the charm like a water faucet. She almost laughed as, while they spoke about the gas mileage on the car she was trading down for, he rotated his shoulders forward in an attempt to magnify the bulk of his already bulging muscles. He was as muscular as Franco and perhaps even better-looking, yet the overall effect was common. Martell's type was a dime a dozen. He had none of the refined elegance and subdued sexiness that made Franco so electric.

Lou Martell leaned over her desk as she signed the final sales papers, his breath hot near the back of her neck.

"There you go." She handed him his two copies and the keys to the Corvette. "Thank you."

He nodded, but didn't move away. "Listen," he said, leaning closer, "if you're not doing anything, you could take one last spin in the 'Vette. We could run over to The Golden Plume and have a few drinks, a few laughs."

"No laughs," she said, "no drinks, no nothing."

He stepped back, jingling the keys in his hand as he pocketed the papers. "Pretty touchy, huh, baby?" He laughed. "I know you women's lib types—not enough action." He walked toward the door. "If you decide you need a little, give me a call." With a sulky grin, he closed the door behind him.

Just in time, she thought as she released her grip on the ledger book on her desk. Another crack like that and she'd have thrown it at his head.

When she heard him drive away, she got up and looked out the window. There it was—the five-year-old Mustang she'd traded the Corvette in for. She sighed. Well, look at it this way: No more car payments, lowered insurance premiums, and, best of all, she'd be able to pay off some of the personal loans John had accrued before he died. Change was in the air everywhere.

No doubt about it.

By Thursday evening she felt ready for a rest home. Joe had given her more bad news. "Sorry, kid, but they're making noises about repossessing the computer equipment."

"They can't do that," she wailed. "Without it we're out of business."

He looked very sad. "Unfortunately, they can do it and they will do it if you don't come up with the back leasing fees."

"What the hell am I going to do? There's nothing left to sell."

"You could start with the stereo system in John's office, for one," Joe said. "That would be good for one month's rent. Dee's CRT unit—you don't do that work anymore, right?"

She nodded. She felt as if she were standing, in very high heels, on a rug and some clown were pulling it out from under her. "It's in your hands, Joe," she finally said. "Sell whatever you need to. Just, please, keep John's office intact. I still haven't been able to bring myself to sort through most of his papers and I don't want anything disturbed." Besides, she admitted to herself, once she'd cleared away the papers and personal things like his favorite Cross pen and those brown marble ashtrays, John would be truly gone and she wasn't ready for that, even if he had brought A-B down around her ears.

So, Thursday evening, hours after Chris had gone home, Stacey wandered aimlessly through the cavernous office. Every place she looked familiar objects were gone, sold to the highest bidder. Joe had called her a little after five to tell her she was set for another month.

"But I don't know what you're going to do after that, Stacey. If you don't bring in more work, we'll be in big trouble."

They'd be in big trouble? She laughed, a sound that echoed in the bareness of the room that had once housed the CRT and the fancy word-processing equipment. It seemed to her they already *were* in big trouble.

"Anyone here?"

Her heart jumped. "Franco?"

He came into the room and hurried over to enfold her in his strong arms. The hassles and headaches of the day evaporated the way they used to after a long swim. His arms became a safe harbor.

"I didn't expect you until tomorrow," she murmured, when his lips moved away from hers. "This is like a present."

"I was in Queens for a meeting," he said, "and decided to drive out and see you. When I didn't get an answer at your apartment, I came over here. Where did you hide your car? I didn't see it in the lot."

"Oh, yes, you did."

He looked confused. She didn't explain it to him, just collected her pocketbook and keys, turned out the lights, and locked the office. Taking his hand, she led him across the parking lot to the small brown car with the golden-brown vinyl top. "This is it," she said as she unlocked the door.

He looked at her, full understanding passing across his handsome face. He pulled her close for a moment, nuzzling the sensitive spot behind her ear. "Let's grab some dinner," he said. "You must be hungry and exhausted." He ran his hand down her spine, making her shiver. "Do you want Chinese food?"

"No. Actually, I'd like to cook for you at home. I just don't feel like being in a crowd. Okay?"

He agreed. He knew how hard it was for her to allow someone this close and it moved him beyond words.

Then, as he had a week ago, he followed close behind her to her apartment.

Chapter Eight

He loved watching her slim, capable hands as they chopped the ripe red tomatoes and stirred the garlic-flavored sauce heating on the stove. Her curly blond hair was piled loosely on top of her head and out of her way, long tendrils escaping and falling down around her ears and forehead. Occasionally she would run the back of her arm across or direct a puff of breath up to her forehead to get an annoying curl out of the way.

"I'm probably crazy to serve my marinara sauce to a native Italiano," she laughed as she set him to work cutting green pepper for the salad, "but I think I do a pretty decent job." She chuckled at the sight of him. He had taken off the jacket and vest to his tan suit, but she had forced him to cover his pecan silk shirt with an enormous canvas apron emblazoned "Never Underestimate the Power of a Woman."

"Actually I'm not a native Italian."

Her green eyes widened as she spooned a taste of the sauce into her mouth. "You're kidding! But you have such a beautiful continental accent."

"I'm glad you like it, *cara*, but I was born here."

She leaned on the counter. "So where did the accent come from?"

"Well, my parents were born in Rome and then I was educated in Firenze—Florence—where I spoke nothing but Italian for six years. I guess the accent rubbed off on me. I've tried to rid myself of it, but . . . no success."

"Don't ever rid yourself of it," she said. "It's so fluid and warm and—" She stopped.

"And what?"

"I don't want to turn your head, but it's awfully sexy, Franco. The one thing I liked about you when we first met was your voice."

"You liked nothing else?" His face was creased in a mock-frown. "Not my wit or my terrific shoulders or—"

She swatted him with an orange dish towel. "Oh, be quiet. To be honest, I thought you were terribly arrogant."

He looked disappointed. "And here I thought I was an irresistible sex object to you."

She stepped around the counter and sat on his lap. "I did think you were sexy," she answered truthfully, "but you were so damned sure of yourself that I decided not to like you." She arched her back a little as he ran his hand across the swell of her breasts in the yellow robe. "Besides, you wanted to join Andersen-Bradley."

"And you didn't want that?"

"No, I didn't."

"And what about now, *cara*?"

The sauce started to sputter and she used that as an excuse to not answer as she got up to lower the flame and put a lid on the pot. She turned on the water to boil for pasta then went back to his lap. She took his face in her hands and asked, "What about me? What did you think of me when we first met?"

He started to laugh, then laughed harder at the truly outraged expression on her face.

"You'd better explain what's so funny, Mr. Borelli, and fast," she said as he tried to stop laughing.

"Honestly?"

She nodded, though she was growing less sure with each moment that she really wanted to know.

"First impression was: God, she's beautiful. Second: How do I get to know her? Third: Forget it."

She frowned. " 'Forget it'? Why 'forget it'?"

"You were closed off, *cara*. When I tried to explain my lateness, you cut me off at the knees with one slice. You seemed barricaded, untouchable. . .and more than a little rude."

She blushed. "I didn't know I seemed that way."

He nodded, caressing her chin with his hand. "You did. In fact, I was ready to call off the deal right then and there but John tried to explain that you'd been under stress."

She stiffened. She forced her voice to stay even. "What did he tell you? The stress about Grandma Lillian?" *Please, God, don't let John have told him about my sterility.*

He nodded. "And remember, he knew the trouble A-B was getting into and I think some of his apprehensions were rubbing off on you."

"Maybe." She put the pasta into the boiling water, then wiped her hands on the dish towel before tearing the lettuce for the salad. "So, what made you change your mind about me after the deal fell through?"

He hesitated. There was so much she didn't know. He watched her as she opened the refrigerator and pulled out celery and little flowers of broccoli to add to the big salad bowl. Seeing her face scrubbed clean of makeup, body wrapped in a yellow robe, her bare, red-painted toes peeping through, he felt a violent surge of lust and love that nearly knocked him off his chair. She had crept inside his brain and into his blood with that strange combination of sophistication and naiveté, the sensuality that could drive a man wild, coupled with a cool exterior that hid the passions inside. How could he explain the curve of his heart?

"It was the night of John's accident."

She put the vegetables down and turned to him, startled by the husky intensity of his voice. He was looking down at his hands, absently picking an invisible speck of dust from the band of his watch as he spoke. He seemed very serious. She was almost afraid that breathing would break the fragile atmosphere in the kitchen.

"I hadn't wanted to break the news over the phone and leave you alone to find your way to New Jersey, so I came here. I had seen a glimpse of what I thought was the real Stacey"—he looked up and gave her a small smile—"but I still expected to find a very different woman here than the one I found."

She tried to think back to what she'd been wearing, how she must have seemed to him, but her memories of that evening were mercifully blurred.

"It was as if the sophistication had been removed along with the tailored clothes and the pulled-back hair. You must have just taken a shower because you smelled clean and fresh and your hair was braided in two ponytails that hung over your shoulders and left little wet circles on your shirt."

She stared at him in amazement. He looked far away as he spoke. "You seemed so young and so untouched, that I hated to bring sadness into your world. And then when you just stood there, barefoot, incapable of finding your shoes, I dug your sneakers out from under the chair and put them on you. It sounds odd now when I tell you," he said, cheeks flushing beneath his tan, "but when I saw you had a small hole in the canvas top of the right sneaker and I saw your toe peeking through—

that silly shade of cherry red—I knew I was lost.''

"I don't understand. What did that do to you?"

He shrugged. "It's hard to say. I guess it proved you were human, not as totally in control as you seemed to be. Whatever—it showed me the real Stacey you kept buried under your office personality.''

He seemed embarrassed by his speech and she walked over behind him and wrapped her arms around his neck, crossing them over his chest. He covered her hands with his own while she put her head on top of his head and breathed in the clean scent of his hair. She was filled with an almost painful sensation of love so intense she was beyond speech. He was as beautiful inside as out.

For a second she thought about telling him the truth about Michael and her condition. However, the timer on the oven rang and she moved away from him.

"Time to eat," she said, making her voice light, pretending she was really interested in the spaghetti.

He caught her by the wrist and pulled her back to him.

"Not now," he said, his voice a low growl. "Later."

It was much later when they finally sat down at the maple kitchen table for dinner. While he'd put on a pair of jeans and sweat shirt her brother-in-law had left at her apartment last summer, she'd thrown out the now soggy spaghetti and cooked a new batch.

"This is an occasion," she said as she took a bottle of champagne from her refrigerator. "Occasions deserve champagne.''

Franco, looking a little uncomfortable in the tight pants, eased himself down onto a chair. "These things are lethal to your circulation."

She gave him a quick once-over, then twirled an imaginary mustache as she leered at him. "I think they look just fine. In fact, wearing them should be mandatory."

He gave her a playful swat on her firm derrière, which was outlined by the clinging yellow robe. "If we're going to be sexual chauvinists," he laughed, "then get the food on the table, woman. Your man is hungry."

She dropped a mock-curtsy and hurried around the kitchen at comic speed, draining spaghetti, piling it on earthenware plates, then pouring the rich, red sauce, fragrant with garlic and oregano, over the top.

"There." She placed a steaming platter in front of him and sprinkled some pungent Parmesan cheese over top. "An Italian meal fit for a mighty Caesar."

"Are you implying I'm a dictator?"

She grinned and sat opposite him. "If the toga fits...." She picked up her fork and twirled some spaghetti around it. "Now, shut up and eat!"

Between them they polished off a prodigious pile of spaghetti, washed down by the bottle of champagne and some Amaretto di Saronno. They stacked the dishes in the dishwasher and by midnight, they were lying on top of her bed with shimmers of silvery moonlight streaming through the open window, illuminating their bodies with a lustrous glow. Their lovemaking had been slow and sweet, nearly reverent. She loved the feeling of her bedroom with him in it. Again she wanted to open up to him, to tell him of her fears and desires, to share with him all the things that she loved. Or almost all. The thought of Michael and what had happened made her quiet for a moment.

There were no guarantees Franco would be able to accept her childlessness any better than Michael had.

"*Cara*, is anything wrong?"

She shook her head, which rested against his warm

chest. She leaned up for a moment and gently outlined his nipple with her tongue, teasing, then caressing. "I was just thinking," she answered, her hand on his stomach, "I wish I had met you years ago, Franco, before—" Her voice drifted away as she pressed her lips to the dark hairs of his chest, as if to force the painful memories from her mind.

"Before what, *cara*?"

She shrugged against his skin. "Before I became such an old grouch," she answered, trying to make her voice light.

He was quiet. She suddenly was afraid she had offended him in some way or—worse—that she had made him curious.

He put his strong hands on her shoulders and pulled her face up to his. She was pierced by the golden arrows of his eyes.

"*Cara, amore,* listen. I feel as if we've always known one another. Be happy we are together now. I like to think we bring the fullness of our experiences here, everything that made us what we are at this moment, everything that has brought us to this joy."

She choked back a sob, but couldn't stop the flow of happy tears that fell, hot and damp, onto his skin. He had unlocked another secret door in her heart.

He stroked her hair and back, cherishing her with words in a language she couldn't understand until she slept curled inside the loving circle of his arms.

The next day when he showed up at the office, it was all she could do to keep from running into his arms. As it was, Chris had noticed the look that passed between them and had discreetly excused herself from Stacey's office where she had been filing some papers.

"Do you think she knows?" Stacey asked as she allowed herself the exquisitely unexpected pleasure of cuddling with him on her office couch.

He tilted her face up to him and grinned. "What do you think?"

"I think we're being very discreet."

"*Cara*, the look in your eyes was unmistakable and I'm sure the same look is in mine. Face it: The world knows we're lovers."

She giggled like a child and tucked her slim legs underneath her.

"What brings you here, Franco? I thought you were in Manhattan today."

"I was. I spoke with your attorney and told him I was going to make a proposition to you." He grinned at her upraised eyebrows. "Sorry, not that kind at the moment. You know the word is out about Andersen-Bradley." She nodded, pulling away from him a little. "Well, I'd like to propose you allow me to invest in A-B to get you out of this jam."

"No." She shook her head. "I don't want you involved in this mess."

"For what reason? Do you still not want a new partner?"

"I'm afraid if you get pulled into this disaster our relationship will suffer. Johnny left us in a pretty bad way, you know."

She was puzzled that he didn't seem surprised but she soon forgot that when she heard his proposal.

"How about a six-month trial partnership? I need a tax shelter and access to a Compu-500. If A-B goes down, I lose my chance on the system. Besides, I have a lucky touch at investing and I don't think we'll come up losers if we give it our all."

She frowned. "I don't understand you. Where does

investing come in? I never *did* understand exactly what you do for a living." She laughed. "That is, if you even have to earn a living. I mean, you had a limousine and all of that. Since we're talking money, where exactly do you stand?"

"Rented limo, *cara*," he said with a chuckle. "My family isn't what you would call superrich, but they are definitely upper-middle class. When they came to America, my father was a tailor and my mother an artist. They combined their talents and opened a line of made-to-order clothing for men. News spread by word-of-mouth and finally they put together a catalog like Horchow's and Bloomingdale's—that type of thing. They've ended up turning a cottage industry into a very healthy living."

She sighed and moved closer to him as he stroked a curl of her blond hair.

"As the only son, I was programmed to take over when Dad retires in two years. But it's never appealed to me. They sent me to Florence to study business after I graduated from Princeton with a Master's in computer engineering.

"While I was over in Florence, I took some money I'd saved working summers and tried my hand at investing. I had some lucky breaks a few years ago when gold hit the ceiling. I'll do anything my father needs me to do but this"—he gestured in the direction of the computer room—"is what I enjoy. What I needed—and still need—is a good investment in a small computer company where I could have access to the machines and have my money sheltered in the corporate structure." He was quiet for a moment. "I can't live my father's life nor can I keep on dabbling."

He ran his fingers through her hair, talking now as

much to himself as to her. "I'm thirty-three years old. It's time to feel connected to something, to be committed to something." He kissed her forehead. In a voice so soft she was sure she had imagined it, he said, "I want to know someone cares."

She got up and straightened the skirt of her turquoise silk dress. Without a word she crossed over to her desk, picked up her phone, and dialed a number.

"Joe?" she said, loud enough for Franco to hear every word. "Could you come to the office? I want you to draw up some papers for a temporary partnership."

"I'm sorry to drag you into this the night before you leave for Florida," Dianne apologized to Stacey as they fixed their makeup in the ladies' room of the restaurant. "But I wanted to see you before you leave and I'd forgotten I had a date with that horror outside."

Stacey retouched her apricot lipstick.

"Tell me the truth," she said. "Does marriage seem so bad after a date like that?"

Dianne grimaced. "That's not the half of it. Grandma called the last date I had 'the man with the seven hands.'" They laughed. "The truth is, Al and I have a lot to work out and we don't seem to be getting anyplace. Maybe when I go back to White Plains and start work next week we'll have more time to straighten things out." She shrugged. "Who knows? We said a lot of things to each other before I moved out, Stace, and some of them are kind of hard to forget."

Stacey, still flushed with the first stages of love, hugged her sister. "Think carefully before you throw all those years away, Di. Freedom isn't all it's cracked up to be. I'm the expert on that."

They went back outside, where Dianne's date was

waiting for them, standing by the bar watching all the women walk by. Stacey shuddered at the thought of her sister even being in the same car with a man like that. Having finally found love, Stacey couldn't understand how her sister could willingly throw her marriage away as she had. Nothing, *nothing*, should jeopardize the miracle of keeping two people together.

Her thoughts returned to Franco. She smiled as she thought of him back at his Manhattan apartment packing. In just eleven hours they would be on a plane for Key West and the East Coast Computer Marketing Seminar, a yearly excuse for sun and fun.

Dianne had said they would cut the evening short, and after a hug in the parking lot, Stacey got into her brown Mustang and hurried home to finish her own packing. Everything had changed in the three weeks since Franco had come into the firm. She had refused to change the name of the company, out of loyalty to John, but had agreed to at least refer to it as *A-B*. She had also discovered that Franco had very definite ideas about business.

"First impressions are what count," he told her the week before. "You never forgot that I had a limo and driver, did you?"

She shook her head.

"Did it ever occur to you I had rented it specifically to make that impression on you and John?"

"Not until you told me you'd rented it." She stared at him. "I automatically assumed you were rich and owned it."

He smiled. "Exactly. It cost me a hundred dollars to rent the car and it made an impression on you that ten thousand dollars' worth of advertising and hype never could."

She was still thinking about the changes he'd brought to the company as she went into her apartment and finished getting ready to leave for Florida the next morning.

She'd known many of these things he told her were true, but she had doubted their value. However, just by trying some of his tricks—never answer your own phone, have everything obviously screened through a secretary, don't place your own calls—business had already picked up a little.

She chuckled as she got into bed, pulling the covers up around her shoulders. Franco was right: It *was* all in how you presented yourself.

"Oh, Franco!" She spun around in delight and flopped onto the sunny-yellow bedspread in her hotel room. "You were one hundred percent right! You have the Midas Touch!"

"Whoa!" He flopped down next to her, peeling back the short jacket to her dress and placing his lips against the tanned curve of her breasts. "You have as much to do with it as I do. Let's face it: We just happen to make an exceptionally good team."

She giggled and threw her arms open wide, then wrapped them around his back. He was wearing a pale gold dress shirt and she felt the heat of his suntan coming through the fine fabric. "We *are* a wonderful team," she laughed. "A fabulous team! We're better than Laurel and Hardy, than Abbott and Costello, than Hepburn and Tracy—"

He put one hand over her mouth. "*Basta!* Enough!" He sat up and stripped his shirt off and tossed it onto the chair next to the bed. "I was watching the people here at the seminar," he said as he lay back down next to her. "They take one look at you and you can see the 'pow' happen inside their heads. The men all wonder how you can look so beautiful and be so successful and the women all hate you for looking so beautiful and being so successful."

She laughed again, then was silenced by his hands as they slipped her jacket off and slid the straps of her sundress down over her shoulders, exposing her lush body to his hungry hands. "Then when you speak—*cara*, when you speak you turn out to be so damned nice and so smart that—boom! They're sunk. You win the deal before you even spell out the terms. *Fantastico!*"

She leaned up on her elbows and gazed at him, her green eyes sparkling. "I never knew I could do it. I always hid in the office with the paperwork and made John handle the customer contact whenever I could get away with it. I never knew it could be so much fun or that I would be good at it."

"Such a waste," he murmured, hands featherlight against her flesh. He cupped her breasts together and pressed his face in the valley between. The stubble of his beard was rough against her soft skin and once again she took delight in the physical differences between men and women.

Her mind raced as he flicked a nipple with his tongue, then covered it with his mouth, teasing until it stood up hard and erect, a deep rose color against her creamy breasts. She arched her back as he moved his mouth to the other demanding nipple, then worked his way down. She slipped out of her sundress and he slid her bikini panties down her tanned legs as his hands stroked her inner thighs. She moaned low in her throat as he kissed his way back up her throat to her mouth. She entwined her fingers in his silky hair and moaned as his tongue flicked and tormented against hers until she was moaning even from the feel of his warm breath against her face. Finally, she pushed his head back down against his pillow, and unzipping his trousers and pulling them over his strong legs, she placed her lips against his tanned skin and branded him with her mark as her hands turned him into stone, then fire, then one, long arching wave of desire.

The seminar lasted three days. They didn't get to see much of Key West during that time—basically, just the inside of the hotel's small convention center and its smoky bar, where some of the best deals were usually made. Stacey was nearly high with excitement. If things worked out according to their forecast, by late October she would be able to pay off the remainder of John's gambling debts and bring the rental fees on the office and equipment up to date. Then, with a little luck, she and Franco would be able to start implementing some of his ideas for acquiring new clients, directing A-B into new areas of computer sciences.

The last day of the seminar was a Friday. After calling Chris to make sure no new crises had occurred in their absence, they decided to stay on in Key West until Sunday night. It was a fascinating little town, full of quaint cottages with gingerbread roofs and trams that bussed the tourists down Duval Street, showing them the house where Ernest Hemingway wrote and James Audubon painted.

At 3 P.M. when the last speaker made his closing address, Stacey and Franco were officially free to play "tourists." They raced upstairs to their rooms and stripped off their business clothes. Stacey zipped herself into a lime-green shorts outfit and bare white sandals while Franco put on a pair of lightweight white jeans and a red T-shirt.

The tropical sun was wicked and she was glad they'd taken time to slather on sunscreen before leaving. A few of the conference attendees had neglected to take precautions and had suffered severe sunstrokes.

They held hands as they took the Conch Tour Train through the old part of the city and inspected the Spanish galleon docked at the foot of Margaret Street near Turtle Kroals. They marveled at how low the clouds in Key West were. They barely cleared the tops of the telephone poles.

Then, tired and hungry as they were, they joined natives and tourists alike on the beach by Mallory Docks, watching the glorious pink-and-orange blaze of the Key West sunset as it bounced up and off the Gulf of Mexico. When the crowd broke up at dusk, Franco and Stacey lingered awhile on the sand, content to be bathed by the cooling Gulf breeze and lulled by the steady lapping of the waters at the shoreline.

"This is almost as beautiful as the Mediterranean," he said, stroking her hair and kissing the side of her neck. "Someday I want to show you the Riviera and the beaches of—"

She chuckled and pressed a finger to his lips to silence him. "Shh. . . it may seem crazy, but to me, the most beautiful beach in the world is at Montauk Point."

"Dramatic and striking, yes, but beautiful? I don't know—"

"But it is!" she insisted. She sat straight and faced him, her green eyes flashing. "Don't the starkness and rough edges call out to something in you, some primitive force? I go there whenever I feel trapped or angry.

Somehow it soothes me.'' She stopped. ''Does that make any sense to you?''

He pulled her to her feet and drew her close to him, green eyes almost on level with gold.

''It makes sense to me, *cara*, since knowing you.'' He bent down to retrieve her handbag from the sand. ''Come, let's go back to the hotel.''

''If we went back out to Montauk now,'' she said later as she ran steamy water into the enormous bathtub in their room, ''do you think it would still be special to us?''

He came up behind her and cupped her breasts through the light fabric of her robe. ''It will be special because it was where we first made love,'' he whispered, sliding her robe off until it was a silky pool on the bathroom floor. He kissed the base of her spine, making her shiver with delight. ''But, for me, *bellezza,* my beauty, joy is wherever you are.''

When the tub was full and scented with a slithery bath oil, he stripped off his clothes and stepped in.

''Cara, andiamo!''

She felt strangely shy as she stepped into the tub with him. He told her to sit facing him, putting her long slim legs on either side of his hips. She felt impaled by his golden eyes. There was no avoiding his gaze, no diverting the intensity of meaning by capturing his face in a kiss or ducking her head against his shoulder. She lifted her arms and piled her tumbling hair on top of her head, unaware of the powerful grace of her torso as she did so or of the way his eyes glazed over with desire.

She burned under his gaze, aching to be cooled by his love. She made a move to come to his side of the tub to caress him fully, but he commanded her to stay put. It was a new Franco, fiercely masculine, and his power inflamed her senses, burning away the last shred of shyness. Touch was different in water. She was surrounded by the wet warmth, thrilled by his hands as they slid up and down the muscles of her calf, stroking the sensitive arch of her foot until she was reduced to pure light, pure fire.

As she stayed a prisoner in his eyes, he raised her right leg, and one hand holding the ankle, one hand gently stroking her, he raised the foot to his lips and kissed her instep then the delicate high curve of her arch, making her moan with desire.

Although roomy, the tub was too small to continue making love as they wished to, so, swaddled in towels, he led her back to the bedroom and removed her covering. She went to lie down on the bed.

"*Cara*, no. I want to look at you."

"Franco, please! I feel too self-conscious." She raised an arm to shield her breasts from his hungry eyes, an odd gesture, for he knew her body intimately already. There was just something so exposed about standing nude before him, faults underlined to his gaze. "Franco, really." She tried to make a small joke. "The more you look, the more fault you'll find. Better leave something to the imagination."

He kissed her quiet. "Allow me this privilege, *cara*. To me you are exquisite. I want to know every inch of your body the way I know my own. I want you to know the power you have over me."

With words like music he described her body, the way it looked through his loving eyes. She seemed to blossom before him, self-doubts and self-conscious feelings vanishing. He made her see her body as a beautiful instrument, a garden of delights, and she wanted to share it with him fully.

Standing there naked, with a powerful beauty and dignity, she raised her chin and lowered her eyes as she looked at him. "I want you to make love to me now, Franco. I can't wait any longer for you."

Swiftly he was next to her, then all over her as they fell backward onto the soft bed. There was no part of her body that didn't respond to his touch, to his burning kisses and strokes of passion. A low rolling moan built inside her as her body arched to accommodate him, to take his very being inside hers, to become part of one another, to forget where one stopped and the other began. She wanted to lose herself with him and be found again and again.

He was an exquisite, tireless lover—each time she thought he had brought her to the very edge of bliss, he would gently bring her back only to take her again and again to that glorious edge of madness and delight. Finally, when they had both achieved a simultaneous explosion of ecstasy, he curled on his side facing her and drew her close against his chest to hold her in the deepness of the night as they slept.

The rude jangling of the telephone pierced the stillness of the room.

"What on earth?" He sat up, half-asleep and switched on the bedside lamp. He picked up his watch and squinted at it. "Four-fifteen."

Stacey sat up, covering herself with the white sheet. Her heart hammered behind her breastbone.

"It's Dianne," he said, amber eyes serious. "She sounds very upset." He handed the receiver over to Stacey.

Dianne's normally cheerful voice was shaky as she spoke. "Stacey, you know I would never bother you if it weren't important."

"It's Grandma, isn't it?" Stacey could feel the truth of her words deep inside. "What happened?"

"Her heart. She had a seizure late this afternoon, then another one this evening. I think you'd better come back, Stace. She's asking for you."

"Of course. I'll call you as soon as we get in."

Within an hour and a half, Stacey and Franco had taken a small plane to Miami Airport and were boarding a DC-10 for JFK International in New York. Franco, as usual, was a tremendous help, but she found herself strangely calm and able to deal with the small details of their hasty departure.

"I guess I've been expecting this for a long time," she said, watching the Miami landscape tilt at a crazy angle as their plane climbed into the early-morning sky and headed north. "She hasn't really been well for over a year and she's been trying to prepare us for this." She sighed and rested her head against the tiny window for a moment. "I just wish I'd been able to do more for her, to make her happier. Everything Dianne and I are we owe to her. Everything."

"I know," he said, putting an arm around her. "When you get to the hospital you can tell her what's in your heart, *cara*."

Stacey turned to him, green eyes wet with unshed tears. "If it's not too late," she answered. "I just pray it's not too late."

When Stacey reached North Shore Hospital on Long Island, Lillian was in the Cardiac Care Unit, awake and asking for her. Dianne and Al were huddled on a sofa in the waiting room. Dianne's face was drawn and sad, but surprisingly serene.

"She's a remarkable lady," she told Stacey as she filled her in on the details of their grandmother's condition. "She says she's dying and is ready. She only wanted to live to see us both grown into happy, independent women. Go to her...she's been waiting to see you." She turned and buried her head against Al's chest.

Stacey nodded to the nurse who sat in the corner, head bent over a novel. Lillian couldn't be dying, she thought, not really. Except for the cumbersome machinery by her side that registered every beat of her heart, her grandmother seemed remarkably healthy with her white hair fanned out on the pillow, green eyes still luminous with her indomitable spirit.

"Stacey." Her voice was whispery, but her words were clear. Stacey bent over and kissed her cheek, then took her hand and sat next to the bed.

"Grandma, what are you doing in here? You look too healthy for this." She forced a smile. "I can't leave you alone for a second, can I?"

Lillian returned the smile and lightly squeezed the young woman's hand.

"Another change for you, child. Don't be frightened, Stacey. I'm not."

"Don't talk like that, Grandma. You sound like you want to die."

Lillian closed her eyes for a long moment, then looked back at her granddaughter. "It's my time, dear, plain and simple. I am very, very tired and in pain. I think this is my time to leave gracefully, as they say. I've made my peace with it."

Stacey choked back the sob lodged at the back of her throat. "I don't know what to do without you, Grandma. Who will be there?"

"One of the things that's made me happiest," Lillian said, voice soft as a summer breeze, "is the friendship between you and Dianne. You two will always have one another for support, that I can be sure of.'' She smiled at Stacey. ''And now you have Franco.'' She pulled Stacey closer, looked deep into her eyes. ''Do you love him?''

''I never—'' She stopped. So swept away by her emotions had she been, that she had never taken the time to think deeply about it. Suddenly it all seemed so incredibly clear to her and so terrifying that it took her breath away. An enormous expanse of uncharted future lay before her; none of the old landmarks were there any longer to guide her. And all of her old secrets still remained.

''Yes,'' she finally said. ''I *do* love him, Grandma. But that doesn't guarantee a thing.''

Her grandmother nodded. ''No, it doesn't. But it does prove you are capable of loving and being loved in return, Stacey. You've become a full human being and that makes me proud that I did my job well.''

Tears fell onto Stacey's hand and she didn't bother to wipe them away.

''I love you, Grandma. I always will.''

Lillian nodded. ''You silly child. Did you ever think I doubted that?''

Chapter Nine

"This will do you good, *cara*," Franco said as he eased his black Buick onto the New Jersey Turnpike and headed south toward Princeton. "I didn't want to leave you alone this weekend."

Stacey nodded and curled up in the passenger's seat to get a little sleep. Lillian's funeral had been held two days before. Although not unexpected, her death was a painful loss of Stacey's past and it left her feeling drained. The only bright spot in the whole thing was Dianne's reconciliation with Al.

She sighed and turned her face away from the window, trying to keep the bright sun from seeping through her closed eyelids.

She'd spent the past two days at Franco's apartment in Manhattan. Despite her sadness, it had been a pleasure to see how he lived—to look at the beautiful antique oak furniture, at the fiery orange quilt on his king-size bed, the artwork on his walls; to see silly things like whether he stacked drinking glasses lip up or lip down. She was fascinated by this previously hidden aspect of his life, evidence he had a life separate from the one they shared.

They were heading to see his family who lived in a tiny town just outside Princeton, New Jersey. His younger sister Leeanna had just given birth to her first child and the infant was being christened that day. It was an occasion that Franco, as godfather, could not miss and he wanted to share it with Stacey, to introduce her to the people he loved, the family he hoped she would become part of. He checked the pocket of his vest to make sure the jewelry box was still there.

The bittersweet irony of a birth so quickly following a death offered a sense of life renewing itself, of continuity. He hoped she'd find comfort in that.

They passed quickly through the smoggy, factory town of Elizabeth and sped south. As always, he felt himself grow more peaceful as they left the industrialized sections behind and went deeper into the rolling meadows of south Jersey. Acres of lush green farmland stretched on either side of the highway. In the distance he could see the sloping red roofs of barns and the tiny brown dots that were milk cows grazing.

About five miles from his parents' home, he woke Stacey up as she'd asked him to do, and pulled into a diner so she could freshen up before meeting Carmela and Giancarlo Borelli. She hurried into the ladies' room while he sipped coffee and read the Trenton newspaper. With quick practiced movements she fixed her makeup, carefully wiping away a tiny smudge of mascara at the edge of one eye. Her apricot lipstick had worn away and she reapplied a light, fresh coat. Her hair was pulled on top of her head in a chignon, but her full curly bangs and side tendrils wreathed her face in a blond froth. She turned sideways to the mirror and checked the black linen sundress for wrinkles, then adjusted the short-sleeved white jacket. Finally, pleased with her appearance, she rejoined Franco and they drove the rest of the way to Haverton Street and the Borelli home.

As they pulled into the circular asphalt driveway of the brick ranch house, set amid tall evergreen trees, her stomach did a quick flip up into the hollow of her throat and her hands grew damp with sweat. Suddenly it all seemed to matter so much—she so desperately wanted his family to love her on sight that she thought she'd hyperventilate with nervous tension.

He pulled in behind his sister's green Saab and next to his mother's pale blue Cadillac.

"This is it." He squeezed Stacey's hand and turned the engine off.

Before she had a chance to answer, a swarm of people burst from the front door and surrounded the car, sweeping them out into a multitude of embraces.

A small slim woman of about sixty with deep brown eyes took Stacey's hands in hers, then enfolded the tall young woman in a warm hug. "Sta-cee. I welcome you to our home. We are so proud to have you here with us today." Her accent was musical and delightful, very reminiscent of the lilting traces in Franco's own voice.

"This is my mother, Carmela," Franco said, bending to kiss the woman's youthful-looking cheek. "And, as you know, Mama, this is Stacey Andersen."

Stacey smiled, her nervousness vanishing, and extended her hand to his mother. "I'm so happy to meet you, Mrs. Borelli, and very honored that you would be willing to have a perfect stranger share this happy occasion with you."

His mother linked arms with Stacey. "My son cares a great deal for you and that makes you welcome in our home anytime. And, Sta-cee," she said, looking up at her, "please do call me Carmela. We do not stand on formality here."

"Franco, my boy." A booming voice made Stacey turn to her left in time to see Franco enveloped in the hearty hug of a man about his own size who had a head of beautiful silver hair. "Is this *biondina bellissima* your Stacey?" His Mediterranean-blue eyes danced as he grinned at her.

"Stacey, this doddering old man here is my father, Giancarlo, who, as you can tell, is ready to retire to a nursing home."

Giancarlo roared with laughter and clapped his son on the back. He was a powerfully built man whose athletic body and lively eyes belied his years.

She extended her hand. In a truly Italian gesture of courtliness, he took it and raised it to his lips, lightly kissing it. The ends of his perfectly trimmed mustache tickled.

"Che bella femmina," he said to Franco. "Excuse me, Stacey—I don't mean to exclude you. I said, 'What a beautiful young woman.'"

She blushed under his delightful scrutiny.

"Grazie."

"Vuole parlare l'italiano?"

She laughed. "I'm afraid that was about the extent of it. Franco has been teaching me some. It's a beautiful language."

"The language of love." Giancarlo put an arm at the back of her waist and propelled her up the path to the front door. "Come, *biondina*, I want you to meet the newest member of the family."

The living room was a magnificent mixture of understated traditional furniture, interspersed with a few well-chosen antiques. It managed to be elegant and homey simultaneously, a combination strived for but rarely achieved. What impressed Stacey most were the personal touches throughout the room: a mantelpiece filled with family photos, needlepoint cushions and crewel-work pillows on the antique rocking chairs near the fireplace. The effect was comfortably beautiful.

Giancarlo led her into a bedroom off the hall, where a tiny, black-haired young woman sat in a boudoir chair, holding a bottle to the lips of an infant with an enormous shock of black hair like his mother's. The woman looked up at Giancarlo and Stacey, then smiled.

"Come on in," she invited. "Gian-Franco is just having his breakfast." She wore a pale-blue dressing gown with a white terry-cloth towel draped over one shoulder.

Giancarlo excused himself to find Paul, the baby's father. Stacey stood, transfixed by the maternal beauty of the lovely young woman and child who were bathed by a curtain of summer sun that streamed through the open window.

"Stacey?"

She nodded.

"I'm Franco's sister, Leeanna, and this is Gian-Franco, our newest member. Please come in and sit," she said, taking the bottle from the sleepy baby. "He's through now."

Stacey was still staring at the infant, whose tiny pink lips were stained with milk. He didn't seem quite real to her; he was more like an exquisite porcelain statue than a human being.

"I'm sorry for seeming so dumbfounded," Stacey murmured. "He's just such a beautiful sight to see that I'm overwhelmed."

Leeanna nodded. "I know what you mean. I had never spent time with an infant before Gian-Franco. When you see how tiny and helpless they are, it is kind of overwhelming, isn't it?"

"I've never seen one so young before." Stacey watched Leeanna put the baby over her shoulder to burp him. "It's no wonder the old Masters painted so many pictures of madonnas with infants. It's a very moving sight."

Leeanna smiled. "Franco said if I'd gone to Italy to study the way he did, I would have become accustomed to infants within the first ten minutes."

Stacey laughed. "Did you have natural childbirth?"

Leeanna nodded. "Paul and I decided on that right from the moment we knew I was pregnant: no anaesthetics, Paul by my side, the works. However, at the last moment there were complications and I ended up having a Caesarean section." She smiled down at the baby. "It's been an experience for the whole family—none of us really knew a thing about infants."

Stacey frowned. She was about to say, didn't Leeanna mean they had just *forgotten* everything they knew about infants, when the young woman stood up and placed the child in Stacey's arms.

"Perhaps you'd like a little practice for when you have your own."

After a second's hesitation, Stacey's arms instinctively curved around the sleepy child. The head was surprisingly heavy as it nestled in the crook of her elbow, tiny lips pursed as if still nursing. Over the years she'd become adept at sidestepping the invitations to hold the newest additions to friends' families: She'd claim a bad cold, beginner's nerves—anything to avoid the slash of pain she knew would slice at her heart at the first touch of an infant's softness. She'd trained her thoughts to leapfrog away from anything that could cause her pain, anything that would make her think deeply and long about her sterility.

Having Gian-Franco thrust into her arms like that had made all of it rush to the front of her mind. She'd expected to be engulfed by waves of inadequacy and loss over what could never be part of her life. However, she felt, instead, an enormous swelling of tenderness toward the infant, but not quite the sadness she'd expected. As she held this child who was not a part of her flesh and blood, she felt the rising of a protective instinct, a maternal surge of affection that had nothing to do with the physical act of giving birth.

Nothing could change the fact that the birth experience would be denied her—that was a fact she could no longer hide from. But perhaps it was possible to finally accept it and put aside the pain and the feeling of diminishment. Maybe there were other ways to view it.

Some things had mercifully faded with time—slowly she'd been able to stop the vivid fantasies of miraculous medical breakthroughs, of new discoveries that would unfold the world of pregnancy to her like a blossoming flower. It seemed every magazine she picked up held photo-essays on famous thirty- and forty-year-old stars burgeoning with their first child, inspiring stories of new fertility drugs and in vitro fertilization that could make the dream of conception a reality for more and more women.

At first she had run to her doctor each time she heard of a new technique, regaling him with facts and figures gleaned from the medical journals she pored over in the library. Although he had been infinitely kind to her, he nevertheless refused to entertain any false hopes for her.

"Don't do this to yourself, Stacey," she could still hear his deep, kind voice say. "Put it aside and turn your thoughts toward adoption. There are so many children out there—"

She understood what he was trying to say to her and

felt that, in time, she could embrace adoption as a viable solution for her. However, looking down at the infant, then up at Leeanna who was now standing next to Paul, her tall skinny husband, she wondered if she were being fair to Franco. The joy on their faces was so beautiful to see that it almost hurt her eyes. Could she deny Franco this elemental experience? She may finally be able to accept her condition but was it fair to ask it of him? Shouldn't she tell him the truth before their relationship went any further? If she loved him, didn't he deserve the choice, even if it meant losing him?

Within an hour, the sprawling ranch house was filled with friends and relatives who spilled into the living room and dining room and sat in deck chairs on the patio sipping lemonade while Leeanna dressed the baby for the christening at noon.

Franco introduced her to a score of people and she tried very hard to keep Aunt Julie and Uncle Anthony from getting confused with Mr. and Mrs. DeGregorio or the Wagner family who had come in from Gettysburg to be there. Many of the people brought their children, who now sat, dressed-up and thoroughly miserable, on the flagstone steps in front of the house, waiting to go to the church for the ceremony.

She whirled around at the touch of a hand on her elbow and looked into the dancing blue eyes of Giancarlo.

"*Biondina*, may I steal you away from my son for a stroll through my garden?"

She looked at Franco, who bowed toward his father and grinned. "I warn you, Stacey, when he starts talking gardening, there's no escaping him."

Giancarlo said something in Italian that made Franco

laugh, then the older man extended his arm to Stacey. "We go?"

She looked at him and smiled, the dimple in her right cheek deepening, then slipped her arm through his. "It would be my pleasure," she answered.

Giancarlo led Stacey around to the side of the house where they followed a narrow path lined with violets in a deep, vibrating shade of purple.

"I was pleased when Franco told me you're a gardener," Giancarlo said as they reached the gate that led into the garden. He opened it for Stacey.

"I have the heart of a gardener but the skill of a child," she said as he led her past oak trees so tall she had to crane her neck to see the uppermost branches. Ringing the sprawling trunks were concentric circles of deep yellow alyssum with their masses of minute round blossoms; shocking-pink begonias, their green leaves round and waxy; and a final circle of tiny zinnias in a blazing rainbow of oranges, yellows, and golds, with one deep red bloom incongruously springing up in the center.

"Are they really zinnias?" Stacey asked in astonishment, bending down to gently touch the scalloped edge of a small flower. "But, they can't be! Zinnias are huge."

Giancarlo bent down next to her and plucked the vibrant scarlet flower from the center. "You have a good eye, *biondina*. These are my pride and joy."

She squinted into the fierce sunshine and, despite the glare, saw the pride on his face. "Where on earth did you find them? They must be very rare." She was entranced by the miniature perfection of the thumb-size zinnias.

"Trial and error," he answered, bending down next

to her. "They are my own hybrid—I just perfected them two years ago." He briefly explained some of the cross-breeding processes he used to come up with the dwarf zinnias. "Finally, last year, I brought them to the point where they bloom at just four inches tall." He sighed. "I was about to take them to the botany department of the university when I discovered a major seed company had already mass-produced a strain similar to mine and was selling them in the new catalog." He shrugged and shook his head.

"How terrible to have worked so hard and not have your work recognized."

He looked at her. "The work I do every day at my office—that is the work I do for recognition. This"—he gestured toward the flowers—"I do for myself. *I* know these are my own doing." He tapped his chest with a weathered hand. "Just that this beauty exists and I exist to enjoy it is reward enough. We hurry people along, forcing them to grow at our own speed. I've been guilty of that myself."

He smiled at her. "You can't do that in a garden," he went on. "Here each flower grows at its own pace, following its own timetable, hurrying for no man. And when all conditions are right, the seedling blossoms into a beautiful flower, right on schedule. And, *biondina*, the blossom is all the more lovely for the wait."

Gently he turned the scarlet blossom around between his fingers, then, with another smile and a nod of his head, extended it toward Stacey. Her hand shook for an instant as she took it, for she realized it was more than just a flower he offered her—it was acceptance.

"*Grazie,*" she said softly. She didn't trust herself to say more. The wave of emotion that flooded her threatened to turn into a flow of happy tears she was afraid she'd be unable to stop.

A smile curved the ends of his mustache as Giancarlo watched her tuck the flower into the right side of her chignon. He stood up, one knee creaking a bit, then helped her to her feet.

"It must be near time to leave," he said, placing her arm through his. "Carmela and Franco will send out a search party if we do not return now."

She nodded. Briefly she touched her index finger to the red flower nestled in her shiny blond hair. "Thank you," she said again. "Thank you for everything."

He patted the hand that rested lightly on his forearm. "You thank me now," he teased as they walked back toward the house, "but where will you be tomorrow morning when I am on hands and knees weeding the vegetable garden?"

"Right beside you," she answered, her voice firm.

He glanced at her, his eyes filled with growing respect as the party sounds of ice tinkling in glasses and happy chatter surrounded them again. "Is 7 A.M. too early."

"A *true* gardener begins at six thirty." She smiled.

He nodded as they walked around the side of the swimming pool. They approached a laughing crowd of aunts and uncles where Franco was the unwilling center of attention.

"Should we rescue him?" Stacey asked as Franco flashed them a wide-eyed look of appeal.

Giancarlo released her arm. "You go, *biondina*. It is you he wants right now. I'd best see if Leeanna and the baby are ready to leave."

Suddenly, in an impulsive gesture that didn't come easily for her, Stacey kissed the older man's ruddy cheek. "I'll be in the garden at six thirty," she said.

He patted her shoulder.

"I never doubted it, *biondina*."

Straightening her shoulders, she took a deep breath and plunged into the pool of relatives, quickly drowning in a sea of names and who was whose second cousin twice-removed by marriage.

"My head is spinning!" she said half an hour later as she and Franco slipped into his old bedroom for a quick embrace. "I can't keep anybody's name straight." She narrowed her eyes and looked at him. "Who did you say you are?"

He laughed and kissed her, long and full. "A friend of the family's."

She chuckled and pulled his head down for another kiss.

"I don't mean to interrupt," Paul's voice, light and teasing, came from the open door, "but it's time to get the show on the road." He winked at Franco and considerately closed the door on the lovers so they could steal one last moment.

"If you think this is bad," Franco said five minutes later as they waited for their turn to back out of the crowded driveway, "wait until the party when we get back. That's when you're going to see a real crowd."

She glanced around at the parade of cars heading for the church in Princeton. "You don't call this a crowd? To me it looks like the Macy's Parade at Thanksgiving. All that's missing are the floats."

He looked at her and laughed, ruffling her bangs with his hand. "*Cara*, these are just family and very close friends. *Everyone* else comes later."

He hadn't exaggerated. By 4 P.M., the enormous backyard where the tents of food were set up near the swimming pool was a mass of solid flesh. Ladies in cocktail dresses made of fine silk mingled with gentlemen in open sport shirts and casual pants, while children sat on the edge of the pool splashing their feet in the cool aqua water.

The solemnity of the church service was over and a festive air filled the yard. Lights had been strung around the supports to the house and over the tents, for no one expected the celebration to end before nightfall. There was to be a buffet later, yet waiters in crisp white suits circulated among the milling guests, offering platters of hot hors d'oeuvres and champagne cocktails.

A bar was set up in the enclosed sunroom and Stacey slipped in to try to get a club soda with a twist of lime. The hot sun and excitement made champagne too powerful, so she decided to switch to something nonalcoholic.

"I wondered where you'd gone to." Franco slipped an arm around her waist and kissed her neck. "Are you all right?"

"I'm having a wonderful time. Everyone treats me like a member of the family. They're lovely people, Franco."

He nodded. "We've had our difficulties in the past," he admitted, "but I don't think anything could shake this family apart. We have a pretty solid foundation."

She thanked the bartender and followed Franco outside. They wandered across the side yard to an enormous weeping willow, where two empty lounge chairs waited in the shade.

They sat next to each other, not touching, but connected nevertheless. The grass had been cut recently and she smelled that heavy, sweet odor she loved. She'd been neglecting her own garden this year—she'd been so busy with everything that the patch had gone unattended. Suddenly her hands itched to dig in the soil, to feel its richness between her fingers. She couldn't wait for morning and her appointment with Giancarlo.

She sighed. "Have you any idea how lucky you all are?" She turned to Franco and for a moment her breath caught. He had his eyes closed, head thrown back against the back of the chair. The sun danced off his dark brown hair, causing fine streaks of deep red to sparkle in the light. Faint circles of fatigue shadowed his closed eyes. She longed to trace her hands across and erase them, to draw her fingers over the planes of his cheekbones and imprint the beloved face forever in her very fingertips.

He opened his eyes with lazy slowness. "How do I answer a question like that?" he countered. "Does anyone *ever* really appreciate how lucky he is?" He stretched. "I used to feel lost in the middle of so many people... there was never a moment when I couldn't hear someone else stirring in the house."

She smiled and glanced over at the large family home. "I'd be surprised if you could find anybody in there—it's huge!"

He shielded the sun from his eyes and looked at her. "We didn't always live here, *cara*. When I was little, before Leeanna came, we lived in a small apartment in Little Italy near Mulberry Street with aunts and uncles and what seemed like hundreds of little runny-nosed kids." He shook his head at the memory. "I hated it. I wanted privacy, time to think, time to dream, and there never was any."

She patted his hand. "What did you do when you needed to be alone?"

He grinned at the memory that time had sweetened.

"I used to drape a cloth over the card table in the living room and take a book and flashlight and sit underneath and read. I could hear my Aunt Alyssa calling me in for supper, hanging her head out the window to see if I was playing stickball down the street, while I huddled beneath the table, not two feet from her, trying to stifle my laugh."

"I had no idea," she murmured. "I thought your family had always had money."

"No, not at all. Father still hasn't relaxed over it. He drives himself very hard and everyone around him, as well. When I graduated from college, he pushed me to come into the company and take a wife—neither request was one I complied with—at least, not then." He grinned inwardly as he thought of the jeweler's box in his pocket. "That's when they sent me to Florence to study. They figured the Old Country would teach me new ways, make me settle down into the business."

"It didn't work?"

He shook his head. "No. It made me more independent than ever, less the son they'd wanted. It's taken many years for Father to accept me as I am, a maverick."

She looked puzzled. "But I thought you were doing some computer work for him."

"Yes, I was. I want to work for him, help make the company better, more efficient, but on a free-lance basis only. I love Father, but he's a very strong man— he'd be trying to regiment my life and I'm too old for that."

"Still," she said, "I envy you your family." She told him then of her childhood dream about someone adopting Dianne and Grandma and her, then spiriting them away to an enormous house filled with family and pets.

She smiled at him through the memory. "All that's missing here," she said, "is the big shaggy mutt."

"Wrong again. We have one. She's just being groomed today."

They were silent for a while, listening to the laughter and voices that filtered out from the patio. "I think you've missed the point of a family somewhere along the way, Stacey. You and Dianne and Lillian *were* a complete family." Seeing her puzzled expression, he tried to explain. "Maybe you weren't the all-American dream of Mommy-and-Daddy-and-two-point-five-children, but you still were a family. You cared about one another, were partners working toward common goals, supplied comfort and support. What *is* a family, if not that?"

He sipped his Scotch on the rocks while she watched the soft early evening breeze lift his silky hair and gently blow it across his forehead.

"Sometimes it takes only two people to make a family," he continued. "Sometimes ten people aren't enough." He pointed toward the left side of his chest where his heart rested. "The magic that makes a family comes from in here—that's all that counts."

She was deeply moved. Why, in all the years she'd lived with her grandmother, had she not seen what he saw so clearly? How much easier it had been to blame her mother for the family she couldn't have instead of enjoying the warmth and love she, Dianne, and Lillian shared. For the first time she felt a stab of pity for Maryann and her endless search for happiness. Despite her mother's string of husbands, Stacey knew Maryann had never known the joy of being part of a family as Stacey had.

It had taken Franco to cut through the layers of childhood hurt and anger to show her what had been under her nose all the time.

If he understood so much about what a family really meant, maybe now was the time to tell him about herself. If he truly believed what he said—and she had no reason to doubt him—he wouldn't be threatened or diminished by her inability to conceive as Michael had been.

She was staring deeply into her empty glass, her eyes fixed on the curled-up twist of lemon peel, and didn't notice Franco rummaging through his pocket and didn't see the small black box until it was placed on the arm of her chair.

"It seems an appropriate time." Franco's voice was sweet music, rich with low tones that thrilled her. He watched as she lifted the lid and stared inside, green eyes widening with shock.

"Franco." Her voice was barely a whisper. "Oh, my God, I didn't expect—" She covered her face and began to cry, powerless to stop.

He dropped down to the grass next to her and cradled her head against his broad chest. "I want you to marry me, Stacey, *cara*, to be part of my life forever. From the moment we met I couldn't envision any kind of future without you in it."

She couldn't speak past the lump in her throat. For the first time in a very long time, she felt protected and needed, fully connected to another human being. All her thoughts of telling him about her condition vanished and she could only nod "yes" as he slipped the sparkling diamond onto her ring finger. "I love you, Franco," she said, lifting her face to his. "I don't think I've ever said that to you before. I love you." Her voice rang clear and true. "I've said it a million times in my heart but I was too afraid to say it out loud for fear you wouldn't care.''

He shook his head in disbelief. "Not care? I would have given anything to hear those words, *cara mia*. *Ti voglio bene*.''

"*Ti voglio bene*," she repeated, moving her lips closer to his. "*Ti voglio molto bene*. I love you very much. . . .''

They waited until midevening before they made their announcement. Only the immediate family remained. Leeanna had put the baby down for the night and was stretched out on the cushioned chaise longue next to Paul, who seemed to be dozing. Giancarlo had adjusted the patio lights so that they now provided a soft glow to the backyard, reflecting yellow and green in the still waters of the swimming pool. Carmela brought out a pot of coffee and she was pouring it into cups while Giancarlo cut slivers of rum cake and placed them on plates.

Franco and Stacey, however, were seated on the old-fashioned glider-style swing at the far end of the patio. Their low whispers mixed with the gentle squeaking of the swing and the early-summer clicking of crickets. Stacey had kept the diamond on her ring turned inward so no one would notice until she and Franco made their announcement. Every now and then she would steal a glance at the sparkling round stone, amazed that this symbol of her future was there on her hand. Her green eyes would search for then meet Franco's gold ones and their faces would be split by matching conspiratorial grins.

Stacey was sure it showed on their faces—could anyone not see how in love they were? She felt sixteen—she felt like she never had felt when she really *was* sixteen: happy and free and filled with the certainty that good things happen to nice people. For the moment, at least, her old fears did not exist. There would be nothing to ruin her happiness this night.

Finally, as Giancarlo passed out the pieces of rum cake, Franco stood up and pulled Stacey to his side.

"Everybody!" At the musical sound of his voice, his parents turned toward him, Paul opened one eye, and Leeanna sat up straight in her lounge chair. They all had a look of such suppressed excitement that Stacey was sure a neon sign "engaged" hovered over her head and Franco's.

When he had everyone's attention, Franco put his arm around Stacey's waist. "I don't think I introduced Stacey to you properly before," he said, holding her fast in his golden gaze. "May I present my fiancée, the future Stacey Andersen Borelli."

The quiet patio came alive in a kaleidoscopic burst of sound and motion. Stacey was swept along in a swirl of loving excitement: tiny Carmela hugging her, the top of her dark, perfectly coiffed head reaching not even to Stacey's collarbone; Giancarlo's exuberant hug and the tears that sparkled in his blue eyes; Paul's hearty handshake; and Leeanna's happy hug and kiss, her skin fragrant with the delicate smell of baby powder. These images were burned deeply into Stacey's heart with a sweetly sharp pain.

And Franco standing proudly next to her, as intoxicated as she was on the love that flowed over and around them like the champagne Giancarlo brought up from his cellar.

"I have waited thirty-three years for this occasion," Giancarlo said as he expertly eased the cork up and out.

Carmela smiled through her happy tears as she held out the fluted wineglasses, their stems as thin as slivers of ice, waiting for Giancarlo to fill them with the sparkling golden wine. She smiled at her son and future daughter-in-law. "I had begun to doubt you would ever marry and make us grandparents, Franco."

Stacey stiffened and prayed Franco wouldn't notice.

"Mother, what's the rush?" he teased. "Stacey and I have only just become engaged tonight. But if you'd like us to oblige. . . ."

In her happiness she had forgotten her earlier intention to tell him of her inability to conceive. A feeling of guilt pressed at her heart. She knew she would have to tell him. *But, not tonight,* she thought as Giancarlo, joyful and carrying himself with an air of dignity, stepped into the center of the loving family circle. *This night must be perfect.*

He turned to face Stacey and Franco and raised his glass.

"There is nothing in life more beautiful than being witness to the miracle of two people deciding to spend their lives together." He looked directly at Stacey and winked. "As I said earlier to a lovely young woman, very often the flower is all the more beautiful for the wait."

She smiled back at him and touched the red zinnia that was tucked in her hair.

He continued. "May your married life be filled with the same joy you have filled us all with tonight."

To the cheers of their family, Franco and Stacey linked arms and sipped from one another's champagne glass in the time-honored tradition of lovers.

Her heart swelled with happiness. There was no space in her heart for worry. Where there had once been fear and trepidation now there was only room for joy. She could think of nothing but Franco, of this wondrous ready-made family she had so miraculously been welcomed into in the space of just one day. As she sat there looking at the faces of these people who seemed to love her, at Franco's face dark with passion, she felt rich beyond her wildest dreams. The success or failure of Andersen-Bradley was nothing compared to this feeling of fulfillment. Nothing mattered but now.

The Borellis had graciously put her and Franco in the same bedroom, a concession, no doubt, to the imminent marriage. For a while after he fell asleep she sat in a bentwood rocker near the window, enjoying the soft breezes that ruffled the white curtains and made them brush gently against her bare legs.

She set the alarm clock for six, yet was awake before it rang. Rising carefully so not to wake Franco, she slipped from bed, showered, and pulled on a pair of jeans and shirt she'd brought with her, then went out the back door and over to the vegetable garden in the far corner of the property. She smiled as she thought of the smile on Carmela's face as she whispered to Stacey the night before that only a rare few had ever been invited to join her husband at work in his garden. It was a very special, very private passion of his.

The grass was wet with early-morning dew. It seeped through her worn sneakers as she hurried along the narrow path into the vegetable garden.

"*Buon giorno, mia ragazza.* You did not disappoint me."

She smiled at the older man, who looked very much as she imagined Franco might in thirty years.

"It's so peaceful and lovely at this hour, isn't it?"

She bent over and breathed in the minty-spicy smell of the tall basil plant. "I notice your son didn't inherit your love of working in the soil in the mornings."

Giancarlo laughed. "Except for business or the baby, neither of my children believes there's life before noon."

He showed her what needed to be done with the tomatoes and zucchini, then explained how he wanted to ring the herb garden with orange and yellow marigolds. Stacey made a suggestion about staking the tomatoes in wire cages, then picked up a small trowel and knelt down to get to work.

It wasn't until much later when she stopped to wipe the sweat off the back of her neck and stretch her aching arms that she saw Giancarlo watching her, a peculiar half-smile on his face.

"Basta!" he said. "You've done enough." He motioned for her to join him at the picnic table. "Come, have some iced tea and then we'll go in and demand breakfast for our labors."

She looked at the sun. "What time is it—around ten o'clock? The time went *so* fast."

Her body felt tired but it was a marvelously satisfying kind of tired. Working with Giancarlo in the garden had established an unspoken bond between herself and the older man that ran deep. He recognized in her a woman with the patience to plant a seed and wait for it to bear fruit.

"Here." He handed her a paper cup of iced tea from the blue thermos bottle he'd brought with him. She drank thirstily and held out the cup for more.

"I like a woman who's not afraid of hard work," he

said as they strolled arm-in-arm back to the house. "Many people look on hard work as an aberration."

"Not me," she said. "I've been working hard since I was thirteen. I don't know any other way to live."

"You had time for college, I assume?"

She shook her head. "Afraid not. Too much work, too little money."

"I never went to college, either," he told her as they entered the cool kitchen. "Now that I think of it, that's probably why I pushed Franco and Leeanna to get an education." He sighed. "Even at this age, I still sometimes wish I had one."

"I think of it too, sometimes. Every now and then I feel embarrassed when someone asks me when I graduated and I say, 'Newtown High School, Class of 1974.'"

They smiled at each other, warmed by the start they'd made toward being a family.

By the time Sunday night arrived, Stacey felt she'd known the Borellis her whole life. They had overwhelmed her with such open and honest affection that her last barriers of reserve broke down and she allowed herself the luxury of being happy. She wondered what she had ever done to deserve such joy.

It wasn't until much later as she was lying in her bed next to Franco, listening to his light snoring, that it again occurred to her: She still had not told him about her sterility.

A tiny shiver of guilt coursed through her.

She hadn't done it deliberately. Wasn't it just an oversight? Why, in the forty-eight hours since they'd become engaged, they'd barely had a moment alone. She'd been swept along in the tide of excitement. After all, it wasn't something she could casually have brought up at the Borellis' breakfast table, was it?

She'd tell him in the morning before they went to the office, she thought drowsily as she looked at her beautiful diamond ring. She closed her eyes, letting sleep take her.

Yes, she'd definitely tell him tomorrow.

Chapter Ten

Her intentions were good but, somehow, the right time never came. Despite the sharp twinges of guilt ripping the edges of her conscience, she managed to convince herself it was circumstances, not her own fears of facing her truth and losing Franco, that kept her silent. She allowed Andersen-Bradley to provide her with the perfect excuse.

A rush of work orders poured in—thanks, no doubt, to their spectacular showing at the seminar in Florida—and most of her time was spent expediting the work, overseeing the temporary computer operator and filling Franco in on who was who and what was what, so he could handle some of the out-of-office meetings. *A-B* still wasn't out of the woods yet, but she began to see a clearing ahead.

And besides work, a wonderful portion of her time was spent in the magical prenuptial world of planning a wedding. She only wished Lillian had lived long enough to be part of their joy. Dianne, though, had happily taken over, designating herself and Al as surrogate parents-of-the-bride and she was kept busy setting up bridal showers and looking into catering halls, for Franco and Stacey had set the date for October 12, just two and a half months away.

Many times in the weeks since they'd become engaged, Stacey had planned to tell him about her medical condition. They'd be strolling along the beach near her apartment after work or sharing a meal at their favorite Chinese restaurant and she would sense that this was the right moment, that this was the time to tell him. But when she'd open her mouth, the words would turn to hot ashes and she'd let the opportunity pass. She had every reason to believe Franco would not turn away once he knew of her sterility, that given the choice he would choose her. Yet, each time they were together and she had the opportunity to reveal herself fully to him, she'd fall silent.

In fact, it seemed that in all the excitement, Stacey and Franco had very little time alone. Twice in late July he had to go out of town to contact clients and she found his absence to be a time of tremendous loneliness. Her apartment, which at one time had been the sanctuary of a very private woman, became cavernous without his presence. The sight of his toothbrush in the stand or his running shoes near the closet door in her bedroom were enough to move her to foolish, sentimental tears and she counted the hours until his return.

Dianne was tickled by the change in her sister.

"I always knew that when you fell, you'd fall in a *big* way," she teased as they lunched at La Crepe after a morning spent searching for a bridal gown. They sat outside in the small al fresco dining area, sipping white wine while their crepes were being prepared.

Stacey was radiant in a lemon-yellow sleeveless jumpsuit, banded at the waist with a wide rainbow belt. Her wild mane of curls was set free, anchored only by two tortoiseshell combs. It lifted and blew softly in the warm August air.

She chuckled at her sister's good-natured teasing. "I never thought this would happen to me," she said, turning serious. "I thought I was strictly work-oriented, married to my job and all that. I never expected someone like Franco to come into my life.''

"Oh, I did," Dianne said as the waitress placed their orders in front of them. "I remember when you were a kid, walking around the house, hopelessly lost in *Jane Eyre* and *Gone with the Wind,* sighing over every love scene. You were a sucker for romance."

Stacey blushed and put a piece of the succulent ratatouille crepe, thick with zucchini and tomatoes, in her mouth. A few moments later she said, "That was my fantasy life, Di. That didn't mean I ever believed it would really happen."

"It happens," Dianne said. "The whole secret is in being smart enough to recognize it when he's staring you right in the face. When I first met Franco, I prayed you didn't have your blinders on. He's someone very special."

"I know."

They concentrated on lunch for a while, listening absently to conversations at the tables around them, watching traffic move down Northern Boulevard's Miracle Mile. The waitress cleared the round table and brought their desserts of orange sherbet topped with a generous scoop of vanilla ice cream served in enormous frosted glasses.

"If I keep doing this, I'd better look for a larger size bridal gown," Stacey laughed as she finished her dessert.

"I have to get a larger size matron-of-honor's outfit as it is."

Stacey looked up at her sister. "You've gained weight? I don't see it."

Dianne met her eyes, then reached across the table and put her hand on her younger sister's forearm. "I *will* be gaining weight, Stace. Al and I are expecting a baby in April.''

Stacey gasped. A brief, sharp pain shot through her but was replaced by a jolt of pleasure at her sister's happiness. She jumped up and hugged Dianne, tears of happiness welling.

"I'll finally be an aunt! I'm so happy for you two, Di. Really." She sat back down. "When you broke up, I was so afraid that was it."

Dianne smiled. "It nearly was," she said. "But when Grandma died, it made me realize how quickly life can change and how important it is to hold on once you've found the right person. But don't think this will solve all of our problems."

Stacey frowned. "What problems? I thought things have been worked out."

"Not everything. I told Al that I still expect to take night classes at the university and we'll share childcare. There's more to life than bearing children, no matter how beautiful that experience is. One day the two of you will be alone again and if you haven't established who and what you are, you're left with one very sad, empty woman. That's not going to happen." Dianne looked at her sister. "I was a little nervous about telling you. I didn't want to make you sad."

Stacey waved a hand in the air. "Your happiness could never make me sad, Di. I'm looking forward to being a doting aunt—I'll probably spoil my little niece or nephew rotten, if you'll let me."

Dianne smiled. "I'm glad you've finally worked things out and come to terms with it."

"It hasn't been easy," Stacey admitted. "Seeing Michael at your house last spring really brought it all home to me. But I think I understand finally that

I am more than the sum total of my internal parts.''

''I'm glad Franco isn't threatened by your condition. Grandma said she thought he'd be able to handle it.''

Stacey felt her blood chill. ''She didn't bring it up that day she spoke with him, did she?''

''Of course not.'' Dianne narrowed her eyes in a gesture much like Stacey's own. ''There *wasn't* any problem with Franco, was there? I know he comes from a background where family ties are terribly important and—''

Stacey cut her off. ''There wasn't any problem, Di, because I haven't told him yet.''

''What!'' Dianne's voice cut the heavy summer air. A woman at the next table turned to stare. Dianne lowered her voice. ''What do you mean, you haven't told him yet? Stacey, you're engaged to this man. Don't you think he ought to know?''

Stacey glared at her, embarrassed because she recognized the truth of her sister's words. She tried to brush away the problem. ''Don't you think you're overreacting, Di? You yourself said he's man enough to cope with it.''

''That's right, I did.'' Dianne's voice was firm. ''But part of marriage is being truthful with one another, respecting each other enough to level with your partner. You can't go into this without telling him about your sterility, Stacey. It's not fair to either one of you.''

''I meant to tell him,'' she answered, her voice slightly apologetic, ''but there never seemed to be the right time. Either we're in New Jersey with his family or we're at work, or—''

''Or you're together alone and you don't want to spoil it, right?''

She nodded, eyes focused on the tabletop. ''Yes.

Damn it, Dianne, you're right. I don't want to spoil it. And it's my business, isn't it?" *My mistake.* "Don't push me, okay?"

Dianne stared hard at her sister. "Okay," she answered finally. "But take my advice, Stace: Don't think you'll ever be happy keeping that secret from him. If you'd really come to terms with it yourself, you wouldn't be hesitating like this. Franco isn't Michael." She touched Stacey's shoulder, adding gently, "I don't think he'll turn tail and run."

Stacey looked at her, green eyes wide and vulnerable. "But can you guarantee it, Di? Can you guarantee it?"

She knew, better than most, how quickly people can change.

The subject was dropped for the rest of the afternoon.

However, as Stacey drove to JFK Airport to pick Franco up on his return flight from San Diego, the issue was never far from her mind. Love had caused her to take a long, hard look at her problem and her true feelings about it. When it first happened she'd been devastated—thanks, in large measure, she decided, to Michael—and that had obscured some very important facts, like: Did she really *want* children? Eliminating the possibility of pregnancy had made the question of motherhood more intellectual than physical and all at once she realized she was not yet ready for parenting. The insecurities of her childhood, her fear of not succeeding, still haunted her.

Seeing Leeanna with her baby had been a powerfully moving experience and had underlined the beautiful connection between natural mother and child. However, when Leeanna had placed the infant in her arms, Stacey had felt a nurturing love for the helpless child she held. It seemed motherhood could be an acquired state. She didn't have to give birth to feel the desire to cherish a small child. Adoption was an alternative—if and when the time came—and she could embrace it wholeheartedly. But the question still remained: Could Franco?

They were planning to drive out to Montauk this weekend—the last weekend of the summer. Maybe she would tell him when they were alone and the mood was right. She owed it to him, didn't she?

But the moment she saw him striding off the plane, tanned and fit in a buff-colored suit, all rational thought disappeared. Nestled against him in the car, nose pressed close to his neck, as they wound their way out to Montauk, she was caught again in a whirling of emotions that left her weak with desire.

He had taken care of reservations and she was delighted when he pulled into the driveway of the same inn where they had first made love on Memorial Day weekend. Had it really been only a little more than three months ago, she wondered disbelievingly.

"It seemed fitting," he said as they unpacked their suitcases in their room. "We began and ended the summer here."

She wound her arms around his muscular chest from behind him and slipped her fingers in between the buttons on his shirt, to feel the warm skin beneath. "Many other things began here too," she whispered against his back. "Let's not speak of endings."

He turned around to face her and, golden eyes dancing in the light from the sconces, untied her belt then slowly, tantalizingly, unzipped her yellow jumpsuit and let it fall quietly to the floor. She stood there, tall and lovely, clad in only a pair of silky bikini panties while he lightly drew his fingers up along her legs, over her rounded hips, and into her small waist, then slipped the lacy lingerie off. Then, his warm hands cupped her full breasts and he bent and buried his face between them, glorying in their lush beauty. She gasped and laced her fingers tightly through his thick hair. "Franco," she murmured huskily, "I've missed you so."

"Be still," he answered and gently pushed her down onto the oversize bed.

She lay there, mind seared with passion, while he stripped his clothes from his strong body. She longed to reach for him, to touch him, caress him, but he kissed her hands and put them at her sides. "Wait," he said. "I want first to make love to every part of you. I've missed you also, *cara*."

It was a sweet torment. She gripped the headboard while, beginning with her feet, he kissed and nibbled her burning flesh. A nip at the back of her ankle made her moan in ecstasy. Every inch of her body was alive with erotic possibilities as he explored the sensitive area behind her knee, the small of her back, and the smoothness under her arms with his tongue and hands. Finally, when he was maddeningly nipping at the sensitive flesh of her inner thighs, she could stand it no longer. With a strength she didn't know she had, she pulled his head up toward hers and wound her long legs around his back, driving him into the fiery core of her being while she met and matched his passion again and again.

"I suppose we should find somewhere for dinner," he said lazily afterward, his face resting against her breasts while his fingers traced a sensuous pattern on her back.

She arched beneath him. Somehow their lovemaking had only increased her desire for him; she felt alive with an all-consuming need that only he could fill. "Not now," she murmured. "Now I want to show *you* how much I love you."

"You're full of surprises, aren't you, *cara*?" he said as she knelt over him and began to slowly massage his feet, her hands coaxing the muscles into relaxation first then building up a mounting excitement as she drew her tongue over his instep. He gasped and began to writhe beneath her and his movements turned her fire into a blaze. She was everywhere and everyplace—her hands and tongue and legs, all tools of pleasure designed to take him to the brink of madness over and over. Finally he grabbed her shoulders and rolled her onto her back as easily as if she were a child. She had pleasured him in ways he'd never known, given him the fullest measure of her love. Suddenly their mutual fire turned into a tender communion as he slowly moved inside her and together they exploded with a sweetness like they'd never known.

After a large breakfast the next morning—they never *did* get down for dinner—they walked the half-mile to East Lake Beach. It was a glorious end-of-summer day. The sun was high and bright overhead, bouncing off the silvery-blue Atlantic Ocean like a million diamonds. The surf was unusually calm and the water was crowded with laughing, shouting bathers, jumping the small waves as they gently crashed against the shore.

They were quiet. So much had been said the night before, albeit without words, that they felt no need for conversation. They found a semisecluded spot on the beach within sight of the lighthouse and stretched out the enormous "I Love Key West" towel they'd bought back in June. Although they were both very tan, they took turns rubbing one another with oil, as much for physical contact as protection from the sun's scorching rays. He had taken his sweet time, stroking the coconut-scented lotion over the curve of her breasts where they swelled over the top of her jade-green maillot, then turned her over so he could do her back. She suppressed a moan as his hands stroked and gently pinched the backs of her thighs then tickled the sensitive spot behind her knees.

"I'll get you for that," she teased as she pushed him down on the towel and poured a cool puddle of lotion on the dark hairs of his chest.

"Hey! Couldn't you warm that first?"

"Don't worry. I'll see it gets plenty warm."

She was true to her word. Aided by the slippery lotion, her hands tantalized up and down his muscular legs, sliding along his sides until he had to grab her hands and make her stop. "You could get us into big trouble, *cara,*" he laughed as she glanced at his virile body in the small black bathing suit. "Quit while we're both still decent."

Since they hadn't slept much the night before, they dozed on and off under the summer sun, lulled by the rhythmic sound of the ocean and the chatter of other beachgoers. Stacey felt totally at peace. Every muscle in her body was relaxed and her mind free of worry. Now and then her sister's words about telling Franco the truth would rise to the surface like a piece of driftwood but she would lift her face closer to the sky and allow the sun to burn the thoughts from her brain. After dinner, maybe—or later that night. Not now.

Before she knew it, it was Sunday night. They had planned one fancy dinner at a restaurant in East Hampton on their way back home and had gotten dressed up for the occasion. They pulled up now in front of the three-story white building that was also home to the family who owned The White Swan Restaurant and parked in the small lot reserved for patrons. The sun was setting behind a small grove of oak trees and bathed everything in a violent hot-pink and orange glow. Franco, dressed in a dark navy pin-striped three-piece suit looked like he'd stepped out of the pages of *Gentlemen's Quarterly*.

She took his arm and he helped her over the driveway, which was really no more than sand and rocks. She wore an airy voile dress of forest-green that clung to her bosom. Her shoulders and arms were bare except for narrow spaghetti straps, and the skirt flowed in a swirl about her knees. She had wanted to pin her hair up in a loose chignon but Franco had asked her not to. "I love it when you let it go wild and free," he'd said, kissing the nape of her neck. "You can pull it back at work, but for me, let it down, *cara*." So, it rose up and around her lovely face now in waves of honeyed gold, streaked platinum in spots by the sun.

She loved the way people turned and noticed them as they entered the elegant restaurant. They both took secret pride in the fact that they were such an attractive couple. And the fact that they were nearly the same height only drew attention to their striking appearance, making them seem halves of the same whole, the gold and the bronze, male and female, each one necessary to the completion of the other.

They lingered over cocktails, dawdled over the entrée, and stretched dessert and coffee endlessly. The White Swan was an exquisite place, open only to twenty diners per night. It believed in giving full and undivided service to few rather than haphazard attention to many. The waiters, although young, were solicitous yet unobtrusive, well-trained in divining a diner's needs before he or she was even aware they had been filled. The atmosphere, from the snowy linen tablecloth to the fragile crystal glasses, right down to the vibrant red geranium plants that ringed the room, was one of understated elegance, and Stacey hated the thought of leaving.

"Do you want more coffee?" Franco asked, lifting the small silver pot.

She nodded. "Just a half cup. I'd like to stay here all night."

He laughed and watched as she rummaged in the zippered compartment of her bag, then withdrew a small package wrapped in silver foil.

"Happy birthday," she said with an impish grin.

He raised one eyebrow and untied the silver cord. "My birthday is in January—not that I don't accept belated presents."

She shrugged her tanned shoulders. "I didn't know you in January. I simply couldn't resist giving you this."

She heard his slow deep intake of breath as he opened the lid of the jewelry box and saw the gold pocketwatch nestled on the black velvet. He looked at her from across the table, amber eyes alive with the glow of loving and being loved. Tears burned in her own eyes and she blinked rapidly to stop them.

"Stacey, *cara*, no one has ever done anything like this—"

"Shush!" She reached over and touched his lips with the tip of her index finger. "Open it up."

He pressed down on the stem and held the watch to the candlelight to read the inscription. "May 27th—the start." He grinned. "Our first night together." He leaned across the table and kissed her, then called the wine steward over to order a split of champagne to toast their love.

It was after eleven when, content and happy, they made their way out to the car. Despite the chill in the air, he kept his suit jacket unbuttoned so that the pocketwatch was visible.

While he fished for the keys he'd stashed in her purse, she leaned against the car and closed her eyes. "I may never eat again," she moaned. "I must have gained ten pounds on that cheesecake."

"Be happy they didn't have Linzer tarts," he said with a laugh. "Then you might have gained fifteen."

She could hear him rummaging through her bag.

"I know I put them in here," he muttered. "Why do you keep so much junk in this thing?"

Wearily, she opened her eyes and took the purse from him. "Let me look. Men seem so intimidated by handbags for some strange reason." Her hand hit on a small unfamiliar package. "What on earth...?"

He smiled broadly at her. "Go ahead, *cara*. Take it out."

Frowning, she extracted a slim flat box, wrapped in shiny white paper and tied with a bright red ribbon. "Franco?"

"We are definitely on the same wavelength tonight."

She removed the wrapping paper and opened the box. Nestled on a bed of black velvet was a small gold charm in the shape of one perfect Linzer tart, an exquisite red ruby in the center, suspended from a fine gold chain. She burst into a crazy combination of tears and laughter as she picked it up and held it in front of her. "You nut," she managed to say. "You wonderful, crazy nut!"

He fastened it around her neck and she looked at him,

his face sultry and dark, filled with happiness, illuminated by the one streetlamp in the parking lot and threw her arms around his neck.

"I love you, Franco, oh, how much I love you!"

And so she didn't tell him that weekend either. And Monday was so busy with catch-up work and Tuesday there was a meeting with her attorney, Joe, and then Wednesday Franco had to leave for Houston on a three-day conference on "Computer Engineering and the Future of Schools," where he was giving a short talk.

"I wish I could be there," she said as they hugged at the boarding gate at JFK. "I'll miss you."

"They're making a tape recording of all the speeches," he said, a groan in his melodic voice. "You'll be able to hear me in all my nervous glory when I get back."

"Hurry home," she whispered as they kissed once more. "I miss you already."

She jumped into her Mustang and drove back to work, throwing herself into a massive project she'd been putting off. Once she got into the swing of catching the duplicate zip codes, she worked hard and steadily, finally completing the project around 7 P.M. Chris had long since gone home and the computer room was empty. Joe had asked her to look again for the key to the elusive safety-deposit box of John's and she'd promised she would.

She walked past the locked door to his office on her way out of the building. It really was time to get in there and dismantle it. Leaving John's office untouched, almost as some kind of unhealthy shrine, wasn't doing anyone any good. Franco was working in a tiny anteroom near the computers instead of being able to spread out in the space he needed. And, with all his talk of making the proper impressions, having to slip him into her office to meet clients when he needed to was getting ridiculous.

That did it. Tomorrow morning she would start packing up John's things for storage. And when Franco returned to the office Monday morning she would surprise him with a place of his own, right down to the name on the door.

"I didn't know John had accumulated so much junk," Stacey groaned to Chris as the two women sifted through doodled-on notepads, packets of sugar, and canceled checks that had piled up in the bottom drawers of his old desk. "There are things that go back to the old office on Shelter Rock Road. He must have just packed up a box of junk from one desk and dumped it in the new one."

Chris picked up one small drawer filled with tissues and matchbook covers and tilted it right into the garbage bag on the floor. "Franco'd better appreciate this work. This is worse than cleaning a child's room."

They were both trying to keep things light and uncomplicated, for going through John's personal effects was much harder than either had thought. Little things—like a Polaroid snapshot of John, Margie, and Jill standing in front of the office the day they'd bought the computer system, or a grocery list in Margie's handwriting marked "Don't forget birthday candles!"—would hit them unexpectedly like a blow to the heart and leave them brooding and silent for a while.

Stacey felt almost disloyal, as if putting these items into storage was somehow denying John's existence. Her life had become so full and so happy that sometimes—for a day or so—John would disappear from her thoughts. Lillian's death, while it made her sad, had been a coming full-circle of a happy life. John's, untimely as it was, was harder to bear. If only he'd lived longer, she thought, perhaps he could have had a second chance at happiness. As it was, now he never would.

On impulse, she snatched the snapshot of John standing proudly by the Compu-500 with a paper hat and streamers on his head, toasting the camera with a plastic cup of champagne. They'd held a big party the day it was installed, inviting all their workers and spouses and families to join them. Lillian had come with Dianne and Al, Stacey tended bar, and John had played convivial host, telling anyone who would listen about the way Andersen-Bradley was going up, up, up. She put the photo in her pocket.

Her stomach growled. She looked at Chris and laughed. "Listen, why don't you call out for a pizza while I finish this top drawer? I think we both need a break."

Chris stood up, knees creaking after being in one position for so long. "Good idea. I'm too big to be crunched up like this." She stretched, rubbing her very pregnant belly. "Give it about fifteen minutes, Stace. I'll set everything up in the kitchen."

Stacey nodded and pulled out the top drawer. She had just finished tossing away the empty Bic-Clic pens and the dried-up markers with no caps when her fingers came across a slippery bump in the back corner. Giving an extra tug, she pulled the drawer completely out, and there, taped in the farthest recess of the drawer, was the safety-deposit key. It was a deep copper color and she recognized it immediately as the duplicate of the one she'd once had for the box in the First Federal Savings Bank. Well, at least this would make Joe happy. If she could just find the papers he'd been looking for, they could tie up the loose ends concerning John's estate. She was in the mood for fresh starts, for putting loneliness and sadness behind her and embracing change the way she had embraced her love for Franco.

If it hadn't been for John forcing her into having lunch with Franco that afternoon at the Four Square Inn, she might never have found him, might still be that isolated fearful woman she'd once been.

"I wish you were here, John," she said aloud. "I wish I could thank you."

By Friday night the office was nearly done.

"It looks darned good, Stace," Chris said as they closed the door and admired the new brass letters, "Franco Borelli" on the dark wood. "You did wonders with it."

"Of course it's not completely redecorated," Stacey said, "but at least it's more Franco's now."

She'd brought throw pillows from her apartment for the leather sofa, placed a lamp from her bedroom on the credenza behind his desk, hung framed prints, and changed the drapes, turning it into a place where Franco could be comfortable and proud to meet clients without the ghostly memory of its former occupant.

"I'm only sorry Franco won't be in on Monday to see it," she said as Chris collected her things from the reception area and the women walked to the parking lot.

"When will he be back?"

"Two weeks." Her voice was filled with regret. "There's some problem with an investment in Rome and he had to fly over this morning and settle it as a favor to his father."

"Come for dinner tonight," Chris said, touching her

forearm. "Tom hasn't seen you in ages and the kids have been asking for you."

"I'd love to," Stacey said, "but can I take a rain check? Dianne is coming down to look at restaurants for the wedding reception."

They made plans for the following week and Stacey hurried to her apartment to change for restaurant-hunting.

While she was changing into a simple blue knit dress, the phone rang. It was Joe. Guessing why he was calling, she told him she'd at last unearthed the safety-deposit key.

"Stacey, if you don't have time yourself why don't you give me that key and I'll go to the vault." He sounded exasperated.

"I'm sorry, Joe, but after all, I just found it tonight."

He chuckled through his annoyance. "I should make allowances for the prewedding crazies, huh?"

She returned his laugh. "Something like that. Listen, the bank is open Saturday mornings. I'll go first thing, okay?"

"I'm going to hold you to that, Stacey. I'll be at your office at noon and we can go over everything. I'd like to get this whole thing cleared up and we can put in the papers bringing Franco in permanently."

"Twelve noon," she said before she hung up. "I promise."

True to her word, by nine fifteen the next morning, she was ushered into the guarded safety-deposit area. The clerk retrieved the narrow box, led her to a private viewing area, and discreetly left her alone.

This whole thing was making her feel very sad and morbid and she couldn't wait for this last vivid reminder of John's death to be settled. Swiftly she fit her key into the lock and flipped open the box. There on top was the old paper that first brought her in as a profit-sharing assistant. She rummaged through family photographs and letters, found—thank God—a copy of John's life-insurance policy, the mortgage for his house, and, at the bottom, a folded-up legal document. Curiously, she opened the long paper.

The "legalese" rambled on and she was about to drop it unread onto the pile of papers she was bringing back to Joe when a familiar name caught her eye.

Franco Borelli!

Chapter Eleven

Her hands shook as she unfolded it the rest of the way to read it. At first, the jumble of "whereases" and "heretofore-mentioneds" made little sense. Then, suddenly, she reached the next-to-last paragraph where it all came clear.

Two weeks before she even met Franco for the first time, John had allowed him to buy out his shares in Andersen-Bradley with the stipulation that John remain under salary and in the same capacity. Suddenly, little bits and pieces fell into place: John's insistence that she and Borelli get along, his constant harping on joining the "big guys," Franco's easy adjustment to the ways of the company—why, he probably knew more about the inner financial workings of Andersen-Bradley than she did!

She carefully refolded the document, put it in her handbag, and gave the safety-deposit box back to the clerk. On wobbly legs she left the bank and got into her car. She had no memory of driving east back to the office. Her body automatically commanded the little Mustang safely back while her mind raced full speed as she tried to understand this betrayal.

How could John have done this to her? How could he have undermined everything she thought they had done together by bringing someone else in as half owner? Her fingers tightened on the steering wheel. No wonder Franco had been so nice to her—through marriage,

Andersen-Bradley would be all his. With his knowledge of investments and computers, he could easily expand it or write it off as a tax loss, however his mood struck him.

She beeped at a yellow Volkswagen in her way and zipped around the startled driver. Damn Franco! Andersen-Bradley was nothing to him—hadn't he himself said he'd been searching for the right business to shelter his money? Was the company she had given her life—her blood—to, going to become a rich boy's plaything? Never! She'd sell out completely, withdraw all her money—what little remained after debts were paid—and leave the dregs behind for him. She'd be damned if she'd work herself into the ground to help him. She glanced at the ring on her finger, glinting beautifully in the sun. She'd take that damned diamond and stuff it down his throat. That continental charm, that sweet-flowing combination of good manners and intelligence—calculated, the whole bit.

She swung into the parking lot and pulled her car into her spot. In her anger, she hit her bumper against the post supporting the nameplate: "Stacey Andersen—Vice-President." The sign bent backward, the nameplate itself hanging off at a crazy angle.

Good! Exactly how it should be. With a vicious yank she pulled the sign completely off and tossed it into the bushes under the reception office window. She wouldn't be needing it much longer anyway.

She had calmed down a bit by the time Joe arrived. Instead of throwing the document in his face the second he sat down, she let him finish his business, then casually pulled the paper from her pocketbook.

"Take a look at this," she said, sliding it across her desk toward him. "I found it in the box with everything else."

She rested her chin in her hands and watched his dark brown eyes widen as he read the form.

"What the hell?"

"Oh, come on, Joe," her voice was thick with sarcasm. "Don't tell me you didn't know anything about this."

He pulled his glasses off and rubbed his eyes. "I swear, Stacey, I never saw this thing in my life."

"Bull. How could John have done this without your okay?"

"Very easily, apparently. He took it to another attorney."

It was her turn to be surprised. "It's legal, then? No loopholes?"

He shook his head. "None that I can see from here. You're engaged to Borelli, aren't you?" Joe looked sympathetic. "He never told you about this?"

She twisted the ring, eyebrows rushing forward in a scowl. "Do I look like I knew about it?" She looked at Joe again. "Are you *sure* you had no idea, Joe? None at all?"

He thought hard. "All I can say, Stacey, is John was in big trouble. I guess he was desperate enough for money to sell out. What other explanation can there be?"

Suddenly she felt too worn out even to think. She put her head down on top of her desk, praying she'd wake up to find the whole thing had been a terrible dream.

"Stacey?" Joe's hand touched her shoulder. "Are you okay?"

She looked up at him and tossed her hair off her face. With a quick motion she opened her desk drawer, removed a coated rubber band, and pulled her thick hair back into a neat ponytail.

"There," she said. "Now I can think clearly."

She stood to her full height, adjusting the hem of her pale blue linen skirt as she did. She walked to the window and looked out at the Long Island Sound toward Connecticut, her eyes stopping on the mast of a sailboat, tiny and insignificant, in the distance. Suddenly she wished she were on it, wished she were anywhere but where she was.

"You know," she said slowly, turning to face her attorney, whose broad face was creased with concern, "I just can't understand why he did this. I thought he loved me."

Joe tried to comfort her. "I'm sure he does, Stacey. I've seen the way he watches you. You *are* getting married, after all."

She threw him a look of utter contempt. "Borelli?" The name was a curse on her lips. "Forget him. He's out of the picture. I mean John. How could he have sold out on me? Betrayed me like this? I trusted him like he was my own father, goddamn it!" She turned back to the window and covered her face with her hand, trying to hold back the angry tears burning her lids.

He stood and watched her, his large hands hanging helplessly at his sides. Law school had never prepared him for legislating emotions.

Finally she regained her composure and sat down behind her desk. In that familiar position she felt some of her old control return, anchored by familiar objects.

"How much of the business do I actually own?" Stacey demanded.

"Sixty percent," he told her uneasily. "You have the controlling interest."

"Then I want to close down A-B," she announced, her words crystal clear and firm. "Let's just sell everything off, pay all the debts, and divide the profits according to percentages owned. Just make sure we leave a month's severance pay for Chris. I want out of here by the end of the month. Let Franco run his own one-man show.''

"That's crazy!'' Joe leaned over the desk, hands clenched. "You can't throw all this away on a whim, Stacey. It's meant too much to you.''

"That's right.'' She stood up and faced him, feeling herself swell with rage. "It's meant too damned much. I know Input Computer has been dying to take over—well, fine. Sell them our school lists, sell them the Compu-500, sell them the damned carpeting and pictures, for all I care. Just get this millstone off my neck and let me go!'' She stopped abruptly and drew a deep breath to calm herself.

"Give it forty-eight hours,'' Joe pleaded. "Give yourself time to sort out the idea.''

"Sort it out? If I give myself time to sort it out, I'll probably give up on people completely, Joe. Let me out while I still have a glimmer of faith in human nature left. Do what I ask and prove I can trust *someone,* please?''

Joe sighed. She'd been through so much lately and this last and final betrayal might be the thing to break her. "You win, Stacey. I'll start proceedings tomorrow. When will Franco be back?''

Casually she flipped through her desk calendar as if the date weren't burned into her heart. "Twelve days. Do you think it can be completed by then?''

"We'll need his signature for some things.''

"Why can't I liquidate my portion without his consent? Remember: Except for Franco, you and I are the only ones who know about this paper.''

"And the other attorney," he pointed out. "You have to do it the right way, Stacey, through the proper channels. Leave it to me. Andersen-Bradley will be dismantled very soon."

He was true to his word. By Wednesday morning, the manufacturers of the Compu-500 had sent their moving men to retrieve the huge system. A used-office-furniture place was coming to give an estimate for the desks and wall systems, and Stacey had offered to make a present of the stereo in John's office to Chris and her family.

"I can't take it, Stacey," the woman said, blotting her tears with a pink tissue. "This is terrible."

"Take it with my love."

They were sitting in a booth in Burger King across from A-B. Joe was still in the office supervising the removal of the system and the women had slipped across the street for lunch. "You know I'm not going to leave you in the lurch, Chris, don't you? You'll get severance and fine references. In fact, Input has expressed an interest in having you supervise their CRT operators after you have the baby."

Chris brushed the offer aside. "I don't care about that. I might use this as an excuse to take that course in woodworking I'd always wanted. I can always make extra money working through a temporary service when the baby gets a little older."

"I hope we stay friends." Miserable, Stacey sipped her diet soda and looked at the woman across the booth from her. "You've been a dear friend to me since I moved out here. I don't know what I'd have done without you."

"Please don't start crying, Stacey. If you do, I'll start again and I don't think I'll be able to stop this time." She patted Stacey's hand. "Of course, we'll stay friends. We only live fifteen minutes away from each other. We can shop together, you can come over for dinner—you know how Tom and the kids love you. Except for work, everything else will be the same.''

Stacey shook her head and adjusted the chignon at the back of her head. "Nothing's the same, Chris. Things change and there doesn't seem to be a damned thing you can do about it. If there's one thing I learned this summer, that was it."

They stared out the window as the computer was slid into the truck and the burly workmen locked the door behind it. Two minutes later, the truck eased into traffic and drove slowly down the winding road, merging into traffic until it was out of sight.

She was truly amazed at how well she'd handled everything. Not once since the first shock of finding out about John's treachery and Franco's lies had she fallen apart. Her emotions were under lock and key and she'd never give anyone the opportunity of getting to them ever again.

Under her authority, Joe had sold all the furnishings, draperies, and carpets, removed the computers. Except on a piece of paper in his office, Andersen-Bradley existed no longer.

Miraculously, she had retained controlling interest, enabling her radical decision to pull out of A-B. She'd made sure Joe kept scrupulous records of every transaction. John's gambling debts were paid off and the score evened with the finance companies. Franco's forty percent of A-B was now represented by thousands of reels disks, stacked neatly in the old computer room. Loaded with names and addresses and buying information, they were worth a small fortune—but he would have to start up his own business. Without the fun of secrets and manipulations, what good would A-B have been to him anyway?

He'd sent her a telegram from Rome saying he'd be back Thursday the twenty-second. Deliberately she didn't meet him at the airport, no craning her neck to see him going through Customs, no waving and smiling. No. Let him wonder where she was. Let him worry awhile and come to her apartment to find out why she hadn't showed up. Better yet, let him stop first at the office and see it empty and desolate, a ghost of what it once was.

Thursday night was rainy and chilly. A dense fog tumbled along the shore, making everything seem raw with a dampness that burrowed inside her bones. She lit a small fire in the fireplace and curled up with the needlepoint cushion she was working on—another unicorn motif to join the display on the sofa. She was quickly absorbed in the intricate bargello background. She'd become very adept at turning her mind into a blank, at not allowing anything painful to filter through.

At five after ten she heard the turn of a key in the lock to her front door.

"Stacey?" That golden voice—how she had once loved it.

"Unlock the chain, *cara,* please."

She got up, smoothing the folds of her yellow robe as she walked barefoot through the narrow hallway. Without a word she unhitched the chain and stood back.

"The fog is thick as molasses," he said as he stepped into the hallway, brushing drops of moisture off his raincoat.

She leaned against the door to the linen closet, eyes

narrowed, watching him. It was funny, but he still looked beautiful to her—that aristocratic nose, the full sensual lips, the amber eyes glowing with hidden promise. Hidden treachery, she reminded herself. No, she wouldn't be swept away again.

He came over to her. She could tell by the look on his face that his antennae had picked up the vibrations in the room. "Are you all right, *cara*? When I didn't see you at the airport I—"

She moved away from him, out of the circle of his imminent embrace. "I'm fine."

He stared at her. "So I see. Is your car out of order, then?"

"The car's fine too. Everything's fine."

He exhaled. With a swift movement he took off his raincoat and hung it up.

"Not in there," she said automatically. "It's wet. Here, let me put it in the bathroom." She practically snatched it from him, hurrying to hang it up.

"Did you stop by the office?" she asked when she came back into the living room. He was standing by the fire, rubbing his hands together for warmth.

He nodded. "I drove by. When I saw the lights were off, I figured you were here." He turned. "Are you going to tell me what's going on or do I have to guess? It's obvious something is wrong, *cara*."

What an exquisite liar he was, she thought. So smooth, so sure.... Had it never occurred to him his little plan might backfire?

Without another word she handed him the folded document, watching his face as he read it. She had to admire him—he was smooth. Even when caught, he betrayed nothing. And to think she had trusted him!

Head still down, he refolded it and tapped it against

the back of his hand. So, she knew of his business deal with John. He'd hoped to be able to break it to her in his own way.

"*Cara*, I'm sorry you had to learn about it like this. I've been wanting to tell you but you've been through so much lately that—"

Her expletive shocked the both of them into silence. She reddened and sat down on the couch. She hadn't meant to give herself away like that. It wouldn't happen again.

"When did you meet John?" Her voice was cool once more, detached. The empty look in her green eyes sent a shiver of fear through him that the fireplace's warmth couldn't reach.

"I met him in February at the Computer Engineers' conference in Cincinnati. He knew Leeanna's husband and we arranged to meet. We hit it off and he knew I was looking to invest in a place with a Compu-500 near Manhattan and—"

"We didn't *have* the 500 back in February," she interrupted. "Try another story, Franco."

He brushed his hair off his forehead and sat opposite her. He longed to take her in his arms, stroke her hair, but knew she would shatter like glass if he touched her. How could he make her understand the frightened, desperate John Bradley he had met?

The warm lights in his eyes were extinguished. He was serious, more than a little sad. "Stacey, look. I want to tell you everything. Why don't you just let me get through the story once, then you can slice it to ribbons, all right?"

She nodded and picked up her needlepoint—anything so she didn't have to watch that once-loved face spin his lies.

"You know John was in big trouble, financially. Joe told you all about his gambling debts, the pile of loans and second mortgages he racked up since his wife died, right?" Without looking, she nodded. "What you don't know is he was being threatened. He had lost a lot of money and taken a few, shall we say, 'personal loans' that he couldn't pay."

She gave a hollow laugh. "I knew he owed money to a loan shark. Are you trying to tell me his *life* was in danger? Come on, Franco, really. You can do better than this."

He slammed his fist down on the coffee table, making the bisque unicorn slide near to the edge. "Are you going to listen or not?"

"I'll listen, I'll listen." Her voice held a cutting edge of mockery.

"He was in much worse shape than you know, Stacey. His family's death had really shaken him up—he was seeing my brother-in-law for psychiatric therapy."

She looked up, needle poised in midair.

"Yes, it's the truth," he continued. "He was trying to get on top of things again and was finally making progress. But when the loan shark started leaning on him, he panicked." He sighed and tapped the wooden surface of the coffee table with one finger. "We made a deal: I became the silent backer, with the promise from him that he'd get the Compu-500 and rent me computer time. He'd still be front-office man, still run the company—nothing would change. When A-B was on top of things again, he'd buy me out. We all would have come out winners."

She snorted. "Come on! This whole story makes you sound like a boy scout. Couldn't you have gotten a better deal with someone who wasn't in so much trouble?"

He rubbed his eyes wearily. "Of course I could have, Stacey. It was a gamble. But I knew about John and I came to care a great deal for him. Did you know about his heart condition?"

She nodded. "He'd had a small attack a few months before he died."

Franco shook his head. "It was worse than that. His cardiac specialist suspected a major blockage. He was supposed to go in for tests the week after his accident."

She was quiet, thinking back to all the jokes they'd made about his diet, all the relentless teasing about weight and exercise—she shook her head, willing the embarrassing tears away. Finally she said, "That makes your involvement all the more unbelievable."

He made one last stab. "Stacey, he told me about you. He felt terribly responsible. He was terrified the loan shark would get to you. He knew all you were doing for Lillian—he even told me something about your past." He saw her shoulders stiffen. "He was afraid he might die and leave you with a company in ruins. It haunted him. He was willing to do anything to get out of trouble and put A-B back on firm ground again. And, as you know, it backfired. His loyalty to you and the way he struggled to set things right again touched me."

He looked at her face, thin and pale, and felt a swelling of emotion that frightened him by its intensity. "When I met you, I understood why he felt as he did. He was going to tell you as soon as some of the more embarrassing bills were paid, but, unfortunately, you know the rest."

"Why didn't you tell me then? What was *your* angle?" Her voice was thin, strangled.

"Because, *cara,* I fell in love with you. You don't

know how often I rehearsed my speech, how many times I told you in my head, then, faced with those trusting green eyes, I just couldn't. Whether you believe it or not, I didn't want to see that look in your eyes that I see now when you speak of John. I wanted his memory to stay beautiful.''

She laughed, a harsh, metallic sound. "Oh, sure. And while you were so busy keeping John's memory lily-white you were charming yourself right into my bed and ownership of A-B.''

He sighed. "I didn't want your damned company, Stacey. Can't you understand that? I could buy and sell three Andersen-Bradleys if I wanted to. I cared about John. . .and I love you. Maybe I made a mistake by not telling you, but I erred on the side of love. Can't you see that?''

She threw her needlepoint down on the carpet and stood up. "No, I can't see that. All I see is that John came damned close to ruining my life and that you used the situation to your own advantage. That's what I see.''

"Have you no compassion, Stacey? Can't you understand the hell that man was living through? How much was he supposed to stand without cracking in some way? From what Paul told me, he was almost insane with grief those first few months. Couldn't you see it?''

"For your information, he held his grief very privately and very well. He never once lost control.''

"Were you blind then, *cara*? Don't you recognize a drowning man when you see one?''

She hugged her arms around her body and walked to the window and stared out. Bits and pieces of memory floated back, taunting her. John's face, gray and desolate when he thought no one was watching him; the way his hands shook when he held his coffee cup; the cigarettes smoked practically two at a time, overflowing his ashtray. She covered her eyes, trying to push the vivid images back. Had she really been so absorbed in herself that she hadn't seen the signs?

She felt Franco gently touch her shoulder. "*Cara,* can't you—"

"Don't touch me." She leaped away as if burned. "You may be right about John, but that doesn't excuse you, Franco. That can never explain to me why you deceived me."

"It was only with love, *cara.* Now I know I was wrong not to level with you from the beginning. But, first John died, then Lillian—I was so damned crazy in love with you I couldn't think straight! Your sadness scared me and I was afraid telling you about this would push you away from me. And, besides, I—"

"Spare me." Her voice was soft, devoid of all emotions. She spoke more to herself than him. "I should have known some things never change, and human nature is one of them. Protect thyself first—isn't that the golden rule?" She laughed. "You're really no different than Michael. You just make a better first impression, that's all."

He stared at her. "Who's Michael?"

"It hardly matters anymore," she answered. "Remember what you said in Key West? Put a buzz in someone's head and don't get out until you close the deal? I had no idea you'd incorporated that philosophy into your love life too. Well, you've been an education, I'll grant you that."

He grabbed her by the shoulders and turned her toward him, ignoring the fury in her green eyes. "People make mistakes, Stacey—I'll be the first to admit mine. I see now it would have been kinder in the long run to have told you everything from the start. But it's too late to go back. Can't you forgive me, rather than condemn me for my mistakes?''

"Is this another calculated assault designed to make the proper impression?"

He let go of her and moved back, hands up in front of him in a gesture of defeat. There was no way he could convince her of his love.

"Have it your way, Stacey, but ask yourself this: Have you been totally honest with me? Think about it and when you have an answer, call me. I'll be waiting."

He started walking toward her front door. In a blinding fury, she tugged at the diamond ring on her finger and threw it at him. It bounced against his back and fell to the floor. "Take that! Maybe you can buy yourself a new computer with it!"

She stood there, breasts heaving, as he quietly closed the door behind him. She didn't move. A few moments later she heard the sound of his car engine catch and start, then the whine of the motor as he backed out of the lot and roared back toward Manhattan.

She felt fragile as a piece of glass.

She went into the bathroom to rinse her face with cold water. Turning on the light, she saw his raincoat, dry now, hanging from the shower rod. Without thinking, she buried her face in the lining and breathed in his familiar smell.

"Damn it," she whispered. "Damn it, *damn it*!"

Why did she still have to love him?

And why did she feel so guilty?

Chapter Twelve

Saturday morning she drove up to White Plains to see Dianne and Al. She knew telling her sister was going to be hard, but she hadn't been prepared for Dianne's loud anger when she heard the news.

"I never thought of you as a coward, Stacey." Dianne faced her over the dining room table where the two women were having dessert. "You're so afraid of taking a chance that you've not only given up your business, but you've pushed happiness away with both hands! Congratulations."

Stacey put her coffee cup down. "If you weren't my sister, I think I'd get up and leave. What was I supposed to do—allow myself to be lied to for the next thirty years?"

"I can't believe you can be so stupid. Where's all the wisdom you displayed when Al and I were separated? Where's all that talk about thinking carefully before you let love slip away?"

"I made a mistake, okay, Di? I just have rotten judgment when it comes to men. It happens to women all the time."

Dianne glared at her. "Don't give me that nonsense, Stacey. I won't buy it. Even Grandma told you Franco has the 'right stuff.' If I didn't have Al, as a matter of fact, I'd be tempted to give you a run for your money." At the brief flare of jealousy on Stacey's face, Dianne grinned. "Don't worry. I was only kidding."

"Who's worrying?" Stacey lied. "He means nothing to me anymore."

"Then why do you still wear the charm he gave you?"

Involuntarily Stacey reached to the chain around her neck. She had no answer. "Okay," she said finally. "Maybe you're right. So what?"

"So go to him," Dianne said. "Tell him how you feel, listen to him. You owe it to both of you, to what you had."

Stacey fingered the chain that held both charm and engagement ring. "I also owe him a few explanations and it's just too late for that now. It's all blown up in my face."

Dianne shook her head. "You should have told him when things got serious, but—"

"Oh, great," Stacey broke in. "What should I have done? Said, 'Hi, my name is Stacey, and I can't have children?' Come on, Di."

"What I was going to tell you is, since you didn't tell him then, you damned well owe it to him to tell him about it now. Even if everything *is* over between the two of you, at least you'll know it was all out in the open at the end and the choices were freely made."

Her jaw hardened. "No, I refuse to do that. Even if he didn't hate me for withholding things, how could I ever be sure now he didn't use me to get to my business?"

Dianne guffawed. "Come on—we both know he didn't need A-B. I don't think even *you* believe that nonsense. You're just covering up your own guilt."

Her sister had painted a pretty unflattering picture of her, one Stacey found very hard to accept. Even though Al was out of town on business, she declined Dianne's invitation to stay overnight, and drove home instead on the dark, deserted highways. She hated to admit it, but Dianne had been right about many things. She did still love Franco but the hard truth of it was they could never have a future together. Not now.

She slept late Saturday morning, glad to be in her own apartment and away from Dianne's sharp criticisms. Many of her barbs had hit their mark, making small punctures in her carefully constructed armor. She, of all people, should have realized just how desperate John was. Had she been too afraid of change to see? Had she just buried her head in the computer room and pretended things were fine? Franco, at least, had had the sensitivity to see through John's bravado. He had seen John's pain and extended a hand, while she had been so busy feeling sorry for herself that she'd been nearly blind.

She toyed with the cup of tea that sat cooling on the kitchen table along with a half-eaten piece of whole wheat toast. With a sigh, she stood up, put the plates in the sink, ran hot water over them, then went into the bedroom to dress and brush her hair back into her usual tight chignon.

She needed exercise badly. Her muscles ached for use. It was raining too hard to jog or rake leaves. So, instead she scrubbed the bathroom floor on her hands and knees in an attempt to exhaust herself so she couldn't think. Without Anderson-Bradley to run to, she was alone with her thoughts—and they weren't pleasant company.

She finished the bathroom and had moved into the kitchen to clean the oven for the first time in months, when the doorbell rang.

''Be right there!'' She stripped off the rubber gloves and wiped some sweat from her forehead with the back of her hand. Barefoot, she hurried to the door. "Who is it?"

"Biondina?"

She started. Only Giancarlo would call her "little blond one." She opened the door and was immediately swept into his embrace.

"Giancarlo! I—I mean, did we. . . I must have forgotten—"

He looked at her patched jeans and faded navy sweat shirt and laughed. "You forget nothing, Stacey. You are dressed for gardening."

She brought him into the kitchen, where he cast an admiring eye over the lush plants at her window. What on earth was she going to say to him?

She made espresso in the machine Franco had given her. "I hope it tastes okay," she said as she put a demitasse down in front of him. "Did I forget we had plans to garden today?"

He sipped the rich brew. "Very good. Not every one can make espresso properly."

"Giancarlo? Did we have plans today?"

He shook his head, blue eyes serious.

"You know about Franco and me, don't you? He told you?"

Giancarlo nodded. "He didn't have to tell me. The way he looked when he said good-bye before going back to Rome told me everything."

She felt like she'd been struck. Now, even if she wanted to, she couldn't tell him anything at all. Not anymore.

"So he didn't send you here?" Her voice was flat.

"No, *biondina*. In fact, I think he would be furious if he knew I was butting into his affairs. You see, neither Carmela nor I carry a burden alone if it can be shared.

Franco, though, has always been solitary, like he carried the weight of the world on his shoulders like Atlas. He's always carried his burdens alone, from the very day we got him. His parents must have—''

Her head shot up. ''His parents? What are you talking about? You and Carmela are—''

He waved his hand in the air, an offhanded gesture. ''I mean his birth parents. As I was saying—''

''Wait! Do you mean Franco is adopted?''

He nodded. ''Yes. As I was saying—''

She interrupted yet again. ''And Leeanna? She too?''

''Leeanna too.'' He waited for her next question to come.

She sat very still, shaking her head back and forth in a nearly imperceptible motion. ''I had no idea,'' she breathed. She looked up at Giancarlo, her green eyes wide. ''Why didn't he tell me?''

Giancarlo shrugged. ''I'm not surprised.'' He patted her arm. ''I don't think he ever gives his adoption a thought. It's never been an issue—he is ours as surely as if he'd been carried beneath Carmela's heart.''

She rested her forehead against her hands for a moment, trying to assimilate what she'd just learned. ''I don't think I understand anything anymore. Leeanna and Franco look so much alike, I—''

Giancarlo sighed and took a sip of his espresso. ''It was so long ago,'' he said, leaning back in the kitchen chair and watching Stacey. ''Now, when I think back, it is like another lifetime.''

She swallowed hard. ''You don't have to dredge up any painful memories,'' she said in a soft voice. ''It's okay.'' Who was she to ask someone else to do what she could not?

His serious face softened. ''They are not painful

memories, *biondina,* unless the very sweetness of them causes a bittersweet pain.'' He paused a moment, then explained, ''Leeanna and Franco are natural brother and sister. They were the children of friends of ours from Italy who had moved to America when we did. Franco was born ten months after Julia and Robertino moved to Staten Island. They called him their American baby. Robertino died in an auto accident when Julia was pregnant with Leeanna.'' He sighed. ''Julia was unable to handle her grief—her family wrote her and asked her to come back to Italy for a while, to recover. She went, but then decided the children should be in America, so she wrote us and asked us to care for the children while she got back on her feet. We had loved both Julia and Robertino so we agreed. Franco arrived in September, Leeanna at Thanksgiving. By Christmas, Julia was dead.'' He exhaled in a long shuddering breath.

''Suicide?''

He nodded, closing his blue eyes for a moment. ''She'd left a note that she wanted Leeanna and Franco to stay with us. Now, Carmela and I were a little''—he shrugged, searching for the right word—''nervous at the prospect of suddenly being parents. We had known for years we couldn't have children and we'd made our peace with it. We had each other, a good marriage, and were happy in our apartment in Brooklyn. We tried very hard to weigh both sides, to come to a logical conclusion, but there was something we hadn't counted on.''

His eyes took on a distant look, as if he were watching a movie only he could see. ''Those two had crept inside our hearts: Our ears were suddenly attuned to that tiny cry in the night, our eyes searching for a smile that meant they were growing used to being safe.'' He lifted his hands and spread them in an expressive gesture. "They had become ours as surely as if our blood ran in their veins."

A sharp pain threatened to choke Stacey as she remembered how it felt to be without a real mother. How long it had taken her and Dianne to take root and blossom under Lillian's loving care. The feelings of insecurity planted in the child can grow into a strangling weed in the adult, she'd discovered. She remembered searching Lillian's face time and again through the years for signs of resentment at the predicament her son's widow had put her in. Stacey had seen anger toward her mother, fury over her way of life, but toward the girls, never anything but loving support. The loving support of a family.

She looked at the man who could have been her father-in-law. "What was Franco like as a little boy?"

"Ah, *biondina,* he would have broken your heart. He came to us at three years old—the skinniest, most frightened child you'd ever seen. So quiet at first, never showing emotion. We said he was like a lake: peaceful on the surface with no hint at the darkness and depths below. He remembered things that must have haunted him."

She swallowed hard at the thought of the child he'd been. "And Leeanna?"

Giancarlo broke into a smile. "She was six months when she came. Franco's direct opposite: open and sunny and transparent as a clear stream."

"I never guessed," Stacey murmured. "I wish I had known."

Giancarlo frowned. "I don't understand. Does this bother you?"

She shook her head, then buried her face in her hands, trying to blot out the images Giancarlo's words had evoked. She'd had glimpses of a sadness in Franco at times, a feeling when he held her that she was not just his lover but his anchor—that he feared loss just as she did. But the understanding had come too late.

Giancarlo gently touched her arm. "Tell me, *biondina*, what happened. You and I have a bond of the soul. Forget I am his father. If you need someone to talk to now that your dear *nonna* is gone, please call me. I want to make those green eyes shine again like they did that day in my garden."

She looked into that kind face and started to cry. At first it was a quiet, pitiful sniffling, then, as her barriers broke down, it changed into big sobs that tore through her body like explosions. Giancarlo wasn't a man frightened by emotion. He got up and put his hands on her shoulders. She buried her face against his side, her tears leaving wet circles on his worn denim shirt. The ocean of pain she had carried around inside her for years broke in a tidal wave, ripping through her throat, leaving her gasping for breath.

The years of secrets and loneliness came out in a barrage of words, much of which was unintelligible. He nodded, handed her Kleenex, offered his shoulder and fresh tea. Finally he led her, fragile and shaky, to the couch in the living room and covered her with an afghan.

"This is good for you, *biondina*," he said as he sat next to her. "There are times when it becomes too much and you need a purging of the soul—to coin a phrase: the storm before the calm."

She laughed, then winced, for her throat was sore from all the crying.

"I'm so sorry you had to be here to see me carry on like a lunatic, Giancarlo." Her hands fluttered to her tear-swollen face and red nose. "I must look a mess."

He tilted her chin and smiled kindly. "You have looked better, but at least you are at peace now."

"Do you know, for a while I think I actually *hated* John for dying and leaving me alone?" She held the mug of tea to her cheek. "I felt so abandoned, so betrayed." She shook her head. "I knew he'd been hurting and I just couldn't reach him. That hurts the most."

"I've learned a few things having a therapist for a son-in-law," Giancarlo began, "and one of them is that grief has certain definite stages and everyone passes through them in their own time until they reach an acceptance of their loss. This anger and guilt are normal and natural, Stacey. You have nothing to be ashamed of."

She unwrapped the afghan and stood. "No, you don't know everything about it." She paced the room. "For years, I've been wrapped up in my own private world, blaming everything on something that happened five years ago. I used it as a means of escape—I see that now, finally—another example that you can't trust things not to change. I just didn't want to deal with the world the way it really is. I buried myself in work and convinced myself it was exactly what I wanted."

She felt torn by the realization. She had not bargained on Franco coming into her life and seeing into her heart, recognizing her hunger for love. How much safer to retreat into her cocoon where she took no chances, risked no pain.

"What could have been so terrible five years ago?" Giancarlo asked, rising from his chair and walking over to the window where she stood looking at the rainy backyard. The trowel was still on the grass, rusted now, almost obscured by the fallen autumn leaves. "Have you a dark and secret past life?" He smiled kindly.

"No dark and secret past," she answered, smiling back at him. "But"—she hesitated—"I've kept something from Franco, something important, and it's too late now to do anything about it."

"Can I help?"

She shook her head. "I don't see how. I should have been honest from the start. Franco isn't the only one who made that mistake."

Giancarlo stroked his hair. "You know, Stacey, when Franco and Leeanna came to us, Carmela and I prayed they would grow up healthy and strong and marry well. To us, a good marriage is the cornerstone of a happy life. You are everything I could have asked for in a daughter."

Her tears started fresh.

"You're everything I could have wanted in a father," she said between gulping sobs. "Your home, Carmela, Leeanna, the baby—everything. I felt so safe and happy with you, like I'd been searching all my life for all of you."

"Franco told me about your childhood. I wish I could have met *Nonna* Lillian. She must have been a great lady."

"She was," Stacey sighed. "She would have loved you as I do."

Giancarlo put his hands on her shoulders and turned her to face him. "And Franco?" His voice was suddenly like his son's. "Do you still love him?"

She nodded. "That's the worst part of all. I *do* still love him, but there's no future for us."

"If you love him, there is always a future."

She walked back to the couch. "You don't understand. We said terrible things. I was hateful, Giancarlo. Hateful."

"If he were in Manhattan, I would call him right now and force you two to speak with one another. Love such as yours is a miracle from God, not something to be thrown away like yesterday's newspapers."

She shook her head. "Thanks for saying that, but there isn't much we can do with him in Italy, is there?"

He stayed for more espresso and they turned on the radio, humming along to some easy-listening music while she reheated the espresso. Was this, she wondered, going to be the pattern of her life: great realizations when it was too late to act on them?

"You know what's really ironic?" she said as she walked him to the front door around 2 P.M. "Franco and I really could have been a dynamite business team. Given a choice, I can't think of anyone else I would want to be partners with."

"Don't give up hope, *biondina*," Giancarlo said, leaning over to kiss her cheek. "When he returns, perhaps then. . . ."

She kissed his leathery cheek. Her nostrils filled with the scent of his citrusy cologne and a rush of memories of Franco hit her square in the stomach.

"Are you sure you won't come to our home for the weekend? We would love to have you, Stacey."

She shook her head. "I can't, Giancarlo. Not that I don't love you both, but it would hurt too much. You understand."

He nodded, face heavy with sadness. "Remember I'm there if you need a shoulder. You're my other daughter."

She hugged him again, dizzied by the memories his scent evoked. Even after she closed and locked the door behind him and waved good-bye from the kitchen window, the tang of his after-shave lingered. Buried memories of Franco's face, clean and ruddy after shaving, flashed before her eyes. She saw him everywhere—in the matchbook cover from The White Swan that rested on her stove to the burnt-orange-and-tan bargello cushion she'd been needlepointing for him. He filled her home the way he filled her heart.

Damn it! To have been so close, to have been just weeks away from a lifetime of happiness. It just wasn't fair.

Sunday morning she felt as if the walls of her apartment were shrinking, pushing against her heart until she wanted to scream. The rain had stopped and a pale early-autumn sun struggled to peek through the clouds. The oak trees in the yard had begun to change color, the greens slowly turning to vibrating oranges and blinding yellows that were almost painful in their beauty.

The phone rang as soon as she awoke but she couldn't bear the thought of listening to any more of Dianne's advice or Chris's well-meaning sympathy. Even the thought of hearing Giancarlo, whose voice was so reminiscent of Franco's, was more than she could handle.

As far as she was concerned, there was no one at home.

By one thirty she was behind the wheel of her brown Mustang, heading east on the Expressway. She'd grown very fond of the small car, comfortable with its easy handling, its understated good looks. She could get lost in the crowd in this car as she never could with the Corvette.

There were few cars on the road. In fact, by the time she reached Exit 63 in Farmingville, the only company she had were two enormous eighteen-wheelers with Nebraska license plates and a man in a white Corvette who kept going even with her, winking and trying to catch her eye.

In the old days when she had *her* Corvette, she could have flashed him a smile and left him in the dust. Now, in the sturdy, but unexciting, four-cylinder car, the best she could do was try to keep her speed at fifty-five and ignore him until he tired of the game. If there was one thing she wasn't in the mood for, it was flirting.

She was old. She was a tired, old woman of twenty-six, well past all the frivolous pleasures of youth.

Even the windswept beauty of the beach at East Lake in Montauk held no magic for her. For the first time, its majesty didn't touch her. The cold mists swirled damp against her skin and she hunched down into the warmth of her sweat shirt, hands buried in the kangaroo pouch pockets in front, her head bent low. The ocean was very choppy; sharp waves whipped up froths of white foam that crashed against the rocky shore, creating a wind that whipped her hair around her face. She pulled a rubber band from her pants pocket and twisted the wild mane into a ponytail, then secured it.

Finally, when for the third time she thought she saw Franco—the first was a fisherman hip-deep in rubber boots, the other a painfully young Coast Guardsman—she knew it was time to go home. He had crept into every part of her life—even her solitary pleasures didn't work anymore. She needed Franco at the edge of her vision, always near her to be happy.

She pulled back into the apartment complex parking lot after 5 P.M., shivering with the cold, hungry and totally miserable.

He had looked for her everywhere. The barren office had been a shock that sent a streak of hot fear through him. He drove to her apartment, only to find her car missing from the lot, then drove past the health spa she belonged to, even drove halfway to Montauk. Finally, in desperation, he called Dianne to see if Stacey had gone away somewhere or done something drastic. Reassured she'd be home later most likely, he settled down in his black Buick in the parking lot, watching every pair of headlights that approached, waiting anxiously for the familiar pair to make a left turn into the driveway.

The chill dampness seeped through the windows of the car and he shivered. Suddenly he heard the high-pitched whine of a four-cylinder engine winding around the curving driveway toward the lot. He saw her pull into her spot, leaving the car at the slightly cockeyed angle he'd grown used to. As she got out of the car, straightening the legs of her jeans and stretching slightly to relax the long limbs that had been cramped in the tiny car, he felt an overwhelming sensation of tenderness and love and desire. The way she carried herself—straight and tall, hiding her fears and insecurities deep within—moved him deeply, struck a familiar chord of loneliness within himself. She had to listen to him. She had to have the chance to open up to him. He got out of the car.

The light above her front door had burned out. She couldn't see the lock clearly and had to bend down to fit the key inside. She stood there, balancing canvas pocketbook, grocery bag, and book, trying to unlock the door when she grew aware of footsteps rustling through the fallen leaves. Immediately she straightened up and turned, her heart beating sharply.

"I didn't mean to frighten you, Stacey."

She sagged against the door as Franco stepped into the tiny circle of light from the next apartment. She stared at him, unsure he was another mirage.

He reached for her key. "May I?"

She nodded. Oh, he was real—very real. If she wanted to—and she did—she could rest her hand on that silky hair, now covered with light mist. Mirages didn't smell like citrus cologne or have that intoxicating scent special to a man. This man.

They went into the hall where she put her packages down on the table near the linen closet. "I thought you were in Rome," she said for lack of anything better, as she put their jackets away.

He stood awkwardly between hallway and living room until she motioned him inside. "I was going to go," he said, "but I changed my mind at the last minute. I was hoping you'd call me."

She blushed, thinking of all the times she'd begun to dial his number, actually dialing area code and exchange. "I wanted to," she said, her voice little more than a whisper. "I was afraid."

A glimmer of hope lit his golden eyes. "I want to explain, *cara*—the company had been signed back to you right after we got engaged. I was going to tell you. I just wanted to wait until you were so filled with happiness, until every corner of your heart was lit up, so you would forgive John—forgive me. I'm sorry."

Her heart soared. She struggled to keep from running across the room into his arms. She didn't have the right anymore. "It's freezing in here," she said instead. "Should we light a fire?"

"Cara?" He stepped near to her. "What's in your heart?"

She put her head down so he wouldn't see the torment. "Sit down. I have something to tell you."

He sank into the sofa, leaning forward on his elbows, watching her face.

"I overreacted, Franco. I'm not happy you did things that way, but I understand your motives now. In a way I guess I always did." She smiled wanly. "I've been guilty of a little secret-keeping myself." She twisted a loose curl around her finger, then tucked it back into her ponytail, trying to choose her words carefully. "There's something you need to know before we go any further."

She told him about her operation and the ensuing sterility and even Michael's reaction in simple language, without a trace of self-pity. He felt a wave of pain as he thought of her five years ago, left alone to adjust to her loss. He watched the beauty and dignity on her face and realized he had never loved her more than at this moment as she revealed her heart to him.

"I've come to terms with it," she said when she'd finished. "But I knew it was a lot to ask of a man—to accept it. I love you so much and I was so afraid you'd leave me."

She finally dared to look at him. His head was bent down, resting in his hands, and she held her breath. He stood up and took her by the shoulders, his expression serious.

"I'm glad you told me, *cara,* but it was no surprise."

She turned bright red. "Did John tell you? Lillian?"

He shook his head. "Neither. When John and I drew up our contract, we ran the normal reference checks and, along with the information on John's heart, it came out in the health insurance papers."

"You knew everything?"

"I knew there had been surgery, obviously, and that it had been serious. Are *you* healthy, no after-effects?"

She shook her head. "I'm healthy as a horse."

He breathed a sigh of relief. "I was terrified you were ill. I didn't want that for you."

"This is bad enough," she said, watching him closely. "We can never have a family."

He smiled. "I think we *are* a family—the two of us, as we are."

She moved into his embrace and felt something in her heart snap into place at long last—like the final piece of a jigsaw puzzle completing the whole.

"It would have been nice to have a child by you," she murmured against his cheek.

He looked at her. "I won't deny a little girl like you would be a miracle. But, in this world, it's miracle enough when you find the other half of your heart."

"What if one day you want more?" she persisted. "Children to raise...."

He kissed her. "There's such a thing as adoption," he murmured into her hair. "It's been known to work out very well."

She looked at him and suddenly had a glimpse of the frightened three-year-old he'd once been. A laugh bubbled up from her throat. "Yes, you could find a little boy with golden eyes." She hesitated a moment. "I hope you know what you're getting into—things *do* have a way of changing, Franco."

"I'll say this once, Stacey, and from then on it's a closed subject: I fell in love with you—Stacey Andersen and everything she is. I want you fertile, infertile, happy, sad, anyway I can get you. Damn it, woman, I've waited long enough to find you. Can you get that through your head?''

She nodded and slipped the engagement ring off the chain around her neck. With great ceremony he put it back on her finger and sealed the commitment with a kiss.

She'd never thought she'd feel him close to her again, be lost in that dizzying swirl of sensation as his tongue traced the outline of her mouth and she drank of his sweetness. She sighed, deeply content.

''Happy, *cara*?''

She nodded, too filled with joy to trust her voice.

Pushing her slightly away from him so he could see the expression in her luminous green eyes, he said, ''I have one more question.'' At her anxious look, he smiled. ''What are you doing October twelfth?''

She grinned and let herself fall into the liquid amber pools of his eyes. ''Sorry, I'm busy that day,'' she said. ''It seems I'm getting married!''

Stacey Andersen Borelli—that was a change she could learn to love.

Epilogue

"We shouldn't be doing this," Stacey said as Franco whipped the black Buick into the lot near East Lake Beach in Montauk. "We should be home packing and cleaning and—"

Her husband reached over and placed a finger against her lips.

"—and spending a little time together before the madness starts."

He switched off the engine and flashed her the grin that, after almost a year of marriage, still sent a warm shiver of joy through her. "Just an afternoon, *cara*. All the packing and everything will still be there when we get back to the apartment."

She nodded, for he was one hundred percent right. The logistics of moving from Long Island to Jamesburg, New Jersey, were turning out to be more complicated than those for the invasion of Normandy.

She took his outstretched hand and they picked their way over the dune grass down to the shoreline. Although it was only late September, the air by the ocean was chilly; it cut right through their light shirts and zippered sweat shirts. A diamond-clear sun peeped through streaks of clouds and a light mist tumbled along the waters that lapped against the base of the lighthouse farther down the unchanging beach.

Montauk was always there for her, a constant source

of strength to draw upon. She breathed deeply of the tangy air. It had been months since they'd been here and her fatigue drifted away as she viewed the rolling waves. She glanced over at her husband's profile, at the random strands of silver hair that were suddenly popping out around his temples. She reached over and brushed some stray hairs off his forehead.

"Counting my gray hairs, again, *cara*?" He turned and smiled at her. "I got every one of them waiting for you to come home from school at night."

She chuckled and rested her cheek against his for a moment as they strolled along in the growing mist.

"Well, it's over now," she said, her voice filled with a pride she couldn't disguise. "I am now a trained computer systems analyst!"

He stopped in his tracks and whirled her around to face him. "You passed the final?" His amber eyes danced with delight.

Her laugh was infectious. "We got the grades last night: ninety-seven point three—I was tops in the class!"

He pulled her close and kissed her, his tongue savoring the soft contours of her mouth. "Tops in the class is only fitting for the co-owner of the new firm Borelli and Borelli, no?"

"Don't remind me," she groaned as they continued walking the beach, arms around each other's waist. "There's too much happening all at once." A peal of laughter bubbled in her voice. "Wife, student, aunt, and programmer all in the same year—it's overwhelming!"

"Not for you, *cara*," he said as they stopped near the boulder that jutted out from the slate-blue waters. "I get the feeling you're just hitting your stride—there's nothing you can't handle.''

They scrambled up the slippery rock and perched there precariously, thighs pressed close together.

Stacey bent her blond head down to rest on his shoulder. He turned away from the restless brooding ocean and looked at his wife. A full wave of hair covered half of her face and he could discern only a curve of cheekbone and tilt of nose. He brushed the hair away, trying to reveal more of her to his probing eyes. He heard her sigh.

''Stacey? Is everything all right? If you're too cold, we could—''

''No, no. I'm fine.'' She nuzzled up against him, her lips pressed against the deep hollow of his throat, filling her senses with the warmth and sweetness of his skin and that intoxicating scent that was his alone. ''I'm just feeling nostalgic.''

An amber light blinked faintly in the distance past the lighthouse.

''Look—over there!'' Stacey directed Franco toward it and narrowed her eyes in an attempt to pierce the thickening fog.

''Do you think it's the *Will o' the Wisp*?'' she asked, her voice soft. ''I've never forgotten how it sailed right past us that afternoon and—'' She stopped as the light grew brighter and they saw it was just a small fishing vessel seeking harbor. ''Not this time, I guess.''

He chuckled and ruffled her hair. ''Disappointed?''

She nodded. ''A little. I would have loved to have seen it once more—just so I could be sure it wasn't the delusion of an extremely love-struck woman.''

''It was an optical illusion,'' he said, logic prevailing. ''A kind of atmospheric sleight of hand.''

Her green eyes twinkled as she looked at him. "Are you sure it wasn't magic?" she asked.

He tilted her face up to his and kissed her.

"No," he answered finally. "*We* are magic."